THE KILLING OF BOBBI LOMAX

Cal Moriarty also writes for film, television and theatre, and previously worked as a private eye. She attended both the 'Writing a Novel' and 'Edit Your Novel' courses on the Faber Academy in 2012-13.

To find out more visit:
www.calmoriarty.com or
http://uk.pinterest.com/calmoriarty/ and follow her on Twitter @calmoriarty.

The Killing of Bobbi Lomax

CAL MORIARTY

FABER & FABER

First published in 2015
by Faber & Faber Ltd
Bloomsbury House
74–77 Great Russell Street
London WC1B 3DA

Typeset by Faber & Faber Ltd
Printed and bound by CPI Group (UK) Ltd, Croydon CR0 4YY

A CIP record for this book
is available from the British Library

ISBN 978–0–571–30538–4

2 4 6 8 10 9 7 5 3 1

For A, always

And for my parents

All that we see or seem
Is but a dream within a dream.
                    Edgar Allan Poe, 1849

Cast of Characters

Marty Sinclair Veteran detective
Al Alvarez Sinclair's long-term cop partner

Clark Houseman A rare documents and manuscripts dealer
Edie Houseman A loyal Faith wife and mother

Kenny Clark Houseman's friend and business associate

Big Tex Bomb Squad detective

Arnold Lomax Widower of Bobbi Lomax
Bobbi Lomax First bombing victim, new bride of Arnold
    Lomax

Audrey Lomax Sister of Arnold Lomax

Elaine
Shona } Friends of Bobbi Lomax

Linda Lomax Ex-wife of Arnold Lomax

Ronald Rook
Roderick Rook } Identical twin brothers, owners of Rooks Books

Peter Gudsen Second bombing victim, Arnold Lomax's former business partner
Betty Gudsen Widow of Peter Gudsen

Marion Rose The Gudsens' beautiful divorcee neighbor

Dougie Wild Las Vegas-based memorabilia dealer

Ziggy Bookman Homeless book lover

Travis J. Winkleman the Third Antiques and artifacts collector
Sanford T. Winkleman His brother, a wealthy Hollywood movie producer

Trevor Angel A dog walker

Alan Laidlaw A Faith Disciple
Robert Laidlaw A judge

The Order of the Twelve Disciples The Faith's Ruling Council

Robert Bright The Prophet
Elizabeth, Rebecca, Ellen His three wives

This is not an exhaustive list.

1

Halloween 1983

Abraham City, Canyon County

Pig of a day, thought Marty Sinclair as he made his way down the back stairs of the precinct and out into the blazing heat of the lot. Two dead bodies in less than twenty-four hours and if the boom that just shook the precinct was anything to go by, one more at least. What a fucking mess. Marty didn't usually allow himself to swear, but for this case he was making an exception. *Carpe Diem.* Make Hay while the Sun Shines and all that. Fuck. Fuck. Fuck. Pig of a day.

Alvarez was already in the car, lights on, facing the street. 'What took you so long, man?'

'Took the stairs. One at a time.'

'Not in such a rush to get to the next one?'

'I'd only just sat down.'

'Who next?'

Marty exhaled. 'Bobbi Lomax was bad, Al.'

Alvarez nodded, muttered something in Spanish under his breath and looked skywards.

Prayer for the dead, thought Marty. A prayer for why would have been more use, especially if it was answered before the Governor called the Captain again. 'Through and through. Like a cannon. She must have tucked it in like this, close to her chest.'

'Thought it was a FedEx or something?'

'Yeah. One of the neighbors drove up, saw her lying there, thought Halloween, the Family, some kind of breakfast-time prank.'

'Trick or treat. Fucker.'

'Until she got out of the car, took a closer look. Could see the lawn clear through her body.'

Alvarez winced. 'Shit.'

'Just married, barely eighteen.'

'No need to ask *what* next?'

'Or where.'

'My ears are still ringing.'

'Almost blew me off the can,' Marty said as he bit down hard on a fresh piece of gum. Cherry menthol filled his head. Not exactly his beloved roll-ups, but it would do. For now. He could see the Prophet, towering above them, guarding the city. Today, it was almost like the gilded statue was mocking them. He chewed harder, turned his head away. They rounded the corner into a wall of traffic stretching the few blocks to the call.

'Fire 'em up.'

Alvarez flicked the switch. The sound was muffled, like they were underwater. 'Thought you weren't in a hurry.'

The traffic parted on both sides, the Red Sea cometh to Main Street. Up ahead a cloud of smoke four stories high signaled to them. Directly underneath it, the tangled remains of what was once a car. Close by stood a large group of gawkers crowded around something sprawled on the street. Body number three, thought Marty as he reluctantly swallowed the gum.

From the opposite direction he could see the fire trucks. No sign of any other cops yet, tied up with yesterday still. The precinct had been like a ghost town. Alvarez threw the car into a space close, but not too close to the hotspot. If the gawkers hadn't trodden on all the evidence, there might even be some left without riding a ton of metal over it.

'Get these people back, Al,' Marty yelled as he jumped out of the car and moved fast toward the crowd. Alvarez matched him, step for step. They both reached for their badges.

'Back it up here now, everyone.' Alvarez's don't-make-me-arrest-you tone, one he'd perfected working the beat amongst Venice's transients through its '60s heyday and into its downward slide. Blood was creeping across the street. The guy's leg was a mess. A hole in his chest. Knelt right beside him was a guy, no more than twenty-five, anointing him with holy oil from a small plastic bottle. He looked up at Marty. Saw the badge. 'Where's the paramedics?! He's still alive. I thought he was dead. Me and this other guy dragged him away from the flames. I went to get the oil, I always carry it in the glove box, then he started moving, talking. I...'

'He a friend of yours?'

'No. I was just crossing the street when ...'

'What did he say?'

'Nothing much, he was hallucinating. I couldn't hear that clear. When are the paramedics gonna get here, he ...'

Marty cut him off: 'What do you think you heard?'

The guy looked confused. '"Sentence first, verdict afterwards."'

Marty had heard that before, couldn't for the life of him think where. 'Was that it?' Marty was knelt beside the guy now, in the warm blood.

'No. He said, "We're nothing but a pack of cards."'

'Nothing but a pack of cards?'

The guy nodded, looked anxiously back down at his freshly anointed patient.

3

Marty leaned in. 'Sir, sir, can you hear me?' Nothing.

'He hasn't said anything for a few minutes. Maybe he's already…'

Marty pressed his face close, whispered in the victim's ear. 'Sir, do you know who did this to you? Sir?' Still nothing. And now it was Marty's turn to be ushered out of the way. Paramedics. As he stood up, the man suddenly seemed to come back to life, reached out to him. Marty noticed the tip of a finger had been blown off, the whole hand badly charred. 'They're trying to kill me,' the soft raspy voice said.

'Who is? Who, sir?'

'Hartman. He's trying to kill me.'

The man's voice was low, raspy.

'Hartman? Who's Hartman?' Marty crouched down lower, nearer the man's mouth as he nodded weakly. 'You got a first name for him?' The man's eyes closed. Marty shook him a bit. 'Sir? This Hartman got a first name? Sir?'

'Not now, Marty.' He recognized Rob Peterson's voice as he felt the grip of his huge hands on his shoulders, pulling him up and away. 'You can ride with us. I'll let you know when.'

Stray spray from the fire hose hit him as it found its target, what was left of the still-blazing car. Marty watched in silence as the evidence got washed deep into the city's sewer system. We're nothing but a pack of cards. The kid had heard it wrong. '*You're* nothing but a pack of cards.'

'Excuse me?' said Alvarez who had snuck up from someplace behind him.

'*Alice in Wonderland*. Used to read it to my kids. You read it?'

Alvarez shook his head. 'Think I saw the movie once.'

'Whoever wrote it was doing a lot of whatever passed for acid back in the day.'

'He could probably tell you who wrote it.' Alvarez beckoned to where the paramedics were gurneying the injured guy towards their truck. 'Got a hit on the license plate, found it blown halfway down the block. If that car's his, he's a rare documents dealer. Clark Houseman.'

'Documents?'

'Yeah. Manuscripts, books, that kind of thing.'

'What the hell has that got to do with yesterday? Peter Gudsen, Bobbi Lomax, they're connected to finance. Property. Gone bad.'

'I know. Maybe this guy Houseman was an investor.'

'One of the disgruntled three thousand?'

'Could be. Or maybe just a passer by?'

'He's convinced someone's trying to kill him.'

'He said that?'

'Yeah. Some guy called Hartman.'

Al beckoned to what was left of the sports car. 'He might have a point.'

'You can't have it both ways.'

'I guess not.'

'Hartman. Could be the best lead in twenty-four hours. He on the list?'

'The investors list.'

'Don't remember seeing it. I'll check later.'

'Sooner the better. I'll run it by dispatch. See if anything pops their end.'

Marty beckoned for Al to follow Peterson into the back of the ambulance, but before Al could step up inside the truck Marty grabbed his sleeve, held him back. 'Al.' Al stepped closer. 'Page me if you get something.'

'Yeah, you too.'

5

Al looked over at Houseman, his arm urgently being pumped full of something by Peterson. Silently, Al looked back at Marty. His eyes said it all. Marty shrugged, shook his head. 'Who knows if he'll make it.'

Al was up in the ambulance now. 'Let's hope he does. We could sure do with some answers. Anything.'

Marty smiled up at him. 'Answers aren't always the answer.'

2

July 4th 1982

Las Vegas

'"Hold your tongue!" said the Queen, turning purple.

'"I won't!" said Alice.

'"Off with her head!" the Queen shouted at the top of her voice. Nobody moved.

'"Who cares for you?" said Alice (she had grown to her full size by this time). "You're nothing but a pack of cards!"'

His head rested on her swollen stomach. It was a good place to be. She stroked his hair as he read. He loved being all the characters.

'He kicked! Did you feel it, Clark?'

'No.' He looked up at her as she wriggled back up the bed toward the headrest. She almost blended in with the walls. Everything was beige and brown and tangerine. He followed her, until they were both leant against the headboard. At the foot of the room's huge palatial bed, their toddler, Jack, played with colored wooden blocks, oblivious to Wonderland and the advent of a sibling. Edie put Clark's hand on her stomach.

'And again.'

'Ssssh, let me feel.'

He waited. Nothing. 'I told you he'd like it, didn't I?'

'You don't know it's a boy. It might be a girl.'

'No, it's a boy. And he'll be a writer.'

'A writer? Maybe a professor?' said Edie.

'Sure, better job security I guess.'

A knock on the door. The sitter. The usual instructions done, they were out and down the dark, narrow corridor, towards the elevator, Clark carrying his attaché case with him. Edie squeezed right up next to him. Edie had never been out of Canyon County before and he wanted to show her a good time. But first, business. And then they'd be able to splash on an upgraded room, a swanky restaurant and maybe even a show.

Downstairs, Edie stood amazed, soaking it all in. It was so noisy. So bright.

'We'll go on the slots later. After dinner.'

'Do you think we should?' Her teeth held onto her bottom lip.

'When in Vegas.'

She smiled, then suddenly gripped his arm and sunk into his side as if trying to make herself invisible.

'You OK?'

She peeked out around him. 'I thought I saw Disciple Arbuth-not's wife.'

'Really? Well, if we see anyone from Mission, here of all places, as long as they keep our secret we'll keep theirs. Anyway, it's business,' he rattled the attaché case. 'Unavoidable – not my fault the dealer's in Vegas.'

'I got us a surprise, Clark.'

'Oh yeah?' Clark loathed surprises.

'I called the concierge while you were sleeping.'

'You did? What is it?'

'That would be telling. You'll see later. I almost forgot you had an appointment.'

'See, you are having a good time despite the fact we're in Sin City.'

She watched the room full of people, money being lost and won, and smiled, reluctant to admit he was right.

'Just be sure, when we get back, you don't let slip where we've been. Not to anyone, especially your sister, or your folks.'

'I won't.'

It was a short walk across the casino floor and through the casino complex to the dealer's. He'd persuaded Edie to stop at a dress store en route, and left her there. He preferred to do business without an audience. A few minutes early, he wandered around the store. It was full to bursting with all kinds of original movie posters, sporting and music memorabilia, the usual slew of Elvis photos, most of which showed him in the Vegas years: overweight, clammy and in a clingy white spangled catsuit. Here, at the back of the store, was a whole different world. It was like he'd stepped into an Upper East Side old-school gentleman's club, all mahogany panels and tan leather Chesterfields. The front of the store, the Elvis and friends section, was full of tourists, anxious to grab a bit of Vegas, a tacky slice of history to take home, something, anything, for twenty bucks. Back here there wasn't anything less than two hundred. Clark gazed in through the mesh of an oversized bookcase. It was locked. Name after famous literary name crammed its shelves. Beside it, a small reading table. He rested his attaché case on it. Snapped it open. As he did so, Dougie Wild, the store owner, larded into view, puffing on a huge unlit stogie.

'Hey, you must be Cliff.'

'Yes, sir.'

Dougie Wild grabbed Clark's hand and shook it. Hard. 'Call me Dougie. You could have just sent these. I've a good courier, very reliable, the rest are all crooks. I'll give you his details.' Dougie looked Clark up and down. 'Vegas is a long way across the desert.'

'It's good to get out of town, Dougie.' Clark would have preferred to call him sir or Mr Wild.

'Good to see who you're dealing with, huh? I'm the same.'

Clark smiled, nodded.

'It's good to look 'em in the eye.'

Dougie took a drag on his huge cigar, seemingly unaware it was unlit. 'What you got for me, then, son?' He looked down at the writing desk where Clark had laid out the books, now unwrapped from their protective covers. Silently puffing, Dougie picked each one up and scrutinized it: spine, binding, inside, back cover, frontispiece, random pages. All of it. Clark knew better than to speak. 'Not bad, not bad at all. Do you ever get any signed copies? Dedicated?'

'Novels?'

'Yeah.'

'Not really. They're not really big on fiction . . . it's not really encouraged.'

'Oh yeah, I forgot. What's the Faith big on then, besides Bibles?'

'Religious documents, manuscripts, hymn books, prayer books – all that kind of stuff.'

'Sounds kinda dull.'

'Hence, I'm selling here not there.'

'Sure, I understand. I remember reading that guy – their Supreme Leader – has a secret vault stuffed full of documents no one's ever seen. Doesn't let anyone in. More secrets than the Vatican.'

'So I hear.'

'Makes you wonder what they're hiding, doesn't it?'

Clark spotted Edie pacing up and down outside. 'How much, Dougie, for the books?'

'Four fifty.'

'Like you said, Dougie, we're a long way across the desert.'

Dougie followed Clark's gaze out the window to Edie. She waved at them, smiling, friendly. Dougie waved back. Winked at Clark. 'Having fun, ain't ya, son?'

'Seven hundred. They're all first editions, Dougie. They're worth a good eighteen hundred dollars retail.'

'You wanna get retail on 'em, son, then you need to go buy yourself a store.' Dougie took out a wad of cash, and with a dramatic flourish slowly and loudly counted $450 on top of the books.

Clark didn't touch it. Instead, he turned back to the bookcase. 'Let's say five hundred — to mark our new relationship — and I'll take that Poe. First edition, I'm assuming.'

Dougie balked, emitting a strange grunting sound through the cigar. 'That's worth five hundred.'

'Retail.'

Dougie smiled. Touché. 'Rob a man, why don't you?' He took a bunch of keys from his pants pocket and moved toward the cabinet.

*

As Edie and Clark moved away from the store, hand in hand, the Poe stashed safely in the attaché case and the five hundred, in fifties, buried in his wallet, a voice called out behind them. Clark turned. Dougie was standing at the door rejigging a display case. 'Hey Cliff, this is Vegas – don't forget, everything that glitters isn't gold!'

Clark looked back, nodded, smiled. 'See you again, Dougie.'

Edie looked up at him. 'Why's he calling you Cliff?'

Clark shrugged. 'Who knows what he's got in that cigar.'

*

Inside the auditorium, the curtain still down, the sound of a happy holiday crowd eager to have even more fun. Clark looked at the sign at the side of the stage: *The Strange Cabinet of Dr Marvin Mesmer*. He turned to Edie. 'Some surprise. A magician?'

'I thought it looked like fun. You like magic don't you, Clark?'

Clark raised his eyebrows at her. He had been doing magic tricks since he was about three. Watching someone else doing them, probably badly, was not his idea of fun. 'OK, but if it's no good we're leaving in the break.'

'There isn't a break,' said Edie. 'It's eighty minutes straight through.'

Clark rolled his eyes, burrowed down into his seat. At least he might be able to catch up on his sleep. It had been a real long drive. The sound of barking woke him up. Human barking. Up on the stage a group of volunteers were being activated by Dr Mesmer. Not so much a magician, but a hypnotist. Judging by the raucous reaction from the crowd, these were their friends up on stage. Clark stared open-mouthed at the spectacle. He watched Mesmer as he touched each volunteer to activate them, connecting with them as he stared into their eyes, enforcing ideas and suggestions with his gentle but authoritative tone which Clark assumed must be peppered with control words. Watched him until two grown men were waltzing beautifully together, joining the woman on all fours, barking, scurrying, snarling as another man and woman swam furiously away from an imaginary shark while the theme tune from *Jaws* played loudly in the background. Clark leaned in towards Edie. Hopefully she was enjoying it. She didn't answer him. Or move when he touched her. Clark shook his head, bemused. Edie was under Mesmer's spell. Whatever that spell was, Clark was amazed that it wasn't a sham. Edie was suggestible. An easier mark. At least he wasn't under. Or was he?

3

Marty watched as the ambulance, siren on, edged its way out through the hastily abandoned cruisers and fire trucks and past the gathering news crews. Al was always better with victims than he was. Hell, Al was better with everyone than he was. Probably why he was still married to wife number one despite the onslaught of four kids and the recent arrival of a high-maintenance mother-in-law from Puerto Rico.

'Hey, Detective, you need this?' Whittaker from the crime lab was a few feet away from him holding out a bunch of evidence bags and a pair of oversized tweezers in the familiar sealed baggie.

'I know beauticians get through less tweezers than this,' said Marty.

'Yeah, and they make more money.'

'Tell me about it.' Marty looked around. The whole street was buzzing now with cops, fire guys. And there were at least ten times as many gawkers. And hacks. Bad news travels fast. Through the noise of all the engines and fire-truck pumps he could hear the hacks calling his name. He ignored them.

Whittaker handed him the kit. 'Me and the boys were still over at the Gudsen site when we got the call. We're gonna be there 'til at least tomorrow. That thing sure did its job alright.'

'The nail bomb?'

Whittaker nodded slowly. 'Yep.' He didn't have to explain its horrors. Marty had been the first detective on the scene yesterday. Al was late in. He'd gone to the dentist. Lucky him. The bomb had gone off in the corridor, right at the entrance to Gudsen's new office, blown him from one side of it to the other. The Forsythe Building was old. Practically ancient for this town. Mid-Victorian. Its strong thick walls had ensured the explosion's shockwaves and shrapnel had nowhere to go but back in on itself and whatever poor fucker was in the vicinity. In that space it was like the bomb was a boomerang, it exploded out and then came right back in again. Gudsen didn't stand a chance. And whoever planted the bomb didn't want him to. Nails in a bomb aren't decoration. They're there to kill. Like switchblades traveling at 900 mph. He remembered Big Tex from the bomb squad telling him that yesterday. Tex loved bombs, talked about them as if they were living breathing things. He could wax lyrical on their beauty for hours. Tex's guys had swept the rest of the building a couple of times before giving it the all-clear. That was before they had got the Bobbi Lomax call and had to take off over there.

One of the nails had gone right through Gudsen's eye, the explosion forcing it into his brain. The ME said he'd died within seconds. Not quick enough, thought Marty, the pain would have been unbearable. Like Bobbi Lomax, Peter Gudsen must have unwittingly tucked the white shoe-box bomb, all tied up with red gift ribbon, into his chest. A fatal move. There'd been no nails in the Bobbi Lomax bomb, close proximity had been enough to kill her. No nails in Houseman's either by the looks of it. The guy was lucky to survive this, thought Marty, particularly if he'd been in the car with it when it exploded. A nail bomb inside a car? Instant death. If that's even Houseman. Guy's got nine lives, if so. When

15

they'd moved him onto the stretcher, Marty had noticed them check for the victim's wallet, for ID. There wasn't one. Maybe it was in his car.

The nails told Marty one thing. Someone hated Peter Gudsen more than they hated Bobbi Lomax and Houseman. Lomax had a husband. Things in the Lomax household had been strained. Financial meltdown, disintegrating business, maybe even bankruptcy on the cards. And his business partner, ex-business partner, was Gudsen. Marty smiled. Too neat, too easy, too obvious. Especially if you add in Houseman and his claims about Hartman. Marty had spoken to Arnold Lomax yesterday, wasn't your typical wife killer, all crocodile tears and blubbed regrets. His tears seemed genuine. But, even so, Marty told him not to leave town. Just to stay somewhere a bomber might not find him, with a random cousin or something. He'd also warned him that with Gudsen and Bobbi Lomax both dead it was probably a wise idea to tell his family, friends and colleagues to get out of town, change their patterns of behavior and generally use extreme caution. So, was this Houseman guy another friend or associate of Lomax? If he was, he obviously didn't get the get-out-of-town-now memo.

Marty followed a trail of what looked like confetti, right up to the trunk of the car, the lid blown clean off. He peered in. A bunch of papers, charred and burned, floated in enough water for a child's paddling pool. Documents dealer? Wasn't that what Al had said? Strange place to put your documents, particularly if they were valuable. And surely they would be if you were a documents dealer. People were dumb. What if someone rear-ended you? 'Hey Whittaker, get some pictures of this for me, would ya?'

'Sure.'

Whittaker moved slowly, cautiously, over from where he was

picking up short lengths of wire and other bomb fragments strewn across the pavement. Just as Marty had, he instinctively followed the main paper trail from the centre of the street to the trunk. Shot off a few of the interior. 'I can't get much in there, Mart, not with all that water. Don't take anything out of there, will you?' Marty shot him his how-dumb-do-you-think-I-look glare. Whittaker smiled, raised his eyebrows: 'I'll have the car taken to the Shed as quick as I can. I'll have to drain the water all out of there, see what we got. I don't want to destroy anything the water hasn't already.'

'Thanks.' Marty bent down, tweezered up a piece of the confetti, no bigger than a thumbnail. He looked at it. Charred around the edges, and on it, handwriting in a sepia-colored ink. 'What do you think this is?' He pushed it towards Whittaker's nose.

Whittaker peered at it. 'Old letter or something. See how brown the ink is, rusty-looking?'

'Yeah.'

'That fancy writing looks like it's a good century old, at least. Might even be older than the city.' He laughed and shook his head at the thought.

Paper older than a city, stored in the trunk of a sports car. Now, that was asking for trouble. Water and paper, never a good mix past the pulping stage. 'Shit,' Marty mumbled to himself as the water reminded him of something. He shouted over to a uniformed cop standing guard near the crime guys' truck. 'Hey! Get on the radio, right now. Get someone from the City on the line. I need to shut down the block, the sewer. Shut off everyone's water.' The kid looked confused. 'This block. The sewer, go through dispatch. Quick! Before our evidence gets washed the other side of the canyon.'

Right then, before Marty had time to dodge it, a news camera was pushed in his face and a microphone shoved towards his mouth and the familiar female voice said urgently, 'With a third victim, the city in fear, its people need answers. Do you have any answers, Detective?' And, before he could even think of answering her, 'Are you losing control of this case, Detective Sinclair?'

'Get off my crime scene, Patricia. If you want answers, justice, it's best you don't destroy the evidence.'

The microphone seemed to be almost in his mouth now and then it was gone. And just as quickly as she'd appeared, Patricia Kent also disappeared, followed by her cameraman, to where, right at the edge of the cordon, the Sheriff had materialized. Marty caught it, just a sleight of hand as a man in a black suit pressed a sheet of paper into the Sheriff's pocket as, around them, a clutch of advisors and City Hall hangers-on pushed forward. Fast approaching them a swarm of hacks, cameras and pens ready, desperate for any broadcastable or printable clue. Marty didn't fully see the face, just enough of the retreating shoulder and slack jawline to recognise the man in the black suit as Duncan Hemslow, the Faith's press officer.

Marty went back to work. A few minutes later he noticed the Sheriff, flanked by the Captain, hold aloft the thick computer printout with the names of all the investors in Lomax's soon-to-be defunct property company. All three thousand of them. When Marty had left the precinct, less than thirty minutes ago, that very same printout was sat on top of his desk. Jesus. On the wind he heard the Sheriff say that these would be their first suspects. Marty wondered if that was what Hemslow's note had said, or if the Sheriff had come to that conclusion all on his own. If the latter, it was a good thing the Sheriff got voted in, because if he'd been relying on his detective skills he wouldn't be running security in a mall. And, thought Marty, relieved, if you get voted in, at least you can get voted out.

Marty's pager beeped, damn thing. He popped it out of his belt so he could read it better. He scrolled across the screen two slow words at a time.

> PATIENT CRITICAL. SEIZURES. BRAIN INJURY. I
> FORGOT: SHUT DOWN THE SEWER!

4

July 30th 1982

The Last Call Tavern high on the cross-county line, scores of miles away from Abraham City, had always been his favorite, a spit-and-sawdust dive where you could drink without fear of being seen by any of the Faithful. And if they were here, like Vegas, you'd be in an immediate secret society where no man spilled another man's secrets. The Faithful were great at keeping secrets. For Clark it was the best thing about them. He was drinking, like he did most every week, with his old school friend Kenny, the kind of guy who looks like he got lost on the way to the surf. They stood up at the bar drinking beer from long chilled glasses and feasted on unshelled nuts they cracked open themselves, dropping the shells on the floor to be ground underneath by another year's customers. Clark was trying to make sense of the Mesmer episode. Kenny looked doubtful. 'Sounds like a bad trip. I've got a buddy could get you pills that would do better.' Kenny always had a buddy that could get you something. Mostly illegal. 'Sounds like Mesmer's in the Order of the Twelve Disciples – they can tell you did something bad, just by looking at you.'

Clark smiled. 'God's Faithful Disciples?'

'Yeah, and they reckon they can do it without hypnosis.'

'So they'd have us believe.'

'Do you think it was real though, man? The hypnosis? Think people can really do that shit?'

Clark remembered Edie being under. He shook his head, lying. 'No, course not.'

Hours later they emerged bleary-eyed and blinking from the darkened bar into the blinding light of day. Across the street, Clark spotted a bookstore. 'That's new.'

'Yeah, opened a couple weeks back – when you were in Vegas.'

'I'm gonna take a look.'

As he moved away from Kenny, an attractive blonde got slowly out of her shiny black Trans Am, walked toward Betty May's beauty parlor. Kenny's eyes followed her. 'Take your time, man.'

*

Clark struggled with an armful of books towards the cashier, but as he moved through the narrow walkways piled to the rafters something on a shelf up high caught his eye. Edging nearer to take a closer look he kicked over a large bargain bin, accidentally tipping several books out onto the floor: *Valley of the Dolls, One Flew Over the Cuckoo's Nest* and some huge leather-bound volume. Clark stared down at it. Interesting. He bent down to pick it up. Slowly, incredulously, he began turning the pages. This is old, *real* old. It shouldn't be in this bin thing in a million years, obviously someone didn't know its value. An original 1638 King James Bible. Cambridge version. English Cambridge. Not Boston Cambridge. A smile crossed Clark's face. Printed in the city after a decades-long face-off between the university printers and the church who wanted full control of the good word. Finally, the university won and they set to printing. A major victory against the church's invidious rule. Clark stared at it. How did it wash up here? It'd certainly seen better days, but you'd look a little tatty after almost 350 years in existence. Clark was almost frightened to move in case he woke himself from this amazing dream. He turned it over in his hand considering its possibilities. He looked around to make sure no one was looking, then tucked it in at the bottom of the pile of books he'd already chosen. On top, he put *One Flew Over the Cuckoo's Nest*.

Clark stood at what passed for the cashier's desk. The teenage assistant looked up, and smiled. Probably pleased to see someone under sixty in the place. 'Did you find everything you were looking for today, sir?' Without waiting for a reply she began ringing up his purchases on the clunky old cash register.

'Yes, I think I got everything, thanks. Great store.'

'Glad you like it, it's my parents.' She picked up *One Flew Over the Cuckoo's Nest*. 'This is great. Did you see the movie?'

'Can't say I have.'

'The lunatics taking over the asylum?'

'That'll be the day,' said Clark.

She had reached the Bible. But Clark knew she had no idea what it really was – all she saw was a dusty old Bible. 'I've never been religious myself.'

'I'm finding, Karen . . .' She looked up, surprised. He indicated her silver necklace, which clearly spelled her name in swirly silver lettering. 'There's just not that many people loving Our Lord Jesus Christ these days. It was in the bargain bin.' He smiled at her. She touched her necklace, smiled back.

'Oh, the bargain bin? Those are two for a dollar.'

'Cool. Don't worry about a receipt.'

While Karen put everything else into a shiny plastic branded bag, Clark picked up a brown paper bag from the counter and carefully wrapped the Bible in it before tucking it safely under his arm.

Outside Kenny stood, almost draped, over the back of the car, still staring at any woman who passed or drove by. Clark half walked, half ran across the street from the bookstore. The plastic bag in one hand, the brown paper bag now clutched in the other. 'C'mon, let's go. Quick.'

'What's the rush, man?'

Clark looked back over the street toward the bookstore. Karen was looking out of the window. He smiled at her, she smiled back. Maybe even waved. Clark threw the plastic bag in the back seat. 'I just remembered I gotta pick Edie and the kids up from her sister's.'

He jumped into the driver's seat, put the wrapped Bible carefully on his lap. Kenny knew better than to ask. Clark reversed the car fast out of the spot, trying not to let the tires screech. As they left the town behind, Clark reached over, took a small breath-freshener spray out of the glove box. Sprayed once, twice and a third time for luck.

Kenny turned, smiled at him. 'Oh yeah, I forgot. You're tee-total.'

They passed a WELCOME TO CANYON COUNTY sign. Clark turned to him. 'Only in the Canyon . . .'

5

Halloween 1983

ICU, Lumina Hospital

The uniform stood aside. He was Ed Grady's kid. Ed had been on Homicide thirty years. Retired last year. Dropped dead the next day. Grady Jnr put his finger up to his lips. Ssssh. Marty looked at him. He nodded toward the corner of the room. Marty could see Al sitting and kind of slumped, his head drooping toward the sleeping patient. 'Hey buddy! Wake up!'

Al woke up fast then, disorientated, stared bewildered at Marty. 'You're in the hospital. But don't worry, you're OK. At least you were 'til you made contact with that metal bar.' Marty smiled at him.

'Funny, man. Real funny.' Al shook his head, rubbed at his fore-head. 'Must have nodded off.'

Marty turned to Grady Jnr. 'Thanks. For protecting both of them.'

'Protect and Serve, sir.' He had Ed's sense of humor. He was a good kid. Marty watched as he pulled the door shut behind him. His slight frame visible in its frosted glass.

Marty moved toward the bed. The patient was out cold, hooked up to a bunch of machines. Marty put his hand on Al's shoulder. 'I thought I'd drop by on my way back to the precinct. This day's not getting any better. And I can't say I'm looking for-ward to tomorrow.'

Al took several large swigs of the Pepsi he'd left on the patient's bedside cabinet. Marty saw him smiling to himself. 'Share the joke.'

Al turned to him, almost whispering. 'I was dreaming about it, that story.'

'What story?'

'*Alice in Wonderland.*'

'Did you raid the morphine cabinet again?' Marty raised his eyebrows questioningly at Al.

'I was chasing that girl.'

'Which girl?'

'Alice.'

'Did you catch her?'

'No, no I didn't.'

'Let's hope that's not an omen for the case.'

'And I thought you weren't the mumbo-jumbo, superstitious type, hey?'

'I have my moments.'

Al smiled. 'I remember seeing it now, a blaze of color, on a screen the size of the world. A treat with my Abuela Perez. Mann's Chinese. Sure was worlds away from ours. She couldn't speak a damn word of English but she laughed and gasped the whole way through, her giant bosom heaving up and down in the dark. I must have been three or four and, man, she lavished me with love and ice cream.'

'You were her favorite, huh? Grandma's favorite?'

'I guess. Some of those lines, I'd totally forgotten, until the dream just now. "Why is a raven like a writing desk?"'

'Why indeed,' said Marty as he watched Al's puzzled face try again to solve the first mystery he'd ever tried to.

A gentle voice interrupted their thoughts. 'Detectives. We have a message for you.' They looked around. A nurse in crisp whites and a tanned face peered in at them. 'A Mr Rogers?' They looked at one another. Who? 'He got a first name?' Marty asked.

'There's none on this.' She was right in front of them now, pushing the note towards them. Marty looked down at it, written in truly illegible medic's script. 'He asked if we'd ensure you didn't leave. He's coming to see you. It's urgent.' Marty looked at Al. Al looked back at him. Blank.

'Not a damn journalist?' said Marty.

'No, they're not allowed in the hospital,' said the nurse.

'That doesn't usually stop them, hey Al?'

A wave of recognition crossed Al's face. 'Rogers. Tommy. Bomb Squad.'

'Tommy, yeah, he could have said that, sure,' said the nurse. 'It's noisy out on the desk this evening.' She looked over at the patient. 'For obvious reasons.'

Marty nodded. He imagined how many calls they were getting. His own pager had beeped almost non-stop all day. 'Big Tex, that's what we call him. Well, you can let *him* in. Big guy. Hence the name.' He smiled at her. She smiled back. A good smile, thought Marty. Soothing. And she was pretty with it. And young. Too young. Maybe that's why she was still smiling.

He watched her as she made her way over to the patient's side.

Marty noticed Al's face was contorted. 'You OK, buddy?'

'I told her. No rice. Nothing spicy. Nothing fried. So she makes me a chimichanga with rice and refried beans. Maria's mother. Man, I been suffering two days. I should stretch my legs, walk around the room a little. Might help. Been sitting half the day.'

'Maybe she's trying to kill you?'

'You think?'

'Got life insurance?'

'No.'

'Don't. It'll just make her more determined.'

Al laughed.

'So, this is the book collector? It was his car?'

'No doubt about it. Clark Houseman. His wife was here earlier. She saw it on TV. Recognized the car. Mangled and everything. She said he always parks in the same place. Walks into town from there.'

'A creature of habit.'

'Guess so. Either that or a cheap SOB who doesn't like paying the city for parking.'

Marty smiled. 'I sent her home to get him some things. Thought it was better if it was only me here if he woke up.'

'Couldn't cope with a hysterical woman, huh?'

Al nodded. 'Not today, not with no sleep and my guts up in my mouth. Besides, maybe he has some information we could use.'

'Something he doesn't want his wife to hear. Is that what you're thinking, Al?'

'Yeah, maybe there's something going on here. With the bombings. Something else, besides financial. You know what I mean?'

'An affair?'

'Maybe.'

'She say anything worthwhile? The wife?'

'Husband is well in with the Church hierarchy. Been running his own business since he bailed out of college. Successful guy. Family man. Devoted to her and the kids. Provider. Y'know. The usual Faith husband.'

'How about the other victims, Al? She know any of them?'

'Nope. First time she saw or heard of Bobbi Lomax was on the news last night. They don't know Gudsen or Bobbi Lomax. And, Clark, the husband,' Al nodded over to the bed, 'he doesn't talk business at home, so she doesn't know the names of any of his business associates either.'

'Maybe he talks business someplace else? Maybe your hunch is right, he's got someone else he confides in?'

Al nodded his head in Houseman's direction. 'She was pretty adamant that he was a devoted husband.'

'That makes her hopeful. Not right. Did you ask her if she heard of anyone called Hartman?'

'She hadn't. What you thinking? He's some spurned husband. Getting revenge.'

'That would make sense. Except . . .'

'There's two bodies in the morgue that aren't Houseman.'

'I put a call out to dispatch. There's nothing on the record and nobody called Hartman in all of Canyon County.'

'Maybe you didn't hear the name right,' said Al.

'There goes our only lead.' Marty exhaled, exasperated. 'What was she like, the wife?'

Al laughed out loud. The pretty nurse turned to him. He shrugged apologetically at her and whispered to Marty, 'Not the type to kill three people.'

'Well, *try* and kill three people. This one's still alive.'

'Just.'

'And you know as well as I do there *is* no type. Haven't you noticed? Everyone but us is completely insane and most of 'em look completely normal?'

'You got that right.' A Texan drawl. Big Tex. They turned to see him filling out the doorway. 'Everyone but us *is* insane.'

'Hey big guy.' Marty stretched out his hand for the no-nonsense handshake he knew was coming.

'Good to see you, Marty. Sorry I missed you earlier.'

'I had to go up to the Mission. Interview some bigwigs. Correction. Make an appointment to interview them. It's a while since I've been up there.'

'This is turning into a habit, hey Tex?' said Al.

'Yeah and not a good one. No offence, guys.'

'None taken,' said Al.

'Three bombings in two days?' said Marty.

'Place is getting like Beirut,' Big Tex said. 'What you boys got so far?'

'A whole bunch of nothing, by the looks of it,' said Al.

'Financials, possible affairs.' Marty shook his head. 'One too many possibilities.'

'As per. That Houseman?'

'Yeah.'

They all looked back to the bed where Houseman lay bandaged and motionless. Tex looked like he wanted to say something. Instead, he just nodded.

'Everyone's telling me all these three victims: Bobbi Lomax, Peter Gudsen, Clark Houseman. Well, they're all stand-up citizens. Who'd want to hurt any of them?'

'Maybe they're just collateral,' Al pitched in. 'Perhaps the bomber's after something else. Someone else.'

Marty looked at him. 'Well, he sure is taking his time getting there. And today, over at the Houseman site there's a whole load of witnesses all saying different things – He was walking up the hill, down the hill. He just got to the car and the bomb went off. He

29

was in the car and the bomb went off. Someone saw him find a package on the seat of the car. Someone else thought they saw it on the seat. Another one thought they saw him drop it and then it exploded. Someone else saw him crouch down and pick it up . . . Hopeless.'

'Well, all of those *could* be true.' Big Tex smiled.

'Sure,' said Marty. 'But not all at the same time.'

Tex laughed. 'You got that right.' He peered around Marty's shoulder to the bed. The nurse had finished, she was moving towards them now, towards the door. Tex smiled at her, nodded politely: 'Ma'am.' If he'd been wearing his Stetson he would have lifted it for her. As she left the room Tex shook his head in quiet appreciation.

'Makes you wanna get ill, don't it, big guy?' Marty slapped him on the back.

'Critically.' Big Tex's eyes followed her outside. 'What about him? Houseman. He gonna live?'

Al nodded. 'They've put him in an induced coma. He was fitting, frothing at the mouth and everything. The docs said he's messed up a bit, internally, also his leg's half blown off, but the chest injury looked worse than it was. He's going to survive if they can keep the brain swelling down and can operate on the leg in time.'

'Good,' said Tex. ''Cos that guy's going to the chair. I damn well hate it when they die before they fry.'

'Tex, you been holding out on us this whole time?'

Marty registered Al's shock, but didn't reflect it. 'OK Tex, spill it.'

6

August 21st 1982

Houseman Residence

Outside, in the street, nothing stirred. Not the neighbors, not their dogs nor that wretched motorbike belonging to Cisco, the next-door neighbor's kid. And, inside, Jack was asleep upstairs. Clark was sat downstairs on the sofa, Edie's hand outstretched in his, her head tilted right back on the sofa's edge. He stared at her. No sign of movement underneath the tightly closed lids. Was he imagining it, or was her breathing getting shallower, deeper? He had no idea what to do with her next. Slowly, tentatively, he said: 'First I'm going to ask you to kiss me.' Edie burst out laughing. 'Edie!'

'It'll never work, I'm not under.'

'You're just not taking it seriously.'

'Well, it's not serious, is it? Just a load of hocus-pocus. I guess I'm obviously not the receptive kind. Or whatever kind you have to be to want to be "under".'

He had to stop himself from telling her she'd been under in Vegas. And that if she'd been under there, she could be under here. It's just he wasn't Marvin Mesmer. Someone with years of practice behind him. He was just a beginner. But he wanted to catch up, to learn, as fast as he could. He'd always been a quick learner.

'Well if you would just focus a minute, stop giggling, I'd be able to do it.'

'I don't want to be hypnotized as me, can't you hypnotize me so I can be someone amazing, someone beautiful? Princess Grace, Farrah Fawcett.'

'Farrah Fawcett?' Clark's face lit up. 'Now there's an idea.'

'Clark!'

'What? You said it.'

'But I didn't mean it. You should love me for who I am.'

'I do. But I love Farrah for who she is, too. *Really* love her.'

Edie threw the cushions at him. One slid along the corridor and landed right at the entrance to his den, its door firmly shut. When he got back into the room he heard Edie's unmistakable purr-like snores. She must have had a day of it with Jack. Well, at least he'd get to watch what he wanted on TV. He sat back down next to her, softly, so as not to wake her up. He clicked the TV on. Pop music blared out. He quickly hit the remote, watching Edie as he did so. He turned down the volume, just enough to drown out her snoring, but not high enough to wake her. It was some variety show. Looked like a rerun. Onscreen, a bunch of beardy guys in satin shirts and tight pants were singing something he kind of recognized. Next to them, in a retro '60s nod, five girls were dancing in miniskirts and knee-high boots whilst a psyche-delic background twirled around and around behind them. Clark stared past the guys, towards the girls to where the background pulled him in deeper. He stared at it, into its centre, as it turned around and around and around. In the room, he could hear Edie's breathing, in and out, in and out, the clock in the corner of the room, tick, tock, tick, tock and, outside, the weeping birch with its long draped branches rustling in the night breeze. It was al-most like a lullaby. He surrendered himself to it and soon he was drifting off someplace, someplace far away in time.

Inside the sparsely decorated room, he watched his boy-self, sat uncomfortable, hunched over, at a small table doubling as a desk. A calendar on the wall marked the year, 1968. The month, December. One of the coldest on record. On the desk were schoolbooks, none of them open. He started to walk towards young Clark, but the sound of an argument drifting from downstairs disturbed him as it crept up through the ill-fitting floorboards. As it got louder there was no escaping it, no matter how much both Clarks put their hands over their ears. Glass shattered. He hoped she wasn't cut again. Clark flung open the door, heavy footsteps on glass crunching along the downstairs corridor. Fast, angry feet on the stairs towards him. He stood, as if frozen, unable to move as his father appeared in front of him. He stopped, glared at Clark, maybe he had gotten too big to hit. Finally. His father mumbled something, Clark thought he could smell liquor on his breath. But he didn't drink. Or, at least, Clark had never seen him. Clark looked back to young Clark sat bent over his desk, too frightened to even look up. Clark closed the door and crept downstairs towards where he could hear his mother sobbing.

She was crouched over, housecoat on. Around her was chaos, tumbled furniture, liquid seeping into the carpet and at her feet a picture frame. Before he felt his feet move, he was crouched down beside her picking up shards of glass splintered out of the frame. She looked up at him. Her face so lined with woe, he feared if she smiled at him it would crack open like the desert floor. He reached out his hand to dry his mother's tears. As he did so, he noticed that his hand was small, a child's. Clark looked behind him to the door where he'd come in. His adult-self was standing there, watching. His mother took his hand, brought it to her lips, kissed it. Tears rolled down her cheeks. He saw that she had the frame's photo in her hand, unscrunching it. She looked right into Clark's eyes. 'He hates me.'

'No he doesn't, Mommy.'

'Hates who I am, hates that my blood's tainted. Your blood's tainted.'

His boy-self had heard other arguments. Knew what 'tainted' meant. Grandpa had three wives, not just one, and all at the same time. He had heard them shout words like 'wrong', 'disapprove', 'embarrassment', 'my position' and a load more. He knew there was a name for it, having several wives, but couldn't remember it. Something beginning with Polly, like the girl's name. He looked up at his mother. 'I hate Father. He makes you sad.' He smiled at her. Hoped she might smile back. But instead, she started yelling at him.

'Clark! Oh no, what on earth have you done!?' His mother's face filled with anguish and she grabbed his hand, pulled it towards her. He could see blood running from it. He watched as she turned his hand over, prised it open. Several shards of the glass had pierced the skin deep and blood oozed from each cut. And then he heard another voice. Another woman. And she was shouting also.

'Clark! Clark! Wake up. Clark!'

Edie was staring right into his face, her eyes wide, urging.

'Clark, you're bleeding. Wake up.'

He saw there was blood on his trousers, on the couch.

He looked down as she opened his bloody palm. The small glass had shattered and broken in pieces. Leftover juice ran into the cuts. He couldn't feel anything. He'd felt more before from paper cuts. Movement on the TV caught his eye, a commercial for painkiller. Pain-free in minutes seemed to be the mantra. Pain-free. He remembered the psychedelic movement on the screen, the lulling repetition of the sounds around him. He looked back down at his hand. A nasty cut. But it was pain-free. Relaxation. Repetition. Suggestion and control. Just like Dr Mesmer. Clark jumped up from the couch.

'Where are you going? Let me dress that for you.' Edie was standing up now, moving behind him, the pieces of broken glass in her palm.

'Not now, Edie.'

'But . . .'

'I'll do it myself, downstairs.'

He could hear her say something, but in a moment he was at the end of the corridor, unlocking the door and down the stairs to his basement workshop. But not before he'd firmly closed the door behind him. And bolted it from the inside.

7

November 1st 1983

Residence of Peter Gudsen (Deceased)

By the time their car rolled up outside the Gudsen home the double shot of Advil was relaxing Marty's stiff neck. He'd slept the night in his desk chair and let Al crash on the makeshift bed made of vinyl-covered cushions Marty had salvaged from a '50s sofa which had been headed for the dumpster outside his building. Marty had used it as a bed for months in his apartment, right after the divorce. That had been the sum of his forays into furniture acquisition. He spent most of his time at the station and when he wasn't there he was over at Murphy's Sports Bar, a block down from the station and the only place serving booze for a good three miles, except the Hilton and that was too pricey. Murphy's had comfortable bar stools, a reasonable selection of low-alcohol beer, a TV and home-cooked food. What more could a divorced man ask for, Marty always said, except for the company of a wild woman and stronger beer.

Outside the Gudsen home there was nowhere to park. The family and friends' cars were lined up along the street and in a cluster outside the overflowing drive. Marty hated being near the bereaved, couldn't bear to hear their questions of why, see their tears, their shaking hands and heaving hearts. It made him re-member and he didn't want to have to remember.

'What do you want me to ask?' Al said, half turned towards him, left hand still on the wheel.

'The usual. But right now, she's a possible suspect, so let's see how she reacts when you suggest there might be another woman in her husband's life.'

'You think it's a case of find the lady?'

Marty smiled. 'It's a good possibility.'

'You're not going with Big Tex's theory?'

'I want to hear all the theories, you know that.'

'We got a lot of witnesses to the Houseman bomb.'

'Contradicting Big Tex, most of 'em. And until Houseman's out of a coma we won't be able to hear what he's got to say about any of it.'

'There's been no more bombs.'

'It's ten in the morning.'

'You waiting for another boom, Marty?'

'Yeah, but I'm not praying for one. In the meantime, let's see if we can beat the ticking clock.'

Marty flicked the car door open. 'See if you can find out from the widow Gudsen about their lifestyle, particularly the luxe. Anything they might be spending their money on or where they might be hiding it, instead of putting it in the bank, out of sight of the IRS and out of the reach of the investors.'

'You think it's fraud? The money thing?'

'Could be. I'd sure like to know how a property company suddenly collapses owing a million to several thousand investors, before it's even built one house.'

'I've already subpoenaed all their financial records.'

'Good. Make sure you get a copy of any wills. Or get the name of the family lawyer. See if it's been updated recently.'

'Anything else?'

'Ask if she's ever heard of anyone called Hartman. But let's see what the widow might say right now, a day into the rest of her life.'

'Hopefully something that might help us find the bomber.'

'Or help find the next victim before the bomber does.'

'Let's hope that clock's not ticking too fast, man.'

'Let's hope. C'mon, let's see what the temperature's like in here.'

*

Inside the hallway a group of young people stood quietly drinking fruit punch. Marty could smell its familiar sticky sweetness from a few paces. A baby-faced boy, his face covered in peach-fuzz, led them through into the living room, Al following behind him, Marty bringing up the rear. Inside, a large group of adults were in various stages of productivity. In the open-plan kitchen several ladies were desperately making quiet small talk whilst cutting, chopping, baking and juicing. A group of young men, members of the Faithful, stood in a line like watchful crows, murmuring quietly next to a telephone awaiting its inevitable ring. On the couch, a pretty brunette in her thirties sat hand in hand with a Faith Father, his black suit and tie his recognizable garb, not just for mourning. On the large armchair next to them an elderly man sat staring blankly into the TV's dark screen, a large white handkerchief crumpled in his hand.

A few paces ahead of peach-fuzz boy, a curvy redhead in Kelly-green slacks and a pale chiffon blouse was moving toward the kitchen area carrying a heavy-looking earthenware dish, its contents smothered by tin foil. Her figure-hugging slacks marked her out as an outsider and when she spoke, in a heavy Brooklyn accent, Marty smiled knowingly to himself and heard her with one ear whilst listening to Al introduce them to the widow Gudsen with the other. Green slacks woman was Marion. She was a neighbor. Opposite. She explained to the women that she'd been over yesterday to give her condolences to Betty. How shocking it all was. Here of all places. Him of all men. Overnight she'd made this pumpkin pie. It was Little Peter's favorite.

Marty figured Little Peter must be one of the deceased's four kids, whose professionally framed pictures took up most of the wall at the opposite end of the room. He recognized the other kids from the hallway. Suits and all. He looked around the room: no signs of ostentatious wealth. A few inexpensive ornaments and a large crystal vase, but that was about it. As his eyes scanned the room Marion walked past him. Marty noticed she wasn't wearing a wedding ring. Big house, the one opposite, for a single woman. A divorcee abandoned in the desert? Or perhaps she had done the abandoning and was looking to get as far from Brooklyn as possible. If so, she'd picked a good spot. Marty thought he'd knock on her door right after. He knew from experience that men don't always confide in their spouses, especially if what they had to impart was detrimental to the family and to their own status within it. If the neighbor was a curvy redheaded divorcee she might well be a pleasurable shoulder to cry on. In a place where everyone knew everyone else from birth and beyond, the New York divorcee might be the best secret-keeper in town.

Al was sitting down now, next to the widow, taking out his notebook and pen. The Faith Father remained, resolute and unmoving, on her other side. As Marty backed away from the couch he heard himself saying, 'Ma'am, I'm sorry for your loss,' and something along the lines of, 'We'll find whoever did this. The detective will just ask you a few questions.' His back to them now, he heard her say, 'I don't know who would want to do this terrible, terrible act, Detective. Peter was a man of God, a good man.'

If only he had a dollar for every time he'd heard that.

8

Clark's Den, Houseman Residence

It was starting to sting now, bad, as he ran it under the workshop tap, cold at first, growing steadily hotter until it was scalding. Clark bit his tongue as sweat popped out of his pores and ran down his forehead.

Trying to hold his hand still under the tap, he crouched down under the sink, reaching blind into the back of the cupboard for the first-aid kit he knew was there somewhere, unused, amongst all the other things he kept there, most of them hidden from anyone that might breach the lock on the door and find themselves in his workshop. Edie knew not to come in here. Ever. But it didn't stop her from trying. Knocking on the door, day and night, trying to entice him to open up with offers of refreshments of all kinds. And sometimes even without the pretence, just to ask simply: 'What are you doing in there, Clark?' It was almost a game now. The only time she'd been in the cellar was when they'd viewed the house and back then the vendor's boxes of junk had been piled so high around the room you could barely see the walls. That was four years ago.

His searching hand hit the familiar cold steel of his electroplating machine. Over the twelve years he'd owned it, his second, it had made him a lot of money, but so had the first until it had burnt out. He was thankful Americans still loved their coins. And even more thankful that they were still relatively easy to alter in order to take something barely worth the metal it was printed on and make it worth hundreds and sometimes thousands of dollars. Last week, as he'd slid the machine back into its hiding place after using it to alter a common 1912 penny he'd already sold to a New York collector as its far more valuable and rare cousin, he'd seen the Target-branded first-aid kit behind it. Now his fingers landed on its plastic carry handle and he yanked it up and out from behind the electro-plater.

Twenty minutes later he was back at the sink, looking for a cloth to clean up the mess he'd made. He looked down at the bandage. The bleeding had taken a while to stop and now little pinpricks of blood were appearing through the gauze and heavily spun bandage. He'd sunk four painkillers with a flat Dr Pepper chaser slugged out of a can that had sat on his work counter for a few weeks, but it was still hurting like hell. He looked down at where the bloodied tweezers sat in the sink surrounded by splashes of blood. He'd pulled two fragments of the glass out with those and it didn't feel like there was any more in there. He'd go to County in the morning, but his amateur job would do for tonight. Tonight he didn't want to wait hours for a few stitches and a morphine shot. He just wanted the pain to go away. Now. Upstairs, he hadn't felt any pain, not until a few minutes after Edie had shook him out of whatever place his brain had ventured to. Perhaps if he could mesmerize himself now, not accidentally but intentionally, he could get the pain to go away again. Even just until the painkillers kicked in. It was a process, he knew that. A process that had structure and order. It wasn't called a routine for nothing. He'd witnessed Dr Mesmer's routine and upstairs with Edie he'd somehow managed to put himself into some kind of trance. To repeat that surely he just had to figure out what the elements were and in what precise order they worked. Clark smiled to himself as he thought that the one element he shouldn't forget was a control word to wake himself up out of whatever altered state he might get himself into. It had been a trip, but he didn't want to be hypnotized forever.

He pulled a sheet of paper out of the notepad on the desk he'd made from an old door and a couple of tea-chests and wrote a list:

1. Contact/connection with subject/self.
2. Voice. Commanding. Alluring/beguiling and V. Imp: monotone.
3. Suggestion.
4. Distancing from the everyday.
5. Control word.

He read the list again, adding 'But not too far' to Number 4: 'Distancing from the everyday.' When he was on his calling in England for the Faith, he had snuck away from the fellow Follower who shadowed him everywhere, met a girl in a Bath pub and dropped acid with her in the back of her father's Mini. It took him a week to recover from that most spectacular of trips. He knew where the mind needed to go. Far, but not too far. He didn't want to be sprinting naked around Mission Square.

He could make it work, he knew he could. After all, order and control were already the fabric of his life. He made another list.

1. Tape deck.
2. Blank cassette or one to record over.
3. Microphone.
4. Earphones.

43

5. Batteries, in case of power out.
6. Mesmerizing lullaby.

He had numbers 1 to 5 not so far from his desk.

Number 6. The mesmerizing word-lullaby might be the stumbling block.

He was sure that it was the music and staring into that spinning vortex that had somehow worked together and mesmerized him. He considered replacing number 6 with music, but didn't think he had anything in his hidden stash of rock music tapes that would cut it. He would have to make up the words himself. Write them and record them and leave a gap of at least five minutes blank on the tape and then put the control word at the end of that time, partly to make sure he would be able to snap himself out of it, but also to ensure that he left five minutes for a short trip to who knew where.

He'd spent ten awkward one-handed minutes assembling everything he needed, including a short, hopefully hypnotic few minutes of self-spoken 'lullaby' that would cover numbers 2 to 5 of his first list. It was all he could do to stop himself laughing as he recorded it, as low and beguilingly moody as he could muster with the pain in his hand racing into overdrive. He sat and waited quietly for five minutes, as the tape whirred noisily in the player, then added the control word once and then, for safety's sake, again with emphasis. *Numismatic. Numismatic.* He figured he needed a word that wasn't in everyday use. He didn't know enough about hypnotism to put his faith in a common word. Didn't want to be accidentally put under by the checkout guy in Wal-Mart, making polite small talk as he eagerly tried to win employee of the month and a set of steak knives.

He added a number 7 to his second list. 'Vortex.'

He started in the centre of the page and drew out from the point where his marker pen dug into the page. Around and around and around until the entire page was filled with a circle that looked like a snail shell.

He listened as the tape noisily spooled back to the beginning, put the earphones in his ears and hit play.

9

The Divorcee

He'd waited thirty seconds before he'd followed her. And now he stood on the doorstep waiting for her to answer his knock. He didn't look over his shoulder, but he knew the hacks gathered in a small tight pack near the cruiser were watching him, curiosity probably killing them. He'd seen the patrolman's hand stay them as he moved past. He'd ignored their shouted questions, which only made them shout louder.

Behind the door, the click clack of high heels on a parquet floor.

'Who is it?'

'Police, ma'am.'

'Oh.'

The door swung open.

'I'd just like to ask you some questions.'

She looked at the badge. And then at him. She smiled a sad, inevitable kind of smile.

'About Peter?'

'Peter Gudsen. Yes ma'am. Detective Sinclair.'

'Please.' She swung the door wide open and watched as he over-wiped his feet back and forth on the doormat. He followed the flow of her hand towards the back of the house as, behind him, she softly closed the door.

He sat at the kitchen table in what looked like a suburban spaceship, all white, chrome and glass. Futuristic, he guessed some might call it. She stood at the counter, a cross between the space-ship's glamorous captain and a kind of domestic Barbarella. 'You have a lovely home, ma'am,' he offered as he took out his note-book and searched his pockets for his pen. Or a pencil.

'Thank you . . .' He could tell she was deliberating over what to call him. 'Would you like a coffee, Officer? Is it Officer?'

He smiled. 'Detective, ma'am. Thank you, coffee would be great.'

'Coffee coming up.' She almost sang it. She already had one of those Turkish coffee pots on the stove.

He'd found a pen. 'Your name, ma'am. If I may.'

'Marion Rose. Mrs. Do you take creamer?'

'No thank you, ma'am. Just strong and black.'

'I'm divorced, but Ms just sounds far too radical for around here.' She laughed as she put the coffees down, pushed the sugar bowl towards the centre of the table. He didn't take any. Instead, he watched as she plonked three cubes in her pale coffee and stirred it almost endlessly.

Marty wasn't one for taking notes. But he liked to have the notebook open, the pen out, lid off, ready. People expected you to take notes, but he preferred to watch them talk. How could you make or break any connection between the speaker and their words with your head buried in a notebook? 'And this is 2346 Kenner Avenue?'

'It is.'

'Did you know Mr Gudsen well?'

'Him and Betty. His wife. Their boys play over here all the time. I have two of my own, Zach and Michael. The age of their middle boys. Especially after Peter started working from home, before he got that office, the one where the bomb . . .' Her voice trailed off and she stared down at her coffee, stirred it again a few times before looking back up at him. Marty was glad for her that she hadn't seen what he'd seen that day. 'We've got a hoop out the back. I told them they could come over any time. Keep out of their dad's way.'

'When was that, ma'am?'

'Please, Detective, call me Marion.'

'When was that? When he started to work from home?'

'Oh, the summer. August sometime. Right after August thirteenth. The day my divorce got finalized. Who said the thirteenth was unlucky?' She smiled at him. It was hard not to smile back.

'Did you socialize with Mr and Mrs Gudsen, Marion?'

'Not that much, mostly through the boys.'

'Mr Gudsen, did he come over here often?'

'Over here? Peter? What on earth for?'

Marty let her find the answer.

'What are you suggesting, Detective?'

'I'm just trying to build up a picture is all, ma'am.' He averted his eyes back to his empty notebook.

'Jumping to conclusions, you mean. They're my neighbors, Detective. That's all. I felt sorry for Betty. Four boisterous boys and all she wanted was girls in candy pink. Don't get me wrong, she loves those boys, would die for them. But a houseful of boys is not what she wanted.'

'So, you think she was unhappy? Mrs Gudsen?'

'Unfulfilled, more like.'

Marty thought they might be one and the same.

'How did her husband feel about that? His wife being unhappy?'

'Do you think husbands notice when their wives are unhappy, Detective?'

He was tempted to look back down at the notebook.

'Do you think Mr Gudsen didn't notice?'

'Peter was a good man, a thoughtful man. But if you're looking for a reason why someone went and blew a loving husband with four kids to pieces I don't have the answer for you. Look.'

She reached out to the windowsill where a bunch of cookery books were piled up high. From beside the pile she took a small leather-bound book, the edges of its pages unevenly cut.

'He bought me this. Just the other week.'

Marty took it from her, opened it up. It was written in some language he couldn't read. He must have looked blank.

'It's Hebrew. The Old Testament.'

He let her continue.

'We're Jewish. It was a thoughtful gift. It's pretty old I think. A beautiful little book. They wanted to thank me for looking after the boys over a weekend last month when Betty's father was rushed into the hospital down in Phoenix. Are you married, Detective?' She looked at the wedding ring on his finger.

'Married?' Something made him not want to lie to her. 'No, Marion, I'm not married.'

'You just like wedding jewelry?' She half smiled, half frowned at him.

'It's easier here this way. I took it off, right after the divorce. Soon put it back on. People figure I'm more reliable with it, I guess. Somehow, it seems to make people more comfortable.'

'Reassures them you're one of them?'

49

'I guess. No one would have cared back in LA. Probably the opposite.' Here it made them talk and he was grateful for it. Stopped him having to.

'You lived in LA? I love it there. It's not the natural state here though, is it? Not encouraged.'

'Unmarried? Divorced?'

'Either. I'm glad I didn't come here to open a singles bar. The Faith seems to have its own.' She threw her head back. Watching her laugh made him forget to ask her what had brought her to a sleepy little city thousands of miles from New York. A sharp rap on the front door ended her laughter. She looked curiously at Marty.

'Expecting someone?' he asked.

'No, I sent the boys to their father's. Peter, the bombs . . .'

He understood. He was glad she hadn't asked him if he had children. It all might have come spilling out.

She was at the door now, opening it. He heard Al's voice. Moved toward the corridor.

'Hey, Marty! We gotta go. Suspect package down at the Mission offices.'

Marty moved fast towards the door. He gave her his card. Al was already halfway down the path.

'Anything you think of, Marion, no matter if it seems irrelevant. Call. They can page me. We really got to stop this guy.'

He could feel her green eyes trying to find his as she looked up over the card. But he didn't look, didn't speak.

He was down the path now. Behind him he heard her call out, 'Stay safe, Officer,' before correcting herself, 'Detective. Stay safe, Detective.'

Al drove up alongside him, barely stopping the car long

enough for him to get in. With the hack pack advancing on foot, they took off.

As they slid into the first corner, Marty turned to him: 'So, Al, how you feeling about Big Tex's theory now?'

10

It hadn't worked the first time – he was too awake, too aware, all keyed up and expectant – and so he'd slugged back some JD he kept stashed deep in the back of the third drawer of his file cabinet and sat back down at his desk. It didn't work the second time either. The silence around him had been broken by a high-pitched faraway sound, Jack he thought, screaming blue murder at the top of the house.

The third time, three grand slugs of JD later, somehow the voice on the tape, his own voice, began to seem further and further away and his brain began to see images, until he found himself sitting in a church pew behind young Clark, aged nine. He could see the white of the collar under his blue cardigan. He couldn't see his legs but he knew the boy was wearing khaki shorts. He had jumped off a tree, snagged them on a branch on the way to the ground. It had ripped the base of the hem. So his mother, having sworn him to secrecy, had rolled them up and stitched a new hem so his father wouldn't notice and then rolled up the other side and stitched that as well, so they matched.

Next to young Clark sat his family, like three shiny pins. All stared, chins forward, listening intently to the Father and his weekly sermon. Except young Clark. His face was down, reading his prayer book.

Clark could hear the Father now, a Faith Bible in hand, repeating the words of the Prophet who had declared their holy book 'the only book on earth, for all man' and said that man 'would ascend to heaven if he adhered to the gospel the Prophet had transcribed'.

Clark's eyes wandered over to the flickering flame of a large altar-side candle. The service was over. Now he watched as young Clark and his family were out into the aisle, moving slowly with the other Faithful. Clark moved out from his seat, into the aisle behind them. They didn't notice him. He shuffled along behind them, toward the light at the end of the aisle, blinding light pouring through the doorway of the Mission. Urgent movement, fast behind him, two young boys broken free from family reins storming through toward the sunlight. As they did so, they bumped into young Clark and he watched as the child's hands reached out to grab the book, but it kept falling, falling, falling down onto the floor where its pages fluttered open. Young Clark froze, like he was cast in stone, or salt. His father, half blinded by the sunlight, bent to retrieve it, but when his hand brought the Bible back into view there were two books, not one. And one had pictures in. It was as if a cloud had put out the sun. Clark watched young Clark, knew that he wanted to run as fast as he could with those other boys, run outside to where he knew the sun shone. Out, out and away.

The Faithful halted in their tracks to stare as his father held the book aloft for all to see. Clark could see his father's lips move, but couldn't hear him. Saw him turn to his mother, as spittle flew from someplace beneath his moustache – his angry mouth twisted and turned, his eyes flared. Clark remembered how it had hurt, his father's hand pressed down, gripping his shoulder as if he knew he would run.

And then the sound came back.

'There's no such thing as dinosaurs, son. NO. SUCH. THING. This filth is worse than fiction. It's blasphemy, that's what this is. BLASPHEMY.'

And now Clark watched as his father dragged young Clark over to the candle, picked up the anointing oil from the altar and poured it over the book.

He saw young Clark reach out helplessly as his father touched the book on top of the candle and held it aloft. Flames began to lick up the dinosaur's tail, consuming Stegosaurus and his friends in penitential fire.

It was February 23, 1964. He didn't know precisely what time, but about the moment the second hand was encroaching upon the 3. That moment, as he watched his burning book arc through the air and land outside on the Mission's concrete path, was the precise moment he had begun to truly hate his daddy and his Faith.

Numismatic.

Clark began to come out of the trance, drawn out by that man's voice. His voice. As he did, through the earphones and the now static hum coming from the tape deck he could hear some other noise invading his eardrums.

Hammering.

It was Edie, bang, bang, banging on the door with what sounded like a jackhammer. He heard her shoulder make contact with the door. What was she trying to do, she was five foot nothing and barely a hundred pounds.

'Clark, Clark, are you alright? Answer me or I'm gonna call 911. Clark!'

Finding his way slowly out of 1964 he couldn't remember if

he'd locked the basement door properly or not. He moved fast as he could up the wooden steps. She must have heard him. She went silent, probably expecting him to open the door. He didn't.

'What are you doing?'

'Research,' he said.

'What kind of research? It's late.'

He didn't answer. Instead, he was looking at the white-painted door panels around the top bolt, smeared with dried blood. His blood. When he'd dragged the bolt shut earlier his hand must have bled on it. And then he realized it was him that was the problem. His baggage. His blood. That's why his hypnotic state was stuck in limbo in his childhood.

Her knock. Soft now.

'Go to bed, Edie.'

'But . . .' He heard her sigh, wait for a moment, and then without saying anything else he heard her move back along the corridor towards the staircase.

Back in the trance state he'd been both himself and his younger self, divided not by place, but by time. Alice had been sucked down into the rabbit hole and found Wonderland, another world where she had been tall and short and then herself again. Clark had fallen into the centre of the vortex and fallen back into hell, but just like Alice he was stuck there as various distortions of himself. Perhaps to escape himself and his past and create a new self, first he had to become someone else? Breathe as them, think as them, even just for a few moments. Fake yourself to find yourself.

He was stood at his workbench now, where the Poe volume he'd gotten from Vegas awaited his attention. Earlier, he'd been crafting a protective cover for it, before adding it to the growing collection of first editions he kept stashed away in a locked cabinet, not too dissimilar to Dougie Wild's. But Clark's cabinet had two locks, not one. Clark picked up the book with his bandaged hand and carefully, with his good hand, thumbed through it.

What if it were possible in the trance state to become someone else, someone that wasn't the younger, fatter or taller you, and by becoming that person, even for a minute, you could *be* them? Just like Mesmer's jockeys and ballroom dancers. Clark's mind filled with the possibilities of that. Put unspoken words in the mouths of the famous, the infamous, write their signatures, their letters, their words. Become them. Perhaps even *create* their words in their style. Surely that was impossible. Or was it? If you could counterfeit coins, then why couldn't you counterfeit people?

11

Downtown, Abraham City

By the time they reached the Mission offices Big Tex was rolling out the cable that connected a control box to his robot, or Baby as he called it. It looked like a cumbersome oversized skateboard with an unwieldy Meccano arm precariously balanced on it. Marty bit down into one of the fresh bacon 'n' cheese burgers Al had liberated, courtesy of a cop-loving waitress, from the diner behind them, right after he'd shooed its customers, necks craning, out of their comfy booths and back up the street away from what could be the center of an imminent blast. Being cleared out of range of flying glass and shrapnel, but out of view of the drama, didn't seem to make any of them happy. Less than thirty minutes had passed since they got the call but every building in the half-block, including the Faith's sprawling HQ, had been evacuated.

Now Al was crouched back down beside him and they watched as Big Tex switched on the screen that monitored Baby on her ops. The picture was fuzzy with lines running up and down on it like you'd see on your TV if you didn't have cable, right before the aerial completely lost its signal and ruined the end of your favorite show. Marty thought it looked pretty hopeless. But he figured it was better than sticking your face into a bomb which might be about to explode, better for the Meccano to take the hit.

The call had come in from a limo driver. He'd had a busy morning shuttling people from the airport downtown and back, for some convention or other. He'd stopped for a coffee when a woman approached him. He shouldn't have taken the ride off the grid, but felt he was having too good a morning to resist. He'd already made a hundred bucks in tips, double the usual, forty of it from a young Korean kid. He didn't feel bad that the kid couldn't understand the currency, mistaking twenties for tens. He'd thanked him for the tip and bowed like some of his Japanese customers bowed. He wasn't sure if they did that in Korea or not. The fact the woman in need of a ride to the other side of town was hot might have swayed his decision to agree to take her far from his airport route, way over the other side of the canyon. But his fantasy as to what might lie ahead for him in lieu of payment and/or tips when they'd got to the canyon was dampened before it had even got to the good bit. As she got in, with him holding the door open for her, she'd noticed a white gift box with a red ribbon tied around it wedged right behind the driver's seat. When he'd reached in to retrieve it he suddenly remembered the descriptions of the bomb packages he'd heard over the dispatch radio. Next he's shouting to the woman to get out, there's a bomb, and they're out running down the sidewalk yelling and warning everyone else. From the payphone up the street the driver had called it in. The woman had hopped in a cab and he'd lost the fare and who knows what else, and now it looked as if his fantasies and his limo would both turn to dust.

'OK, Baby. Do your thing,' cooed Big Tex in Baby's direction.

Marty, Al and what looked like most of the precinct were crouched down behind a slew of squad cars which had slammed to a halt across the street, blocking it off. Marty peeked around the exhaust of one of the cars as Tex toggled what looked like the gear stick of an old racing car, pushing and pulling it in the direction he wanted Baby to go. After a hesitant start, Baby was now racing at a speed of about five miles an hour toward the open rear driver's-side door, where, in the footwell, Marty could see a white shoe box and cascading red ribbons, exactly like the bomber's other packages. Baby slowed down about twenty yards from the cab and began to inch forward. Marty guessed that was to do with not causing too much ground vibration that might set the bomb off before Baby and Tex got a closer look.

Marty looked around at Al. He was crouched down, back to the cruiser, chin tucked into chest and his hands over his ears, expecting the worst. Marty tugged Al's hand away from his ear.

'What did she say, the widow Gudsen?'

'You want to know *now*?'

Marty smiled at him. 'Talking will make you less tense.'

'She said a bunch of stuff. Not sure if any of it will be any use. But basically, she didn't know much about her husband's business. She was in college, met Peter the husband through friends in the Faith. He was a senior, tipped for the Faith's top job even back then.'

'Interesting.'

'Yeah, I thought so. Although that widens our suspects to jealous colleagues from the Faith.'

'Correct. Ideally, we'd be narrowing the search, not increasing it ten-fold. What else?'

'She really had no idea, or she should win an Oscar, about their finances, business transactions. None of it. Said she was totally shocked when she heard on the news yesterday that the business was going to fold. Gudsen had never mentioned it was in any trouble, although she did say he'd been very stressed about something for the past couple of months.'

'But didn't know what?'

'This, I'd imagine.'

'Maybe this. Maybe that. Could be anything. What about another woman? Or Mrs Houseman?'

'Nothing. She said he wasn't that kind of man. Very devout. They were both virgins when they married.'

'Maybe he was a slow starter.'

Al smiled. 'She doesn't know any Mrs Houseman, or Mr Houseman. When I asked her if Gudsen went out a lot, unexplained places, maybe even at night, she said he'd had even more meetings at the Faith's offices in the past few months, mostly in the evenings, than ever before. She figured that was a good thing.'

'Well, at least, that's what he wanted her to think. The Faith, not unfaithful.'

Marty smiled at his own joke. Al continued. 'She didn't know of any offshore accounts or unusual transactions. But, as she said, Gudsen dealt with all that, even the household expenses, gave her housekeeping.'

'Cash?'

'No. Check. Monthly. Into a dedicated account for the house. Four hundred bucks, for shopping, small emergencies, that kind of thing. Wrote a check direct to the cleaner himself once a month.'

'They sound duller than ditchwater.'

'Yep.'

'Somebody didn't think so, or they wouldn't have blown him to smithereens.'

'I asked the widow where he kept the check-books, it'd be good to get a look at the ledger, you know, in the back, see if he kept it up to date, see where any monies might be getting siphoned off. She thought just domestic ones, maybe, not business he would keep in the house. But . . .'

'She didn't really know.'

'Right. In his desk drawer, maybe. It was locked. All the other drawers were open, but no sign of the key. When she was looking I thought I saw a couple of safe keys, tied together with a little scrap of ribbon, in amongst a pen set in one of the other drawers. I don't think she even saw it and if she did, it didn't register.'

'Doesn't know what it is?'

'Perhaps.'

'She a suspect?'

'I doubt it.'

'Well, I guess we narrowed the suspect list, huh?'

'By one.'

'It's a start. We'll get a search warrant. For the house,' said Marty.

'What, on a victim's place? This guy was going places, with the Faith.'

'Maybe this financial stuff put paid to that.'

'And maybe it was the cause of him getting killed.'

Marty thought that was definitely a possibility. And maybe so did the Faith. They were known to invest heavily in projects brought to them by the Faithful. The higher up the Faith tree, the more likely it was they had some kind of financial hold on you by way of investment. From what Marty had seen at the Gudsen house there was certainly a Faith presence, over and above a simple show of support for a fallen Brother's widow. He'd seen the Faithful loitering by the phone, and he'd spotted one guy sat in a car parked opposite the house, clocking the comings and goings at the entrance. They were easy to spot. They didn't mingle, they observed. Mingling was not their thing.

Marty stuck his head around the edge of the car again. As he did, he could see in the monitor Big Tex's Meccano hand reaching down to a corner of the ribbon, pushing towards it as if it was going to tease it open. Marty nudged Al to cover his ears back up, and covered his own. As he did so, out of the corner of his eye, he saw a young Korean guy, clad in the uniform of the Faithful, pushing through the police line outside the conference centre, an equally young cop trying to hold him back. Marty took his hands from his ears, looking to the guy and the box, just as the Meccano snagged the ribbon, lifting it up, the ribbon not strong enough to hold the dangling box together. It fell open and the vase inside crashed to the floor and smashed into tiny pieces.

'What fool left that fucking vase there!?' yelled Tex to no one in particular as he took off fast towards Baby.

Al stood up, brushed his trousers down, turned to Marty who was doing the same: 'So that puts Houseman, Hartman and half the city back in the frame.'

Marty moved past him, head shaking, moving toward their car. 'Come on. We don't have time for this false alarm crap.'

'Where we headed? The hospital?' said Al.

'No point. Houseman's still in a coma. I told Grady Jnr to let me know if that changes. We're back to the better side of town to visit with the grieving widower. He seemed pretty genuine yesterday. But maybe he knew what was coming, had time to prepare. So, let's try and find out why the high school prom queen married an ageing businessman. And how that may or may not fit into the investigation. Especially if there was a good life-insurance policy out on her. The kind of settlement that might help a guy onto a plane headed towards a place we can't extradite from and with a chunk of change left over so he doesn't ever have to come back to this place.'

'You think Lomax tried to bomb his way out of trouble?'

'Why not? I've seen crazier. It would sure deflect attention – even for a little while.'

'I'll second that. But what about the others? Houseman and Gudsen.'

'Gudsen's the business partner. Most likely he knows where the bodies are buried.'

'And Houseman?'

'Maybe he was their silent partner.'

'Maybe.'

'No evidence of that so far, though, hey?'

Al shook his head.

'Some kind of collateral damage then,' said Marty.

'That could make sense.'

'And if not Lomax the Old Fool, how about the Old Fool's ex? She can't have been happy to be cast aside for a wannabe beauty queen fresh out of high school.'

'She wasn't.'

'Messy divorce?'

'Carnage.'

Marty looked at him. 'Maybe literally.'

'Mrs Lomax the First was mighty pissed, sued him for the house, the company, everything – but he had it all tied up in trusts, offshore corporations everywhere. At least that's what he claimed. She didn't get a bean.'

'And now we know why. It was a bust.'

'Where the hell did all that money go?'

Marty shrugged, 'You got the court papers through already or did Mrs Gudsen spill all that?'

'Neither. The whole saga was in the papers. But I'll get the family court transcripts and check.'

Marty looked surprised. 'It was in the locals?'

Al shook his head. 'No. *Nevada Herald*. Last year. Lomax is a property tycoon. Was, anyhow. Local boy made good.'

'And look how that turned out.'

'Folks were interested.'

'Or just plain nosey. Guess the Faith wanted to keep it out of their press.'

'That's why I read the out-of-state press – it hasn't been censored,' said Al.

'Not by the Faith, anyhow.'

'You got that right.'

'Make sure that kid doesn't go anywhere, Al.'

Al followed Marty's gaze over to where the young Korean follower was sat slumped down on the curb, his head in his hands.

*

They got a translator pretty quickly, considering. An older Korean guy. Faith, naturally. He looked ready to give the young guy shit. But Marty just wanted to know if anyone had given the kid the package. No. Anyone asked him to leave it in the back of the limo? No. Where did he get the package? Seoul airport. The lady behind the counter had wrapped it for him when he'd told her it was a gift for his host family. What was he doing in America? He was a new member of the Faith. Obviously expanding their territories. After his plane had been delayed, he'd been so worried about being late for the start of the conference that he'd headed straight there instead of to the host's house first. He'd totally forgotten about the package until he got to the registration hall and ran back out, pushing through the crowd until he saw 'that man', Tex, about to blow up his $200 gift.

Tex was pissed. He liked to blow stuff up. Particularly if he'd been waiting hours to do it. After, as the kid stood with delayed shock, sobbing on the sidewalk, Big Tex gave him a lecture on securing your belongings at all times. It didn't matter the kid could barely understand a word.

Welcome to America.

12

September 10th 1982

Canyon County

He'd been stood in the dark for what felt like a lifetime. Engine and lights off. He hardly dared breathe, but he had to wait there until they settled again, then maybe one or two would edge back towards the fence. If so, he might be able to just reach over and grab one. No such luck.

Instead, spooked maybe by his scent or something, a whole gaggle of the fuckers were shifting quickly again now, heading for the coop. He couldn't wait any longer: he had to move fast up and over the fence.

He was on the outskirts of the gaggle now, felt the beginnings of even hastier movement and frantic noise amongst them. He was primed to react, but so were they. More so than him. And faster. He pushed forward, reached down amongst them, deep into the huddle. One was all he needed. His hand connected with a neck and he pulled its wriggling body out of the melee around him. They were all squawking and fleeing, flapping their useless wings in a concerted effort to frighten off this predator in their midst. He waded out through the racket back towards his car. As he did so, he placed his hands tightly around its neck and it wriggled furiously, evolution must have warned it what was coming. Soon its body went limp.

He headed for the car, back up the track to where it was parked close to the perimeter fence, its dark silhouette barely visible. He was grateful for the fact there hadn't been the usual September rain, otherwise the entire field around the coop would have been a giant shit-fest. Grateful because he'd remembered to wear his old tennis shoes, knowing he could just sling them in the washing machine when he got home. Get them washed and dried under the boiler before Edie and Jack got home in the morning. When he was working on one of his special projects, any nights he could subtly persuade Edie to spend at her sister's – and take Jack – were like a gift from the gods. He liked to work knowing he wouldn't be interrupted by the unpredictable rhythms of other people's lives.

He had a clean trash bag ready. He shoved it inside and slammed the lid of the trunk back down. He had to get out of there fast before the squawking woke the turkey farmer and brought him, armed and irritated, out of his house.

*

He plucked the best feathers out of its left wing. He was right-handed so it had to be the left wing, that way the feathers wouldn't be in his sightline as he wrote. The long, fine feathers had the sturdiest of tips. He'd washed them and dried them, slicing them like a flower stem diagonally across the base, and now he was dipping the first one into his ink-pot, squeezing and drawing it out, careful not to waste any of the precious ink.

Probably the ink had been the most perilous ingredient to obtain. Following instructions from an old ink recipe he'd found in a library book, he had been burning pages he'd ripped out of another book when Edie and Jack had come back early from a Faith-organized Saturday playgroup. Jack had eaten too much cake, guzzled too much OJ and trampolined until his brain hurt. Triple whammy. He'd been violently sick in the Mission side hall and Edie, apologizing profusely, had hurriedly bundled him out the door and into the car as some of the other Faith mothers kindly took to cleaning up the mess.

When he'd heard them pull up to the garage Clark quickly slammed down the hood of the barbecue, sending smoke seeping out the sides of it. He'd yelled out to Edie he was just cleaning it in case she got the idea he might be prepping a cook-out. Not today, he had more pressing things to attend to. She didn't look like she believed he was cleaning anything, but he didn't have time to worry about it. As Edie ushered Jack through the front door and upstairs towards the bathroom Clark quickly wrenched open the barbecue hood before all the ash from the precious pages evaporated to nothing. He gathered up as much of it as he could. This would be the base ingredient with which he would make his ink. He'd sliced the blank back pages out of an 1840s book he'd found in the folio section of the university library. That way the carbon and thus the ink would be genuine nineteenth-century, not some hokey late-twentieth-century version. It was true what he'd told Edie: he had cleaned the barbecue, right before he'd burnt the papers in it. He didn't want 1982's burger fat sullying his pristine, freshly made 1849 ink.

Over the past month he'd spent a few days in various university libraries across the state acquiring copies of the author's signature, plus samples of his handwriting: verified, genuine copies. He had found ten in all, from various stages of the author's life, and he had traced them out again and again and again. Then he'd homed in on a particular year, a year when the author had been most prolific in his letter writing, and Clark had focused on perfecting

– as near as possible – the signature of that year. He noticed that each period in the writer's life had generated slight, almost imperceptible, changes to the signature. As little as a decade later it was very different to how it used to be. After he dispensed with the tracing he concentrated on generating the signature himself over and over. Almost five hundred times. It was vital to perfect the signature first, before embarking on anything more ambitious. He wanted to be ambitious. But he would be patient.

But he couldn't get the signature down. Every time the damn 'tell' gave him away. Every time there was a hesitation mark somewhere in the signature no matter how hard he tried to relax, free his hand, his arm, his shoulder of tension. He knew from his research it was what forgery experts looked for – and always found – it was the one thing that marked out the forger from the forgee. Hesitation. No one ever thinks about their signature, they just do it. It is one of man's rare hesitation-free zones. Even crossing the road doesn't come without either hesitation, thought or some awareness of danger unless you are completely distracted. Genuine signatures just flow. But no matter how much he attempted to discard mechanical thought, when he placed his efforts under the microscope, there it was: the hesitation, every time, even the faintest of tremors, but a tremor all the same and so he would start again. Until it was perfect to the human eye he wouldn't bother to dig out the high-grade microscope he'd bought at the city university's yard sale last year, for he knew that under its unforgiving gaze the hesitation would look less like a tremor and more like a devastating earthquake marked out on a seismograph.

When he wasn't prepping the technical side of his plan, for every moment of the past month Clark had completely immersed himself in the author's life. He felt that if tomorrow he had to write a PhD proposal he would know more about the author's life than the professor assessing it. Now with his research complete he had everything. It had taken over a month, but it had to be done right. Perfect, that's what it had to be: perfect. He knew what he had to do next. What he didn't know was if it would work or not.

He had already recorded the tape he would use to hypnotize himself. Not the same tape as before, but a different one, unique to his subject, the very subject he knew he must become, just like Dr Mesmer's subjects had – temporarily – become jockeys, expert dancers and, even, dogs. Clark didn't like to think his little experiment might go awry and he might spend the rest of his life as man's best friend. He really hoped that wasn't possible.

He had prepared a safe word. So even if somehow his life became a living resurrection of the author's, if he followed the plan as he had clearly set it out on the tape then the name would be repeated by himself and others, and that repetition would hopefully release him from a hypnotic life of surreal servitude to the strange ghost of a long-dead author.

For authenticity's sake, and in the hope that it would help him get under quickly and deeply into the mind of a man who last breathed in 1849, Clark had voiced the recording with heavy traces of a Bostonian accent. Even though Clark's was a strained twentieth-century approximation of the accent, not a nineteenth-century version, he hoped it might still have on it the lick of the pilgrim fathers.

On the desk in front of him sat a first edition of one of the author's collections – Clark put his hand on it as if he were at a séance, attempting to summon the soul of the author from within it. He turned up the headphone volume and closed his eyes. As the tape instructed him, he began to follow the clearly defined

instructions it had taken weeks to hone, and soon he began to repeat the words of a familiar poem:

> Once upon a midnight dreary, while I pondered, weak and
>> weary,
> Over many a quaint and curious volume of forgotten lore,
> While I nodded, nearly napping, suddenly there came a
>> tapping,
> As of some one gently rapping, rapping at my chamber door.
> "Tis some visitor,' I muttered, 'tapping at my chamber door –
> Only this, and nothing more.

Minutes later, as instructed, he took up the turkey quill, dipped it
in the ink and wrote the name.

Edgar.

Allan.

Poe.

Edgar Allan Poe

The words written so close up to one another there was barely
room for the paper to breathe between the lines as the quill
traveled high and writ large:

Edgar Allan Poe
Edgar Allan Poe

Clark filled the sheet of blotting paper in front of him and had
just begun to write on another when the control word halted him
mid-flourish.

Raven.

He looked down at the page. Even without the high-powered microscope he could see the tell. He had figured out that in his previous attempts at mesmerizing himself he had been unable to let go of him, of Clark, kept getting stuck in his childhood because he was still doing things that he, Clark Houseman, did. Things like drinking JD. And so, he had thought of a simple switch that might unblock him from his own past and perhaps help him get deep into the lives of others. He would switch his tipple for theirs. In the glass he was about to take a hit from was cognac: pricey French cognac – Poe's favorite – from a company that had existed for over three hundred years and which Kenny had gotten him a case of, from one of his booze-mafia buddies.

He took a swig from the glass, then another. It warmed his mouth and his throat as it traveled into the far reaches of his stomach. Soon it would be in his veins. He pressed rewind, then play. As he did so, he stared at the hand-drawn vortex he had pinned to the wall in front of him and, once again, he repeated the words of the poem until this time they became their own rhythm: napping, rapping, rapping, tapping, napping until the drawn lines of the vortex seemed imprinted on his mind.

Clark soon felt his entire being alter – everything from his posture to the way he held the pen shifted and resettled until he felt like he owned the quill, the ink and the signature that flowed from it. Each time his hand moved across the page more confidently than the last, until it moved completely without hesitation.

Clark Houseman was dead. For now. Edgar Allan Poe was alive and living in his body, his resurrected lifeblood coursing through Clark's veins, down into his fingers, into his grip and writing upon the page as Poe himself. Poe's hand now wrote the familiar words over and over and over.

Edgar Allan Poe. Edgar Allan Poe. Edgar Allan Poe.

Raven.
Raven.

Clark looked down at the page, saw what he had done. He needed to see, see it quickly up close just to make sure, but he was sure it was right, at least to the naked eye. He searched the workbench next to him and the floor around it for what seemed like the longest time until he found the university microscope buried under a pile of research material. He grabbed it, shoved the paper under the glass and peered down into the latest batch of signatures, checking through each line, every movement, every flourish of the quill. And when he was done he checked each and every one again.

They were perfect.

Flawless.

There were no hesitation marks.

Not one.

He had done it.

He wanted to yell it from the rooftops. But he couldn't risk telling another living soul. This was no party trick. This was his life. His new life. If he could replicate this success with other characters, other personalities, not just Poe, and write real script, real documents, not just the signatures of historical characters, authors, even presidents, in doing so he might be able to rewrite history itself.

Rewrite history.

Clark smiled. Sat back down at his desk. The Bible he'd picked up near the Last Call Tavern was sat there – he had been meaning to write a family history onto its inside cover pages, related to some figure in the church. With its age and that added provenance, if it could be even halfway verified, it might fetch maybe as much as twenty five hundred bucks. But now, now he had a different idea – he would give the Faith exactly what they needed. History. And in doing so he would write and rewrite their history. Write and rewrite it so they wouldn't know what to believe any more. He leant back in his chair and stared at the vortex. His hands settled on the back of his head and he smiled.

He would fuck with the Faith, maybe enough to destroy it, or die trying.

13

November 1st 1983, 4 pm

Residence of Bobbi Lomax (Deceased)

They could have been at a college party. Almost everywhere he looked there were teenagers or those who looked just like them. Most of them had probably never even thought of the Grim Reaper before, let alone felt his shadow brush so close against them, but death couldn't silence them and judging by this room it seemed to make them even more intense.

As Marty moved through the rooms he heard them wonder aloud and to anyone who'd listen why someone so young, so beautiful, so *talented* could be taken like that, all the time silently thanking the Lord and any other deity who might be listening that it was Bobbi who was dead, not them, simultaneously promising to live a Good, Honest, God-fearing Life now that they had been spared. Promises that would be forgotten long before Bobbi Lomax was pushing daisies.

Audrey Lomax, sister of Arnold, sister-in-law of Bobbi, was red-eyed, tissue in hand. Audrey said, far from taking refuge someplace else, Arnold couldn't bear to leave the house, but 'Poor, poor Arnold couldn't face sleeping upstairs' in the bed he'd shared with Bobbi as man and wife, 'can't even bear to go upstairs no more' as images of his life with Bobbi played on permanent rerun in his head. Earlier, she'd found him sleeping in the downstairs guest room, clutching their wedding photo, him and his

Bobbi together under the flowered arch he'd had built specially in their garden for their wedding ceremony. Marty looked outside: the arch was there, young thin branches wound around it. But the cold snap had destroyed any sign of flowers.

Marty counted fourteen framed pictures of Bobbi Lomax in the dining room alone. There must have been hundreds of photos scattered around the house. There was a fine line between love and obsession and it looked as if Arnold Lomax had an acute, maybe chronic, and possibly fatal case of one of them.

Arnold Lomax, fifty-six going on eighty-six, shuffled into view, his hair still wet, ruffled from towel-drying. For a moment the room fell silent. Young hands reached out to his sagging shoulders, patting him, urging him onward; accompanying voices were sorry for his loss, many of them breaking and cracking as they uttered barely a word or two. Lomax nodded as he passed, his head bowed down, watching the movement of his barely shuffling feet. Marty thought Arnold Lomax might very well throw himself into the grave currently being dug for Bobbi at Crystal Heights Memorial Cemetery. He knew Al would press hard for answers as this might be their only chance.

Marty was sure that he wasn't alone in thinking that this display of grief meant that Arnold Lomax was not guilty of the killing of Bobbi Lomax, his wife of three months, nor that of Peter Gudsen, his former business partner, not to mention the maiming and what could be the murder of Clark Houseman – it's just that sometimes guilt and grief can be the mirror image of one another, especially when mixed with a splash of make-believe.

Marty knew only too well that people with little or no theatrical experience can, overnight, become consummate performers, especially if it's the only thing separating them from the death penalty. Two days prior, Marty had spoken to Arnold in the street outside the Lomax house. At that stage, until forensics had been all over the house inside and out, Arnold hadn't been able to go inside and he certainly couldn't go anywhere near the scorched lawn where his wife's once desirable body had lain, now grotesquely altered far beyond anything he would have remembered. Marty had thought his shock and grief genuine. Today, as Marty looked around the room, the absence of anyone aged over twenty or so told him that Arnold's friends had deserted him, along with all of his family except his spinster sister. What Marty wanted to know more than anything else right now was: why was that?

He stepped out onto the patio area at the back of the house. He'd seen a couple of girls he'd recognized as Bobbi Lomax's bridesmaids from the picture in the newspaper, watched them take a bottle of Coke and a handful of plastic cups and head out back. Coke is nothing without something added. So now might be as good a time as any to join them.

One girl had the vodka bottle half out of her bag when she caught sight of Marty heading straight for them.

'This a private club,' he said, reaching to take a cup out of the blonde girl's hand, 'or can anyone join?'

They knew he was a cop. He'd heard word go around when he and Al had arrived and while he walked around the rooms, waiting for Arnold to appear, the whispers seemed to precede him, followed almost without a beat by the stares. Blondie poured Coke into his cup. The other girl kept her hand on the bottle, deep inside her bag. He took a sip. 'Tastes kind of weird, lonely somehow, needs a companion, huh?' He held up the cup, smiled at them. The blonde one smiled back.

'You on duty?' she said.

'Right now?'

She nodded.

He feigned a look at his wristwatch.

'Looks like the end of my shift. My buddy, in there with Arnold, he's on duty.'

'You're not gonna bust us?'

'What for? Underage drinking in a state drier than the desert?'

The girls looked wide-eyed at one another and were about to protest their innocence.

'I think there's some county by-law says it's not an offence if your friend just died,' he said as he pushed the cup toward the dark-haired girl. 'Or you're here to pay your respects. And maybe find her killer in the process.'

The blonde girl smiled at him, nudged the other girl's elbow. 'Go on Elaine, pour him some. He's cool.'

Cool.

Now it was Marty's turn to smile.

Elaine looked dubiously at him as she poured. He could tell she was still half expecting to get the bracelets on and be shoved into a car headed toward the precinct.

Marty turned around, made sure there was no one else watching them in their tucked-away spot. There wasn't.

'To Bobbi.' Their plastic cups met. 'To Bobbi.' The girls swigged, Marty brought his to his lips but didn't drink from it. They wouldn't notice. They were on a mission to get loaded, but he had stuff to find out before they did.

'You gonna ask us questions 'bout her.'

'About Bobbi?'

''Course, Bobbi.'

'Not really,' said Marty.

'Don't you wanna ask us stuff, questions for the investigation and all?'

'I've never been fond of questions,' said Marty.

The cups were filled again. And before the third go-round of the vodka bottle and the second time he'd refused a refill, Marty had learnt that Shona had been at junior high with Bobbi, and Elaine, the brunette, had known her from back when Bobbi's mom had been alive and they'd lived right next to each other over on Smith Street. Elaine and Shona had met at a make-up class held over at the community college on Tuesday evenings. They'd invited Bobbi in as their model on a few nights last term, right before the wedding. She'd asked them to be two of her seven bridesmaids and they'd both done her wedding make-up. 'There weren't anything out of the ordinary,' said Shona.

'She was just the same old Bobbi. But all grown-up and en-gaged,' Elaine added.

'And then married, soon as you know it.'

Elaine was hoping to go out to Hollywood in the spring, train to do make-up for the movies. Bobbi was excited by that. She loved modeling, the little she'd done, and she would have died to become an actress. Elaine caught herself when she said this. Grimaced. 'You know what I mean.' Marty nodded.

'Arnold supported her going off modeling?' Marty was rolling a cherry menthol. Usually he pre-rolled them for the next day, right around midnight, tucked them into his button-down shirt pocket, but everything had been so crazy the past couple of days, living at the station, it had shot his routine to hell.

'Oh, he would have been supportive. He adored her. She was his princess.'

'Queen. I think you're a queen if you're married, isn't that right . . . ?' Shona nudged Marty, 'Detective.'

'Marty.'

'Detective Marty, isn't that right?'

Marty shrugged, he didn't know if princesses became queens or not. He thought it would help if they married a king. But Arnold Lomax was no king. In the wedding picture in that morning's *Desert News* Bobbi Lomax had worn a tiara and a dress that was whiter than white. Next to her was her newly wedded husband, thirty-eight years her senior. He had worn the desperate smile of a man who had been a king a long time, a man who knew the jig was very probably up.

Liss had worn a tiara once, for her eighth birthday party. He had seen the picture a thousand times. Had it in his wallet. She had been Marty's little princess, but she had never become a queen.

The girls talked on and on about Bobbi, mostly about how beautiful she was, about how her mom had died so young 'n' all: thirty-six. Marty didn't think that was young, just unlucky. Hit and run. Drunk driver. No dad to speak of. They'd caught the driver. That was years back. He was probably out by now. How heartbroken Bobbi had been when Johnny, the school jock she'd been secretly engaged to, had thrown her over for her best friend Melissa-Fay; how she'd started working in Arnold's office as a clerk on Saturdays and how they'd fallen in love. Both girls said they'd been a bit creeped out by it at first, Bobbi was barely eighteen, but they'd met him and – they both giggled, they were five vodkas in now – turned out Arnold was quite hot for an old guy. Kind of like Tom Selleck. Marty didn't know so much about old. He thought he might have a few years on Tom. Arnold had told Bobbi he'd been 'emotionally separated' from his wife for years,

Bobbi was just the catalyst to him divorcing her, not the cause. The divorce was in the papers in one of the salons Shona did a few hours in a week. 'That bitch made Bobbi out to be some kind of gold-digging tramp. And Arnold out to be some kind of pervert: Bobbi was younger than his own kids, how could he 'n' all that.'

'Did you ever meet her?' said Marty.

'Mrs Lomax? Never,' said Elaine.

'Wouldn't want to,' said Shona. 'After all the mean things she said.'

'She sat outside here some nights watching them. And if Arnold came outside to ask her what she was doing, she'd just drive away. She said she had friends high up in the Faith and she was going to make him pay. No matter how. That's why they changed the locks and recoded the alarm.'

'Did they call the police?'

'What would they do?' Shona asked.

'Their job,' said Marty.

'I don't think Bobbi wanted to make a big deal out of it. She hoped it would all settle down after they got hitched.'

'And did it?' said Marty.

'I think she still came around. Just not as often.'

'Someone even said they saw her up on the balcony at Mission. At the wedding,' whispered Elaine, although not as low as she thought.

'So, the ex-Mrs Lomax thought Bobbi was a gold-digger?'

'Well, she got it wrong,' said Elaine mid-glug.

'Bobbi was no gold-digger, Marty. She liked nice things is all, and Arnold, he loved to spoil her. She was his princess. Queen. She was his queen,' said Shona.

'And did he keep on spoiling her?'

'Never quit.'

'Bobbi never mentioned anything to you about finances? The company losing money? Arnold being in any kind of trouble?'

'No.'

'We hear the funeral's gonna cost twenty *thousand* bucks.'

'Elaine!'

'What!? It's what I heard. At the salon from Mrs Loudacre, the funeral director's wife.'

Elaine took the bottle out of her bag again. It was empty. Marty stubbed out his cigarette gently on the brick wall of the porch. Half left for later. The girls were still smoking theirs.

Through the gap at the edge of the net curtains he could see Al getting up and Arnold's sister moving closer in to her brother on the couch, offering him another tissue as his eyes wandered to his retreat. Behind them two of the Faith's more devout brethren stepped forward to support him and half walked, half carried him back towards the guest suite.

Marty gave each of the girls his card. Elaine tucked hers into her bag under the empty vodka bottle.

'Thanks for the cigarettes, Detective Marty Sinclair,' Shona said, looking at the card. 'Did she die quick?' She looked over to where right near the garage the neatly manicured lawn was scorched back to earth and police tape annexed it from its otherwise immaculate surroundings. 'I can't bear thinking of her laid there hurting 'til that neighbor found her.'

Marty had read the autopsy report. He doubted Shona knew that it had taken Bobbi Lomax two hours to bleed out. Probably at some stage she'd been able to call out, maybe loud, maybe low, but nobody heard, and if they did they didn't come until something piqued Mrs Wilson's curiosity and made her slow down her car and crane her neck as she passed the Lomax house on her way from mid-morning service. He turned to Shona, her anxious eyes looking up at him. He nodded. 'Yes. It was quick.'

As Marty walked away he heard Elaine ask Shona: 'Hey, do you think that creep Davey Douglas has any weed?'

14

October 1982

Abraham City

He had been there since before lunch. Parked up a good distance, five cars, along from the store. He could watch the people trailing in and out, from up, down and across the street, but there, outside the empty store, in his nondescript car, he knew no one would notice him. He pretended to read the newspaper, but with his eye on his new digital watch and the small notepad in front of him.

The average time spent in there was twelve minutes. Some just a few, others twenty minutes, with only two people arriving whilst someone else had been inside. But that had been the lunchtime rush. Now it was much quieter. He wanted it as quiet as possible. Wanted to ensure that he wasn't interrupted. The second the old guy in the golf sweater left he would make his way inside. That way, if it all went well, and malicious fate didn't intervene, he would have them and the store to himself for twelve vital minutes. Or thereabouts. That way there wouldn't be any diversions that would keep him in there longer than he needed to be or break the spell he needed to cast. More importantly, should it all go wrong there wouldn't be any witnesses to his failure. People seemed to remember failure as if it were branded into their memories. Part of human behavior, he guessed, to remember the negative, from back in the day when all strangers came with a public health warning and were best killed, rather than befriended, just in case they meant you harm.

Clark looked down at his attaché case on the passenger seat next to him. This wasn't coins. But it wasn't an entirely brave new world either. From years secretly building up a respectable collection of literary first editions, he liked to think he knew what he was doing. But, with the forged signature of the author on the title page, Clark knew he would have to navigate his way through the deal like a Zen master whilst wearing the mask of a wide-eyed ingénue.

He didn't know what they knew about Poe. But he knew what he knew. Most importantly, he knew them. He had to start in a familiar place, a place where he was trusted, rather than a new punk in a new town. But failure here would engender suspicion and doubt. He could afford neither. They could snuff out his plans before the flame even took hold. He smoothed down his tie, picked up his case and got out of the car.

At the jingle of the door's bell, Clark saw Ron Rook turn around from where he was returning a coin tray to its place amongst the rows of them on his side of the store, where he offered up centuries of domestic and international coins to collectors and gift-givers. The Rooks had been in business since back when Ron's great-great-granddaddy had built the building and started Abraham City's first general store.

Clark had been buying and selling coins here for over ten years before Ron and his identical twin, Rod, had taken over the business after their daddy, Ron Snr, had succumbed to a diabetic coma.

Clark was a good customer and an even better seller – he was always greeted with a wide smile, but no handshake. Ron and Rod Rook never shook hands with the customers old or new, despite, or perhaps because, both wore gloves in the store morning, noon and night, from when it opened to when it closed, 9.30 am until 7.30 pm, six days a week. Resting on the Lord's Day. But even on the Lord's Day the gloves stayed on. Not white cotton as in the store, but tan leather to match their brogues. For all Clark knew they still had on the white cotton under the tan leather when he would see them at Mission, back in the day when Clark still went to Mission. Even the covers of their antique Bibles were tan leather, as were the patches on their matching tweed hacking jackets. Ron and Rod Rook looked like the men that time forgot. With their neatly groomed moustaches, pince-nez and trim, meticulous appearance they wouldn't have been out of place in Victorian England.

'Morning Ron.'

'Clark, been a while. Where you been?' said Ron.

'He's missed you, for sure, Clark Houseman. There's holes in his collections. Where *have* you been?' asked Rod.

'Oh, you know, keeping busy,' said Clark. He had been so distracted by his preparation for this that he had let his normal routine go, and almost lost his place in it. He made a mental note to never stray off people's radar again.

'Edie had the baby yet?'

'Next week, Ron, according to the hospital.'

'May the Prophet guide the child safely into the world,' said Rod.

'Amen,' said Ron from his side of the counter.

Both men looked at Clark.

'Amen,' Clark said, hoping it didn't sound as reluctant as it felt.

Rod took his place behind his counter on the opposite side of the store. His side teemed with religious books and ephemera.

The store was divided equally down the middle, flip-sides of different coins, whereas the twins were the flip-side of the same coin.

'Have you got something for me, Clark? Looks like you have. Some delicious rare coin or other.' Ron nodded towards Clark's case.

He knew they trusted him. But he also knew they were fastidious and sharp. Both of which might be his downfall today. Over the years he had sold Ron some of his greatest counterfeited coins and nearly all of his genuine ones. And now this, of all things, had to go right. Be absolutely perfect.

'Oh, I've something, Ron, you're right about that. But, sad to say, it's not for you, but for your brother.'

'Really?' said Rod. 'What is it?'

Rod peered over the counter towards the case, like an excited child, as Clark brought it up to rest flat on the glass display cabinets that divided him from the twins. The twins were stood together now, like a mirror image, right opposite where Clark had settled in the book half of the store. They watched expectantly as Clark placed his briefcase on the counter, slowly rolled around the tumblers to the correct numbers, and then clicked open both locks at once. Theatre and suspense were always good for a sale. He propped the lid of the case open and slowly removed something from inside, holding it up, swathed as it was in rolls of white muslin. He began to unwrap it very, very slowly.

'Is it a book? A pamphlet? A *Bible*?' said Rod.

'It is . . .' Clark hoped the silence would sound like a drum roll. 'A book. A collection, to be exact.'

Clark held the slim volume up.

'By an exceptionally important American author.'

Ron looked disappointed. 'You don't usually sell books, Clark,' he said as he peered over his pince-nez.

'No, you're usually buying them from me,' said Rod. 'I hope that doesn't change.'

It was true, Clark had spent or traded an inordinate amount of money on Rook's first editions, ever since he sold his first coin, a forgery, to their father for fifteen hundred dollars when he was just fourteen. The penny Clark had altered had only cost a dollar, and he'd gotten the electro-plater for Christmas. He figured fifteen hundred was a pretty good return on a buck and a few teenage hours spent altering the coin. Collector's magazines had respected his wish for anonymity and called it 'an astounding find'. He grinned like the Cheshire Cat for most of the summer until it came time to go back to school. His mother, believing him when he said he'd found the coin on the street, had hidden the $1500 in her sister's account so his father wouldn't know there was spare money he could fritter away, or donate to the Faith in a vain attempt to curry favor at Mission. Instead, it had paid for Clark's dorm the first year of college before he upped and quit, preferring to forge or forage coins than sit in a lecture theatre. He had already wasted a year on his calling for the Faith and didn't want to waste another moment of his life in another institution.

'Don't worry, Rod, I'm still buying, that won't change. It's just this was such a special opportunity I couldn't pass on it – it could be good for all of us.'

Clark handed the volume to Rod, whose gloved hands were already reaching out for it.

'A collector down in South Carolina, a guy I get a lot of coins from. His grandmother died. He doesn't know a book from a rhino. He knew I knew something about 'em, so he FedExed all the old-lookin' ones up to me last week, for my opinion. I didn't even have time to look at them 'til yesterday evening.'

Rod held the volume in one gloved hand, supporting it, cradling it like a newborn baby, and turned the pages gently with the other. 'Well, I love Poe, for sure,' he said. 'And "The Raven", first edition. 1845. Wiley & Putnam, of course. I haven't seen one this fine before. It's a beauty, Clark.'

And then he saw it, the inscription on the frontispiece. Clark saw a light go on somewhere at the back of Rod's eyes, his gaze suddenly more focused than before.

'"Michaelmas, Providence, 1848."'

Clark could barely watch as Rod picked up his magnifying glass and peered down onto the page.

'"For My Beloved Sarah – Love. Ever. Yours. Edgar Allan Poe."'

Rod looked up, trying desperately not to let Clark see how excited he was.

'How much you looking for, Clark?'

Clark smiled, but before he could answer he heard a woman's voice outside thanking someone for a lovely lunch and then the familiar door bell jingled behind him as someone entered. He wanted to turn around, to see who it was. If Rod rejected the book, he didn't want anyone else in the room eavesdropping, re-membering faces, details. Failure.

Ron looked up from his cataloguing. 'Afternoon, Mrs Rose.'

Clark couldn't help himself. He had to look, it was an unfamiliar name, but it might not be an unfamiliar face. Someone from Jack's kindergarten? A teacher? He couldn't remember a Mrs Rose. A mother, perhaps? As he turned the very attractive redhead smiled at him. He nodded.

'Afternoon, ma'am.'

She smiled a wide smile. 'Good afternoon.' She turned back to Ron. 'And good afternoon to you, Mr Rook.'

'What may I help you with today?' said Ron.

'Just a small gift for Zachary. It's his birthday Thursday.'

'Sure, let me see what I can do. He had the 1924 penny last birthday, didn't he?'

'He did, what a good memory you have.'

'Like an elephant,' said Rod, not looking up from leafing very very slowly through the Poe volume, page by page.

'Perhaps this time '25 and '26, they're about the same cost total as the '24 – is that what you're thinking of, Mrs Rose, a similar spend?'

Ron pulled out a tray and pointed with his gloved hands to the two pennies.

'I'm sure he'll love them. Thank you.'

Clark looked over at the coin counter. Mrs Rose smiled back at him. Clark wondered if the '25 penny was one of the 1923 ones he'd altered last year and sold to dealers far and wide, including Ron. If it was, it was pretty much worthless.

'Clark, how much you looking to get, did you say?' said Rod.

Clark turned back to where Rod was still clutching the book. 'Thirty-three hundred should cover it.'

'That's too much for this, Clark. It's very good to fine.'

'You just said it was fine,' said Clark.

'But it's got some very small foxing and a tiny amount of sun damage. You know that reduces the value, a lot, even if it's border-line.'

'What I do know,' said Clark, 'is that Poe spent Christmas in Providence, Rhode Island in 1848 with his fiancée Sarah – and that, as this was his last published book at the time and she was one of his biggest fans, and a fellow poet, this inscription is where the book's value really is. But if you don't agree, I got to get the best price for my South Carolina contact, so I'll have to send it down to Phoenix Books, see what they'd give . . .'

The mention of a rival focused Rod's mind.

'Sarah . . . ? The fiancée?'

'Sarah Helen Whitman. The poet.'

'Of course. I'd forgotten. Poe was running around with so many women his last year, it's easy to forget their names.'

What Rod should have said was: I know that, Clark, I'd hoped you'd forgotten, or probably didn't even know, you being a relative newbie in the collectors' book trade. Clark moved his hand towards the book, as if to take it from Rod. Rod's gloved hand moved it an inch or two out of Clark's reach. Done. Now Clark knew that there was only the deal to be finalized.

'Twenty-four hundred cash,' said Rod.

'How about two thousand cash and twenty-five hundred in first edition trades?'

'You just said thirty-three hundred.'

'That was cash, Rod.'

'Two thousand cash and fifteen hundred in trades.'

'Two thousand in trades. You know you've marked retail up fifty to eighty per cent.'

'Two thousand, and seventeen fifty in trades.'

Clark nodded agreement.

As Rod took out his cabinet keys, Clark turned to Mrs Rose. 'Excuse me, ma'am. You might want to pick the 1928. It's a little pricier, but I hear it's running scarce, so it might be a better investment for your son, Zachary, is it?'

She nodded. 'Yes, my son. He'll be eight.'

'Something towards college, maybe,' said Clark.

'Thank you, sir. That's kind of you. How interesting about the '28. May I have a look at that one, Mr Rook?'

'Sure can.' Ron handed it to her.

'How much is this one?'

'More expensive, almost double. Two hundred and forty-seven dollars, even.'

'I'll take it. Why not? Like the gentleman said: it's an investment.'

Rod Rook finished opening up the first edition and high value cabinets and left Clark to choose whatever he wanted, to a retail value of $1750, while he went out back to the cash safe. It was the trades Clark really wanted, although the cash was good. He had his eye on a couple of the Faith's early religious pamphlets and a first edition of *The Wind in the Willows*.

*

Outside on the pavement, Clark watched as the early winter's snow fell on the city. It had already covered the peaks for a month. The bulky wedge of cash in his inside jacket pocket and the very carefully wrapped volumes in his hand told him, should he have any doubts, that he had done it.

15

The Former Mrs Arnold Lomax

He guessed she'd had the same hairstyle for a good twenty years, since back when they were fashionable. It nested on top of her head, like the beehive it was named after. But this one must have been sprayed with an entire can of lacquer to fix it in place. Marty thought when her hair ran loose, it must fall all the way down to her knees.

She hadn't seemed surprised to find them on her doorstep when she'd come back from shopping, and had made them lemonade from one of those frozen packets.

After some small talk, they began. She told them she'd married Arnold when she was eighteen, same age as Bobbi Lomax as it turned out. Although, that time, Arnold was also eighteen, not fifty-six. They'd met at a Bible evening organized by the Faith. 'If it wasn't for my kids, Detectives, I'd wish I'd never gone that wretched night.'

'What makes you say that, ma'am?' said Al.

'Well, I'm pretty much homeless and knocking sixty. My house, you been there, I guess?'

The men nodded.

'The house was owned by a corporation, or in some corporate name. Turned out Arnold was renting it off the corporation, we never actually owned it. I wasn't even a tenant listed on the rental agreement. He threatened to have me evicted if I didn't leave of my own free will.'

'Evicted?' said Al.

'Yes. It wasn't either of our property, you see. Although I know it was Arnold's company, it's impossible to prove if it's offshore.'

As she spoke, Marty realized that it was likely Mrs Lomax was the one who had tipped off the Feds about Arnold and his financials.

'Mrs Lomax . . .'

'You boys can call me Linda, I'm trying to forget I was ever a Lomax. Toying with the idea of going back to my maiden name. Deed poll if I can ever afford it.'

Marty spoke quietly now, hoped it would make him her confidant. 'Did you contact the Federal authorities about your husband, Linda?'

'They say I'll get a reward. Five or ten thousand, something like that. I can't say I don't need it. He cleaned out all the savings accounts and everything. And they said on TV that even all the company money has vanished into thin air. I think Peter Gudsen must have found out about the missing money somehow, raised his concerns with someone over at the Church.'

'Why do you say that, Linda?'

She looked down at her feet. 'I know it was wrong, I just couldn't help myself: most nights, I followed Arnold from work. One night, I thought he was going to meet Bobbi someplace, he drove right across town. Instead, he met with Peter Gudsen, over at Shaker's Diner out near the freeway, and right after the meeting, Peter went over to the Mission offices. Perhaps he had another meeting. I just thought it was odd, that late.'

'Did you follow him, ma'am? Peter?'

'No. Peter was a wonderful man. Kind. His daddy, Derek, got him that job with Arnold. I was at high school with Derek. Guess Peter felt obliged to keep the job for as long as possible.'

'Except perhaps when scandal might threaten his career with the Faith?'

'Except. It was ten pm, Peter's meeting over at the Mission offices. Who has a business meeting at that time?'

'How do you know that?' said Al.

'I'd come to my senses outside the diner and headed back here. I was going to my son's for a long weekend in Palm Springs. He'd sent me a plane ticket. I needed to pick up my prescriptions – ever since Arnold kicked me to the curb I'm on all kind of meds. Arnold and Bobbi deserved one another. A home-wrecker and a grade-A asshole. Excuse my French, Detectives. I stopped at the drugstore, picked up the tablets and as I'm driving by the Mission offices on the way back here I see Peter Gudsen getting out of his car. There's a man loitering outside the entrance. He's waiting for him.'

'Did you see who it was?'

'I was stopped at the lights for a little bit, but I didn't recognize him. But Peter had his full Faith uniform on, I guessed he'd been to a meeting or Mission before he met Arnold. But maybe it was for that meeting. Ten pm meetings. I just thought it was odd.'

'That's the kind of time you don't want anyone to see who you're meeting,' said Marty.

'Especially downtown, it's like a ghost town that time of night,' said Al.

'Maybe having lived with Arnold's "meetings" at all hours of the day and night makes me over-suspicious. Maybe it was nothing to do with Arnold's sinking business, but one thing I do know is, the man and Peter, their handshake was kind of abrupt. You know, not friendly, kind of forced.'

'An errant member of the flock, perhaps? He was of stature in the Faith, wasn't he? Peter Gudsen?' said Marty.

'Yes he was. And I don't know what Peter would be doing with another errant sheep. Unless the Faith had tasked him with someone in need of a shepherd. Arnold was probably enough trouble, I'd have thought.'

'Are you saying that you think Peter knew in advance that Arnold's business was fraudulent in some way?' said Al.

'No, but I'm thinking that if he had suspicions he would confront Arnold and then inform the Faith. He was devoted and I think Arnold and the Faith had many dealings over the years. Maybe in this latest venture also.'

'So you think that the Faith had investments in Arnold's business?'

'Businesses, don't you mean? Arnold had so many businesses spread all over that it cost me twenty thousand dollars in accountants' fees just to try and make sense of it. And by the time I had, all the money had disappeared somewhere else. From the records my accountant found Arnold had been doing business in this way for over thirty-five years, straight out of business school. Knowing Peter, it was probably more a case of him wanting to try and stop any small investors, people who had staked their entire futures on this investment, from losing it all, not the Faith's investment. The Faith has plenty of money. Over ten billion a year, if you believe what you read in the *LA Times* and all the rest of them. Saying that, the Faith would not be happy for the bad publicity and bringing inquisitors to their door. Not happy at all.'

'Enough to try and silence Arnold?'

'You think Arnold was the target, not Bobbi?'

'What makes you think Bobbi was the target?' said Marty.

'Because she's the one who's dead.'

'It was a bomb, left – we think – right outside the front door, Linda. Anyone could have picked it up,' said Al.

'Well, who would want to kill Peter Gudsen?'

'What if you're right, Linda?' said Marty.

'About what?'

'That Peter Gudsen told the Faith something was awry with Arnold Lomax's property deals? But if he did, and assuming the Faith was invested heavily in those deals, then word may have got back to Arnold. How do you think Arnold would have reacted to being betrayed in that way by his business partner, even an ex-partner?'

'Oh, he would have been livid. Look what he did to me and I was the one who was betrayed, not the other way around. You think Arnold killed Peter? Oh my . . . what about Bobbi, do you think he killed her?'

'We're not saying he killed anyone, Linda. We're just putting the alternatives out there,' said Al.

'Arnold's a sneaky, cheating son of a bitch, but a killer? No way.'

'Have you heard the name Hartman? Heard your husband mention it?' said Marty.

'No. Why?'

'It's just a name came up, that's all. When you were married to Mr Lomax do you know if he had a life-insurance policy out on you?'

'No, I can't imagine so. I was a home-maker, I didn't bring in any income, what would be the point of insuring me?'

'To help pay for the funeral? Put the kids through college, that kind of thing,' said Al.

'We never discussed it. I hate talking about death.'

'Would it surprise you to know, Linda, that a policy was taken out on your life in 1954 by Mr Arnold Lomax with the Northwestern Insurance Company?' said Marty.

'What?' She spun around in her seat towards Marty. 'Arnold never said anything about that. How come my accountants didn't find it?'

'Maybe they weren't looking properly.'

'How much was it for?'

'One hundred and twenty-five thousand dollars. That policy continues to this day.'

'Today? But we're divorced!'

'Insurance is like gambling. You can bet on anything as long as you can pay the wager,' said Marty.

She sat still now, silent. Trying to take in this information. Then, realizing: 'Did he take one out on Bobbi?'

'Yes, ma'am. With the Golden Gate Insurance Company in the sum of two hundred and fifty thousand dollars.'

Linda Lomax burst out crying. Marty and Al looked at one another. Was it because Arnold had insured Bobbi for twice as much as her? Or was it more a fear–shock thing because, worth way more dead than alive, Bobbi Lomax had ended up very, very dead, while the less-valued Mrs Lomax was still alive – but still worth $125K to a man with a rapidly disappearing portfolio.

Marty nodded to Al to move over to the couch to comfort her, while he made towards the kitchen to fetch her a glass of water. But he would hold back a few minutes until he couldn't hear that sobbing any more.

After some soothing chat from Al and a few drenched Kleenex she seemed recovered. Marty had forgone the water – instead, he'd made her some hot sweet tea. It was a small kitchen, everything had been to hand and relatively easy to find in the lightly stocked cupboards. He guessed it must have been a release to cry. But if he started he didn't know if he would ever stop.

16

December 2nd 1982

He closed the door of the den, as quietly as he could, and turned the key slowly in the lock so it made only the tiniest murmur as it slid into place. Along the darkened corridor he could see the flickering lights of the television. He could hear the sounds of cops chasing bad guys. He knew that she would be sat in there, just like every Thursday night at this time.

He stood in the doorway now, watching her, the empty bassinet on the floor beside her, the baby suckling and Edie's eyes closed, asleep. Edie's favourite, that new cop show *Hill Street Blues*, played on regardless. He thought she must have a thing for Captain Frank, she wouldn't even go to her sister's if it was on. Sis was far too devoted a Follower to have a TV, especially one with cable. Clark had registered it under his Cliff Hartman alias. He didn't put it past the Faith to have one of the Followers inside the local TV company running checks on anyone starting a new account, getting the heads up if any of the flock were straying from the righteous path. The Faith had spent years trying to prevent the cable companies from doing business in Canyon County and beyond, figuring people might replace worshipping in Mission to worshipping the box 24/7 from their armchairs and give up Mission altogether. The Faith certainly didn't want their ten per cent of the flock's income getting diverted en route to their coffers, and especially not by things they'd banned. To avoid snoopers Clark got the TV guide, and the cable bills, sent to the post office box in Arizona he'd set up in Hartman's name with a driver's license he'd spent an afternoon crafting up at the university, using their colour Xerox machine.

Edie insisted on Clark hiding their TV every time her sister was due to visit. The TV had been hefted in and out of the yard store and replaced with a large vase of dusty plastic flowers more times than he cared to remember. Clark watched as the actress playing the bad guy's lawyer, cheekbones you could slice Parmesan on, pushed her glasses back onto her nose and gave the DA a verbal slap-down in front of a vexed-looking judge. As things escalated in court, Clark turned the sound down, so as not to wake Edie. When Captain Frank reappeared onscreen Clark turned the sound back up, then made his way slowly and quietly over to the small table underneath the window. He put the neatly wrapped package down and clicked on the table lamp. The light, the click of the switch or Captain Frank's voice had woken Edie and she was pulling herself upright again now, balancing the baby on her lap as she wrestled her shirt closed with her other hand.

'Clark, I didn't hear you, how long have you been standing there?'

'I just came in.'

'What time is it?'

'Quarter of ten.'

'Oh, I must have dropped off.' She looked around him to the TV. 'I've missed most of it. I could have slept for a week.' She beckoned over to the table. 'What's that?'

She sounded groggy, that was good.

'What?' Clark said.

'That package. On the table.'

'Oh, this?'

He picked it up and gave it to her. This was it, the start of it.

He gestured for her to hand him the baby. Little Lorina, Lori for short. He had told Edie that he thought the name was pretty, delicate. He hadn't told her that the little girl who had inspired his favourite story, *Alice's Adventures in Wonderland*, had a sister called Lorina, named after their mother. He couldn't tell her that, because her very next question would be how he knew such an odd bit of trivia and he could never reveal that to her. Not ever. He could say that the Prophet's work is in the minutiae, the painstaking minutiae of creation. She would like that, invoking the Prophet, but he feared using the word 'creation', feared it would draw her attention and show his hand.

Lori gurgled. He put her over his shoulder. He didn't want her to gripe too much and ruin everything, so he bounced around a little on the spot, patting her on the back, to allow Edie to keep her eyes firmly on the book. Pretending to be engrossed in the TV, Clark watched out of the corner of his eye as Edie unwrapped the Bible from all the layers of protective wrapping he'd used, intent on adding a little suspense into the proceedings, and smiled to himself as she began to flick slowly through its pages.

'Oh, Clark, it's beautiful. How old is it?'

'Three hundred and fifty years. Give or take. 1638 – it's from England.'

'England? I wonder how it got here.'

'Maybe on the *Mayflower*. One sailed in '39.'

'Shame it can't talk.'

Clark was glad it couldn't.

'I'm taking it to Rooks Books tomorrow. I should get a good price for it.'

'Do you really have to sell it?'

'Do you really want to eat this week?'

'But haven't you got something else, one of your coins?' Edie said, silently reading all the pencilled names in the back page, names that he'd spent two weeks researching from microfiche archives at the smaller of the state's two universities, over two hundred miles from home. They had copies of many of the original manuscripts and records held in the Faith's Historical Records Office at their own university, less than three miles away from his house, but he couldn't be seen there, or anywhere local, researching this. Not yet. Edie hadn't liked him being away, but he told her it was one of his multi-state buying trips. She didn't care for coins, so he knew she wouldn't ask to see anything and, even if she did, he had a stash in the basement, so he could show her those.

'I already told you. The recession's really biting, the coin market's not doing so good. I'm trying to diversify. Don't put all your eggs in one basket. Remember?' She'd liked the idea. She didn't much understand why anyone would buy coins and old Faith bank notes as they weren't much to look at. Couldn't hang them on the walls or anything. Well, you could if you liked ugly things. Edie liked pretty things, pretty people, and she really liked babies.

'Oh, Clark, look, how sad.' She held out the Bible to him, pointing to the inside back page with her finger.

'Edie, support it with both hands.'

'Sorry.' She righted the book. 'You see here, this little one, Anna-Beth Bright, she died aged six. And this one. Little William Bright, "died this day April 15th 1832". Just two months.'

'They lost a lot of kids back then, Edie,' he said.

'It must have been awful.' Edie looked closer now. 'It makes me sad, I could just weep thinking about it.'

Please don't. His mother had cried a lifetime of tears.

'All these children and, oh, three wives. They're all listed here. Marriage dates and all.'

'And none of them died before the husband wed the others?'

'No, doesn't read like that.' She looked again. 'Not as far as I can see . . . 1826 was the first marriage, 1834 the second, and the third one just a year later. He was a bigamist. He could have divorced.'

'Obviously didn't want to.'

Clark thought back to his own mother and how it was ru-moured her granddaddy in the tail end of the 1890s had denied the Faith's rules and also taken several wives, all at the same time. It had made his mother an outcast, even though the granddaddy was long dead before she had even been born. Defying the Faith's edicts was the very worst of sins. And its Followers would punish subsequent generations for it, for as long as your father's sins lived in their memories.

'Clark, did you see – one of them was thirteen, another four-teen?'

'The kids?'

'No, the wives. The second and third wives. That's . . .'

'Terrible?'

'It just doesn't seem right.'

'The world was a different place back then.'

'You're right.' She looked skyward. 'Lord, forgive me, who are we to judge?'

'Judge not, lest you be judged,' said Clark.

'Amen,' said Edie. 'Where did you say you got it, Clark?'

He hadn't.

'A collector.' It was a lie. It couldn't take her much longer to notice now, surely, and then she would remember everything that happened.

'Robert Bright married Elizabeth, Rebecca and Ellen.'

She looked up at him. The penny was dropping. He smiled at her. 'Robert Bright?' She looked back down at the Bible. At the names. 'Elizabeth Earnshaw . . . Rebecca Hardy . . . Ellen Mays. It can't be?'

She looked up at Clark again.

'Robert Bright, born Tallahassee, Florida, sometime between Christmas and New Year 1801. No records exist for the precise date.'

'Robert Bright? 1801? Oh my goodness, Clark.' She was trying to whisper on account of baby Lori but her voice rose anyhow. 'Clark. This is *his* Bible?'

'Not his, I don't think. But the immediate family. One of the wives, I'd reckon. And it looks like two very different hands. Both kind of girlish. All the dates match up. As far as I could find, anyhow.'

'Robert Bright? Our Prophet? Clark, when were you going to tell me?'

'I didn't want you to get your hopes up.'

Clark moved to swap the baby for the Bible, but Edie ignored him, started reading the page, pointing out the various passages where in the same pencil – and one of the same hands – Clark, fuelled by Kenny's home-brewed beer and seized by Mesmer, had marked passages in the hand of Rebecca Hardy, second, polygamous wife of the Prophet Robert Bright. Rebecca had accompanied her husband on a calling to the Crystal Arch, where on a searing hot desert day she transcribed the lucid dreams and waking visions of her bigamous husband Robert Bright, twenty years her senior, a former snake oil salesman lately of Kansas City. Rebecca's notations of his dreams and visions, in a language no one could decipher except her and her husband, became commonly known as the Testament of Faith and came to form the cornerstone of the Faith's beliefs.

'Could it be, really?' Edie looked inside its cover pages, scoured the penciled writing for something that might disprove her theory. He could tell, she couldn't see his hand in any of this. His creation. Gently, she closed the cover, her hands clasped together on it as if waiting for morning service to begin. 'You can't sell this, Clark. It would be wrong. You have to donate it to the Church.' He could tell that she was disturbed to see in print the very thing the Faith had spent over 150 years trying to erase from the collective unconscious. Their founder had three wives. All at the same time. For Robert Bright's lifetime and that of his son and successor Robert Jnr, every male member of the Faith had enjoyed the delights of at least several wives at once. Women, however, were allowed just one husband.

'Edie, for all I know this might not even be anything to do with the Prophet. Perhaps some family members filled all this stuff in later. Y'know, like an In Memoriam.'

'It looks pretty old.'

'It is. Sure. It's worth something, even on its own. Without the inscriptions, or any connection to the Prophet.'

'But, if it is the Prophet . . . or his family . . . what will you do?'

'I'll ask the Rooks tomorrow. See what they say. They'll know better than me.'

'You can't sell it, Clark.'

'I'll have to see what they say about it. It could be a fake.'

'A fake?'

'Sure. It could be.'

'Why would anyone fake a Bible?'

'I mean the writing. Not the actual Bible itself, that's real enough.'

'But why?'

Clark shrugged. 'People fake stuff all the time, make it worth something.'

'Shouldn't you take it direct to the Faith? This should be in a museum, Clark. The Mission's museum.'

He knew that she would tell the world. Tell her world. And when she told her sister, she would tell her world and so on and so forth until a ripple of news became a tsunami, one which would reach the Faith maybe before the Bible did. At least, that's what he hoped. He wanted the buzz about it to precede him, to herald his arrival in their orbit.

He took it back off her now. Swapped the baby for it. He watched as, cradling Lori, Edie picked up the bassinet and headed towards the door and up the stairs.

Clark wrapped the book back up in its protective packaging, clicked off the table lamp and followed her.

17

'That's so kind of you, thank you,' said Linda Lomax as Marty placed the cup down in front of her on the small white doily. 'You've both been so kind, I feel as if I should tell you something I did. Something bad. Really bad. I haven't been able to go to Mission since.'

Al shot Marty an expectant look.

'How's Arnold?' said Linda.

Marty raised his eyebrows. 'Ma'am, if you want to call a lawyer . . .'

Linda looked up at him, a Kleenex clamped tight in her fist. 'Can't afford one, is the truth.'

'Still. Do you want to take a moment? We can step out.'

'It's OK.' She picked up the hot tea and took a sip.

Al looked at Marty, one of the what-the-hell-are-you-doing looks he gave him on occasion, but mostly when Marty put the law and the doing-it-right side of his personality between them and closing a case. They hadn't read her the Miranda, she didn't even have the bracelets on, and she hadn't been downtown, or booked in, let alone processed. Anything she said now wouldn't even count, but it might help them close the case. Confessions were good that way.

But Marty knew from the way that she'd asked after the errant Arnold that Linda Lomax still loved the old fool. Took one to know one, he guessed. He also knew those shaky hands couldn't set a tilt bomb into action without blowing her up in the process. Hers were not the hands of a bomb-maker. Bomb-makers need nerves of steel and hands to match. Generally, that ruled out ageing middle-class mothers with a dependency on housewife's heroin. Besides, he'd checked the kitchen cabinets, one of the few storage places in the tiny apartment, and there was no sign of bomb components. No pipes, no blast caps, no nails, no fuses, no stray wires, no mercury, no sulphur and no batches of fireworks that could be gutted for their explosives. But never say never. She could have trained with Baader-Meinhof for all he knew, and he quickly suppressed a smile.

She blew her nose, sighed as if the weight of the world was lifting from her shoulders. Al shifted forward in his seat, pencil poised over his notebook.

'Arnold had a safe, in the house. In his office. Nothing fancy, no electronic codes, tumbler codes, nothing like that. Just a good ol'-fashioned lock with a key. Two keys, to be accurate. It was under his desk, must have weighed a ton. One of my friends, her brother-in-law owns a locksmith company.'

'A locksmith company?'

Al looked a bit confused, his head was all set for the full I-did-it confession. Marty knew it wasn't coming.

'Again, Linda. If you would like a lawyer, we don't want you to incriminate yourself.'

'I don't care any more. Look where I am. Prison might be nicer.'

Marty doubted it. At least this place had a pizza joint underneath.

'There I might have some friends. All my so-called friends are now friends with Arnold and her. Business. Money. That was a mistake, wasn't it, seeing as how he doesn't have any business left.'

'And no money, by all accounts,' said Marty.

She smiled at him, turned to Al. 'A locksmith. You can write that down. But I won't say who or where. He told me what to do.' She looked up at Marty, she was looking for release, for absolution. He could see it. He could trade absolution for information.

'Did it involve a plasticine cast?' Marty asked.

She smiled proudly and her eyes lit up for a moment. 'Yes, yes, it did. It was the day Arnold told me about Bobbi Edwards, as she was then. Told me that they'd been screwing – and that he wanted a divorce, and I was gonna be thrown out like trash. I knew I had to get into that safe, had to find out what he'd got. I knew he'd lie, hide stuff. He rarely let the keys out of his sight. But sometimes out on the lawn he would practice his golf swing, dress in that full ridiculous golfer's outfit and leave the keys on a hook in the kitchen, as they got in the way of his swing. He'd be only about ten yards away from the kitchen door. So, I called my friend, got the locksmith's number and he told me what to get.'

'Plasticine?' said Al.

'Plasticine. There's a kids' toy store just ten minutes' drive from the house, so without even telling Arnold I was going out, in case he changed the locks, I jumped in the car and went and got some. He was still out on the lawn hitting balls when I got back and so I took a small Tupperware dish, put the plasticine in it and pressed down one safe key, grabbed another Tupperware dish and got the second one done. I thought I made sure there was no plasticine left on either of the keys, but I might have been wrong.'

'Why do you say that?'

'Because the next morning after the locksmith had made me the keys – perfectly, they fit right into the locks – when I opened the safe there was absolutely nothing in it.'

'Nothing?' Now it was Marty's turn to look disappointed.

'The SOB had cleaned the safe out. Completely. All I could think of was that he had found a bit of the plasticine on his keys, suspected something and taken everything to the office with him that morning.'

'Did he mention anything about it to you?'

'No.'

'Maybe he'd already cleaned it out, before he told you about the divorce. Taken out anything incriminating.'

'Like my life-insurance policy, perhaps?'

'Looks like Mr Lomax might have had a lot of things to hide, he'd be crazy not to be cautious.'

'So, after, when they were married – I was still watching them, stupid I know. My son called me from Palm Springs and told me her and Arnold were going to change the house locks. He's still in touch with Arnold, but not that often: we have a little grandchild, Arnold Jnr, he's two next month. I just call him Junior.' She looked over to a small shelf which was rammed with baby pictures.

'Cute,' said Al.

'He is, isn't he? It was my last chance. I had to get back in that house. I knew damn well he'd lied to the lawyers, the accountants, everyone including me and his own kids. Arnold Lomax would never leave himself penniless. Not unless the real Arnold's been abducted and replaced with an incredibly dumb alien.'

'I think he's an astute businessman, you're right, ma'am,' said Marty.

'I'd been watching them a few months. Crazy time. But I'd

learnt their patterns. Hers, particularly, as he was out at the office most of the time anyhow. I don't like to speak ill of the dead, Detectives.'

But she would anyway.

'Even Bobbi Lomax, but that girl was a space cadet. We had an alarm system, a good one, she never put that alarm on once. Too many digits to remember, I guess, all three of them: 911.'

Marty smiled.

'So you went back into the house?'

She nodded. 'Morally, that was at least half my house. I don't care what fudge Arnold made of those land records, it was. I was expecting the safe to be full again, that he'd have put back all the papers he'd been hiding from me and whoever else.'

'And it wasn't?'

'No, it was still empty, except for this time at the side, leaning up against the wall so you couldn't see it unless you cranked the safe door completely open, was a slim black notebook, a small one.'

'Really?' said Marty.

'I thought I might have missed it before. But I couldn't have: I'd run my hand around the walls of the safe in case it had any hidden compartments. Wishful thinking. I didn't even want to open it, at first. Who knows what he'd written in it. It's a bit like reading someone's diary.'

'Never know what you'll find,' said Al

It was true: Marty had read Liss's diary, frantically searching for clues. There weren't any. Not that turned into anything real, anyhow. He wanted clues he could follow like crumbs leading away from the witch's cottage and out of the forest. Or was it the other way around? He couldn't remember.

'What did it say, Linda, this notebook?' said Al, pencil ready.

'It was a whole bunch of numbers, a kind of ledger, and what looked like dates, payments in and out, that kind of thing. And in the final column was Arnold's signature on each line and next to it a signature I couldn't read.'

'Could it have been Peter Gudsen's signature?'

'No. I saw Peter's signature on a lot of things. His was very legible. You could read the name easily. Isn't that what the banks say, for security, write legibly so it's less easy to forge?'

'They do indeed. I do that myself,' said Al.

'Was your lawyer able to use any of the information in the ledger, Linda?' said Marty.

'No, I called him. He also asked me where I got the ledger and when I didn't answer him, he guessed I hadn't just come by it. Said we wouldn't get another go-round based on it unless I was prepared to tell him where I had got it. He'd have to tell the divorce judge, something about 'full discovery'. The case had already settled, a few months ago, not that I got anything, this was just all a couple of weeks back.'

'A couple of weeks? Really? Do you still have it, this ledger?'

'No, I don't,' she shook her head. 'When I found out from Peter's dad that he'd quit working with Arnold and that there might be some financial fall-out I went to visit with Peter at his new office. I gave him the ledger. I knew that whatever had gone on over there hadn't been his doing.' She closed her eyes, moved the Kleenex back up to her face. 'May the Prophet protect that poor boy's soul.'

'You gave the ledger to Peter Gudsen?' said Al.

'Yes.'

'Did he know what it was?' said Marty.

'He was shocked when he looked through it. He said it was just what he'd been looking for.'

'Did he say why?' said Marty.

'No, he didn't. He was always very discreet. I was just happy that I could be of some help to him. Even if it just helped him disassociate himself from whatever catastrophe Arnold had cooked up around them.'

'The keys, for the safe, did they have a ribbon around them, tying them together?'

Linda Lomax looked at Marty, astonished. 'Yes, a red one, how did you know that?'

'A red one.' Marty looked at Al.

Al nodded, understanding.

'Did you give those keys to Mr Gudsen?' said Marty.

She hesitated a moment before answering.

'Yes. Yes, I gave the keys to him. And the ledger.'

'Where did you get the red ribbon, ma'am?'

'The ribbon?' She shrugged. 'Probably an old roll left over from Christmas, why?'

'Where is it now, this roll?'

'Probably back at the house. *My* house.'

'We'll check. But you didn't keep a copy of the ledger? Please, ma'am: even if it was just a page, it's very important.'

'No. I honestly didn't.'

'Do you think you could recognize the signature, if you saw it again?'

'I don't know, possibly.'

'Can you remember any of the letters in the signature? Even what you think one might have been, if you can't say for sure?'

'I don't know. It was tiny.'

'But it was written a lot of times on the pages?'

'Yes, fifteen or twenty times, at least. Over a few of the pages. The same one.'

'And the dates, can you remember any of the dates?'

'All over the past year.'

'And the sums?'

'I can't remember the particulars, but I do remember the last line said 666. That's why I remembered it.'

'666?'

'Six hundred and sixty-six thousand. Owing.'

'Arnold owed that much, on one account?'

'No, whoever signed that owed Arnold the money.'

'Owed Arnold? Really?' said Marty.

Linda nodded.

'That's a chunk of change,' said Al.

'Tell me about it. I would have liked to get my share of that.'

'Did you ask Arnold about any of this?'

'No. He called asking me where it was, all irate. Asking how I'd gotten into the safe. Wouldn't he like to know. I told him I didn't know what he was talking about.'

'And what did he say?'

'That there were two copies of it. And I should get a life. Then he slammed the phone down.'

'When was that?'

'The afternoon I took it.'

'And he hasn't mentioned it since?'

'No. We're not in contact.'

'Then there probably are two copies of it. Otherwise, if it's important to prove someone owes you almost three-quarters of a mil, important enough to keep in a safe, you'd kind of need it.

Shame we don't know where either of them is.'

'Big shame,' said Al.

'I saw Peter, at the Mission offices, last week. After I'd given him that ledger.'

'Just last week?' said Marty. He hadn't been much looking forward to his planned meeting with the Faith, but now he couldn't wait.

18

December 22nd 1982

Rooks Books

Outside the months of snow had swamped everything. Inside, though, it was warm and cosy. The books and the Rooks liked it that way. Clark had ensured he went there every week, without fail. Different times, but usually Thursdays or Fridays. Mostly with coins, a good balance of buying and selling. But on one occasion there'd been a book. Henry James, signed first edition, inscribed to his dear friend Edith Wharton. London, 1916. James, his hand weakened, lay dying. Clark, its creator, had thought it was a bit much, overdone, too much of a confection, but Rod had loved it and paid way over the odds. He had a collector friend in London was a big Jamesian and was sure he could flip it fast for a tidy profit.

On his side of the store, Ron, with a tray of Venetian gold ducats in front of him, was peering down his pince-nez, giving descriptions of each one into the handset he hugged tight between shoulder and ear. Rod was staring, stock still, at the Bible in his hands. 'Absolutely unbelievable. Where did you get this, Clark?' It was the first time he had spoken for a good few minutes.

'A collector.'

'Where did he get it?'

'Somewhere on the road. Nevada someplace, I'm sure he said.

He sold vacuum cleaners, door-to-door. Traveled all over. To relieve the monotony of the never-ending loops, he took up antiquing, book collecting. He picked this up in a little antique store. Over thirty years ago, he thought. And now he's retired, the wife wants them to downsize, move nearer their pregnant daughter. He gave me a lot of interesting stuff. At a deal.'

'He didn't realize it might be connected to Robert Bright, maybe even his Bible? *The* Robert Bright?'

'Not a clue. The family's not Faith. I won't tell you how much I got it for, but let me tell you it was a steal. Probably what he would have paid for it thirty years ago.'

'What's his name, the collector?'

'Come on Rod, I can't tell you that. You know the collectors like to fly under the radar. Don't want the Federal Government stiffing them for thousands in taxes on their *investments*.'

Clark knew that mention of the Federal Government would shut that line of enquiry down immediately. The folks of Canyon County were not natural friends of the Federal Government, having been chased into the canyon by them over two hundred years prior on account of their creative, but unlawful, money-making schemes, which often involved selling the same tract of land to thousands of investors, or selling barren land as fertile.

'May I take a closer look?'

'Sure. Take a good long look. I'm here soliciting opinion, Rod: you know how much I value yours. I hope it could be genuine, but history's a bitch.'

'It sure is.'

'I thought it might have been an In Memoriam-type thing, written in after the family had passed, by one of the kids or grandkids.'

'That depends what family branch it ended up in and when. It's likely none of the descendants would have wanted to broadcast their womenfolks' involvement in polygamy.'

It was always better not to be too confident, not to go all guns blazing into hard sell. It was always better to take your foot off the gas, back away a little, give them enough space, enough time and silence to allow the want side of their brain to take over the reason side, and when it did they would have convinced themselves it was the real deal. That way, if reason defeated their want, you'd been the first person to express doubts. It was a win-win situation for you, always.

'So you think the writing was contemporaneous?'

'That would be my guess, Clark. Written at a time when no one had anything to lose by writing about their place in a practice the Faith would stamp out a couple of decades later.'

'So, before polygamy was outlawed?'

'I think so. Let's get a better look.'

Rod took out a cushioned stand and a set of rosary-like beads minus the crucifix. Very gently he lifted the Bible and placed it on the stand, open on the front inside cover. Then he draped the beads over it to hold the page open as gently as possible without too much weight, to avoid flattening the page in the wrong place and weakening it, breaking the book's spine or leaving its pages vulnerable to tearing. Rod took up his magnifying glass. And bent double towards the Bible.

Clark could barely look.

He moved over to the coins. Ron was still on the phone, negotiating a price back and forth with the buyer. They settled on a thousand plus tax. They were getting a rare couple of medieval ducats for that: a pretty good deal. If they were genuine.

Clark smiled at Ron. Ron beamed back at him and turned the tray around so Clark could get a better look. Nice examples. Mostly gold, beaten and battered into wafer-thin coins from a time before it was all done by cast and machines. Even though it was five hundred-plus years ago, the Venetian Mint's records were themselves a treasure trove for collectors and scholars, even revealing the names of the men who had beaten these coins into shape from molten gold: Piero Luigi and Dante San Antonio. Their names preserved forever in the Mint's ledgers.

As Ron read out the Rooks' address to send the check to, Clark moved back over to Rod, who was making some notes on a small jotter. Notes were good. That meant possibility, not instant rejection. Rod looked up over his pince-nez: 'It's wonderful, Clark.' He seemed reluctant to close it up and hand it back. That was another good sign. 'From what I can tell, Clark, these dates are right. Did you check them also?'

'Of course.'

'Pencil's impossible to date.'

'Of course.'

'So that doesn't help.'

'Although I hear the FBI have been trialing some carbon and lead tests.'

'Sooner the better.'

Clark hoped the Bureau would take a good couple of decades to perfect that, as his creations were beginning to rely on it.

'I thought the two different types of handwriting were interesting,' said Rod.

'Well, if it belonged to one of the wives, it might have been one of the kids writing in it? Maybe after the mother passed.'

'Traditionally, it'd be the wives who wrote in it, and no one else. Educated wives or, at least, ones schooled in their letters, as it would have been then.'

'So you're saying this might be the handwriting of two of the Prophet's wives. Two?' Clark hoped he sounded surprised, but he wasn't. He had been both of those child-wives. Rebecca and Ellen. Three nights ago. He had written in charcoal pencil because he knew it was impossible to date and because it was likely that, on the road, the Prophet and his band of Merry Women would have had access to charcoal pencils more readily than ink.

'If this is all genuine – and not, as you so rightly said, perhaps an In Memoriam added later – then this is a very interesting find, Clark. An important find. Controversial. But important all the same. The three wives and no record of any divorces means these were bigamous, of course. But I think you'd find a buyer, no problem. You'll have to get provenance on it.'

'Naturally.' Clark had already planned for that and it involved Edie and the baby, representing a solid Faith family unit, and a long trip to a small suburb of Reno, probably with a diversion en route for the slots. 'How much do you think it might be worth?'

'I'd pay four thousand,' Rod said, smiling. He was slowly removing the beads and turning the cover page back over the Bible, but when he picked it up Clark recognized an expert's instinct, a refined curiosity crossing Rod's face.

'That's funny.'

'What?'

'There's some kind of bump here.'

'It's old, Rod, it's bound to have a few bumps,' said Clark.

'No, underneath the cover.'

'Not going to affect the value, is it?'

'Feels like there's something in here.'

Rod held the book closer, staring at it, prodding at it with the eraser end of his pencil.

'Here.'

'Careful, Rod, it's old, don't rip the pages none.'

'There's something in here. Feel.'

He handed it to Clark.

'Oh, yeah, I see what you mean.'

'Do you want me to find out what it is?' said Rod.

'I don't know if we should.'

'Now, don't worry, Clark. I'll be gentle.'

Ron was by Rod's side now, peering down at him as he used the tip of a scalpel to prise open the book's spine and moved the knife slowly from side to side under the cover.

'What's all this?'

'Don't interrupt him, Ron. I don't want a chunk out of my Bible.'

'There's something in here.' Rod didn't look up from his task.

'What is it?' said Ron.

'That's what we're trying to find out,' said Rod as both the other men stared down nervously at him. 'OK, I've tweaked a little opening. There's definitely something in here, looks like a piece of old paper.'

'Maybe it's an old treasure map. Oh, I love treasure,' said Ron.

'Don't you have enough to keep you going?' said Clark, nodding his head in the direction of the rows of coin trays.

'You can never have too much treasure, Clark.'

'Do you want me to open it right up?'

'Rod, are you sure you should?' Ron asked.

'Can't you see what the piece of paper is?' said Clark.

'No.'

'We think this Bible might have belonged to one of the Prophet's wives, Ron.'

'Really? Which one?'

'Rebecca,' said Clark.

Ron looked suitably astonished. 'Rebecca. His amanuensis?'

'That's the one,' said Rod, nose to the task. 'His second wife. I'm in. See, told you it'd be OK.' He picked up a set of tweezers, lifted up the Bible's leather covering and teased out the piece of paper from within.

'Careful, Rod, careful,' said Clark as he watched.

Moments later, almost with a flourish, Rod was holding up a piece of parchment with strange symbols all across it.

'Maybe it is an old treasure map, in some strange language,' said Clark.

'That's no strange language.'

'It isn't?'

'No, Clark, don't you recognize it?'

'It looks kind of familiar.'

'That's the language the Spirit spoke to the Prophet in, and the only way the Spirit would let Rebecca transcribe his words.'

Clark stared at the paper. 'It looks like a bunch of symbols: hieroglyphics. I remember it from Sunday School, now. It's been a while.'

'The Voice of the Spirit has many similar characteristics, but it is its own language. We are not meant to fully understand it. Just feel its power,' said Ron, gazing at the manuscript.

'The Spirit chose the Prophet to hear his words, and for Rebecca to transcribe them. The Voice of the Spirit came unto the Prophet while at the Crystal Arch, a language only he heard, and, as he repeated the Spirit's words, Rebecca transcribed them into a written language. She said later she could not control her arm, her movements. The Spirit was within her and he controlled her, to bring the Voice of the Spirit to the world through the vessel that was our Lord Prophet so that he would enable us, the Children of Satan, to be delivered from ourselves.'

'Amen,' said Ron.

Rod must be practicing for his new role in the Faith. Clark must have heard that sermon thousands of times. Or at least, the over-long, tedious sermon it was a very small part of. 'Amen,' said Clark. And, as both Ron and Rod had, he raised his clasped hands to his chest as a mark of respect to the Lord Prophet.

'Clark, I think this could be part of the Testament of Faith. The original.'

'The original? The one that Rebecca transcribed?' said Ron, his mouth so open it was catching flies.

'Possibly,' said Rod. '*Very* possibly.'

Want over reason, thought Clark as he watched Rod stride over to the telephone.

'I need to get an expert down here.'

'Now?' said Clark.

'Right now,' said Rod.

'It's almost eight pm. Who's going to come out now?'

'For this?' said Rod. He was punching in numbers out of an address book. 'Any sane person. This . . . this could change lives.'

'Who you calling?' said Ron.

Rod ignored him, put one hand over his ear and pressed the handset up against the other.

'Clark, where did you say that traveling salesman got this?'

'Nevada. Reno, I think.'

'Reno. That's where Rebecca Bright went after Robert Bright's death. Her family were from there. That must be how it got there.'

Want over reason.

Want. Want. Want. Over reason.

19

November 2nd 1983

Abraham City Police HQ

'Rise and shine, I got breakfast.' Marty opened his eyes and saw a foil-wrapped taco being waved in his direction. Al dumped the taco and a large carton of OJ down on Marty's desk. Marty had the floor last night; Al had slept on his chair, feet up on his desk, until one of the rookie detectives, Hobbs, woke him up a few hours ago. Al was back at his desk now, facing Marty. From all the stuff piled on top of both the desks it was hard to see where one ended and the other began. The only thing that set them apart was that Al's had an electric typewriter on it. Marty couldn't type for shit and Al was pretty fast. He would have made someone a great secretary. Still might.

'Where is everyone?' said Marty, twisting himself up off the floor.

'Someone ran a stop light, over by the freeway.'

'Drunk?'

'I'll let you know when they find 'em. They smashed into a drugstore and then took off. A passing trucker said one of them went out the windscreen, was bleeding bad, so sometime soon he's gonna need a hospital.'

'Or the morgue,' said Marty.

'I put the call out. They wiped out the drugstore.'

'Robbed it?'

Al shook his head. 'No. Fireball. Place is incinerated. Lucky the two of them didn't fry.'

Marty smiled. 'Maybe they just took a wrong turn.'

'Yeah, straight to county jail.'

Marty picked up the taco. Unwrapped it.

'Casa Alvarez.'

Marty, his mouth full of its flavors, said, 'Five-star. Thanks, Maria.'

'We got the name of the driver off the engine plate, that was about all that was left. I sent Hobbs and Carvell over to the owner. It was stolen, earlier in the night, off some old couple. They're headed back.'

'Why didn't you wake me?'

'For that shit? Did you want the call?'

'Not really. Sleep's better than chasing down a couple of punks. When did you make it home?'

'Just after. I thought I'd see the kids before they headed off to school. They were fighting over something or other. I shouldn't have bothered.'

Marty rolled up the silver foil, tossed it into their shared wastebasket. 'I'm glad you did.'

*

By the time Marty had showered and was headed back to his desk the room was full again, ready for the morning briefing. Not that there was much to report, but Marty wanted a word with Gary Hobbs first. On Day 2, after the Sheriff's press briefing, Marty had tasked Hobbs and his partner, Carvell, with interviewing the one per cent of the disgruntled three thousand who had lost the largest investments in the Lomax company, figuring that they were probably higher on the motivation Richter scale than the rest of the list. It would be good to see what questioning might bring. Marty stopped at Hobbs' desk. 'How's it going, Gary?'

'The bomber, right, not the drugstore cowboys?'

'Yeah, the former.'

'Well, it's promising, that's for sure. Might all turn to crap soon, but right now it's promising. We got four guys flagged up we could bring in, I was going to do some background checks on them last night, but then the cowboys finished that.'

'What did they say, in the interviews?'

'Yeah, well, Mart, that's it: they didn't show up for the interviews.'

'You gave them notice, right?'

'Sure. Carvell did the ring-around. Gave them all appointment times. And these guys were just no-shows.'

'They know each other, you reckon?'

'Small town, Mart, most everyone knows everyone or knows someone who does. Between us yesterday we knew most of the investors.'

Marty smiled, it was too small a town. He had never figured out why the crime rate here was so high. He guessed no one here had heard the expression, 'Never crap on your own doorstep'.

'Next time, pull the records and do the research before you get them in.'

Hobbs nodded. He knew it was a screw-up. He was only two years as detective and in his defense this was the first time Abraham City had ever had anything that might be described as a murderous bombing spree.

'Anyone bring a lawyer?'

'No. And we saw twenty-four investors. All men. Two were away on business, out of the country.'

'When did they leave?'

'Before the bombings, according to secretaries and wives. They're going to contact them and get them to call me. I said it was urgent. The ones we spoke to yesterday were all seasoned investors, seemed resigned to the loss of their money. It's crazy: some lost almost a hundred grand. Didn't even bat an eyelid when I said that was good motive for murder. Win some, lose some was the general attitude.'

Arnold Lomax had certainly lost, that's for sure. Not to mention his wife and Peter Gudsen, and Houseman all mangled and still in a coma.

'Just the four no-shows? Nothing else suspicious about any of the others?'

'Not at interview. You want us to dig deeper now?'

'No, wait. Track down the no-shows first.'

'Yeah, hopefully it's one of them because otherwise we got about two thousand, nine hundred and seventy others to interview.'

'Put a BOLO out on the no-shows. And when you do their backgrounds put any of them with military experience to the top of your list, particularly ordnance.'

They'd be top of the list for property search warrants also. But first they'd need probable cause.

Hobbs was a promising detective and he was connected, Abraham City style. Which had its advantages and disadvantages, but as long as the information was flowing into the department, not out of it, it wasn't a problem. Hobbs' father, Eric, was the Senior Brother in the Supreme Chamber, a kind of Disciples B-team should one of the Disciples shuffle off the mortal coil without much notice and before they could call an internal election with bishops attending from all around the world. Disciple was a job for life, not something anyone ever quit from.

'Thanks, Marty. We'll get on it right after the briefing.'

'Forget the briefing. Start it now. You and Carvell. Grab a couple of the other guys and get it done as soon as.'

'Sure thing.'

*

Marty was back at his desk now, not that he could see it for paper and throw-away coffee cups.

'Somebody just dropped this off for you, sir.' It was Campbell, one of the young uniforms who worked the reception desk. He held out a small white box. Marty looked at the kid. Didn't take it.

'At least it doesn't have red ribbon around it,' said Al from his desk opposite.

'We had it checked, sir. It's OK.'

'Maybe the guy changed his modus operandi, Al.'

'Or just ran out of ribbon,' said Al smiling.

'Aren't you and Tex just gonna fry that Houseman guy?'

'Maybe. There's not been any bombs since Houseman on Halloween. That's over forty-eight hours. There was only thirty-three hours between the second and third ones, and just fifty-two minutes between the first two, Lomax and Gudsen. So maybe it's over.'

'We won't need that new computer if you keep that up, Al.' Marty took the package off Campbell. 'Thanks. I think.' Marty began to search the desk for a scissors. The package was so bound up with masking tape the sender must not have wanted anyone to open it up. At least not fast. 'What's your point?'

'My point is, man, that no matter what way you look at it the guy is lying low, either lying in the hospital or lying in wait for his next one.'

'And we don't know which?'

'Doesn't look like it. Not for sure.'

'Rome wasn't built in a day.'

'Yeah, but nobody blew it up, either,' said Al.

'Yeah, but they did set fire to it.'

'And fiddled while it burned.'

'What you trying to say, Al?'

'I'm trying to say I wish we had the answers already.'

'Answers aren't always . . .'

'Yeah, yeah I know. I need a piss. Good time to ship out anyhow: it was nice knowing you.' Al got up and moved towards the restrooms.

Marty had hacked his way into the package. Inside was a bulk of bubble wrap, already split open with his heavy-handed scissoring. He prised it open. Right at the heart of it all was a tiny book. He looked at it, flicked through it. It was the Old Testament, in Hebrew. Just like the one that Peter Gudsen had bought for Marion. He looked down at the discarded outer packaging. He could see a small envelope. He opened it up. Inside was a handwritten card.

Detective Marty, I think Peter would have liked you to have this.
Take care of it, and yourself. Yours, Marion Rose.

Above the handwriting was a heavily printed line and above that it read: FROM THE DESK OF MRS MARION ROSE. Underneath was printed her home address and a telephone number. He looked at the phone on his desk. He could call her, right now. What would he say? Here in the precinct, with everyone listening in. Thank you would be a start. He picked up the handset.

'Hey Marty.' It was Johnny Carvell, stood right next to the desk. 'I almost forgot. I took a call for you last night. Some guy called Burkeman. Said he's got some information about the bombings. He's gonna call you back.'

'That it?'

Carvell shrugged. 'That's it.'

'I don't know any Burkeman, that the name?'

'Yeah.'

'Did he say what it was about?'

'The case. He'll call back. He was en route to Cali.'

'What did he say about it?' You always had to drag everything out of Carvell.

'That he had some information.'

'And you didn't think to take it down?'

'I asked. He wasn't very . . .'

'Forthcoming?'

'Yeah, that. Said he only wanted to talk to you. He sounded high or something.'

'It gets better. A high informant heading out of state.'

'The gift that keeps on giving.'

'Did you get a number?'

'I told you: he's traveling.'

Marty hung up the receiver. Hobbs was beside Carvell now.

'Hey Marty, I can go over to the Faith for you later if you want

– once we've done the checks,' said Hobbs. 'I heard you had to cancel your appointment with Laidlaw.'

The Faith jungle drums reach far.

'Postponed it. A bit later. High noon. Don't worry. I got it.'

'If you're sure. I don't mind.'

'I'm good. Thanks, Gary. Keep an eye on Carvell here and the rest of them. Page me when you get something interesting.'

'Sure.' Gary Hobbs and everyone connected with the Faith knew that Alan Laidlaw, the second highest member of the Order of the Twelve Disciples, blamed Marty for the loss of his daughter, Sherri. Lost her to another place, another state, far away from here. But mostly Alan Laidlaw directed his venomous, all-consuming hatred at him not because of Sherri, but because he had 'lost' his only granddaughter, Liss, while she was, ostensibly, in the care of Marty, her father.

Just after that, Sherri had moved to Vegas with that lawyer she'd been having an affair with for over a year. He had a small law firm off the Strip specializing in contracts for cabaret artistes. Cabaret. She had taken Drew, her and Marty's son, with her.

Marty had heard rumors in the Precinct that old man Laidlaw believed he had something to do with Liss's disappearance. For sure, some people didn't look at Marty the same way any more. And it wasn't just pity.

20

The Mission

Not for them the theatre of sweeping through the high entrance with its magnificent gilded gates that opened onto the Faith's glorious cathedral and its towering golden spire. Instead, the Rooks' discretion decreed they not head that way, not this time of night with tourists and the Faithful gathered at the gates, pushing their Kodaks through the wrought iron to catch the twinkling multicolored light show that lit up the golden spire as it reached out shimmering to heaven. Clark silently agreed. It was never a good idea to catch the attention of the camera-wielding curious. Instead, the Rooks' Oldsmobile Cruiser rumbled towards the side gate and parked right alongside the only other car in the lot.

Clark was so near now he made sure to control everything, his breathing, every movement of his limbs, his speech. Nothing could give him away. The Rooks trusted him, he knew that. They wouldn't be looking for a tell, but their contact might be. Who knew how many documents he saw a year claiming to be this and that? How many he and the Faith rejected? But Clark couldn't have the taint of rejection. Not now. Not when he was so close.

With Rod leading, the three of them soon found themselves through the Mission's discreet side door and inside, near the back of a closed and probably locked door marked 'Sacristy' with a bronze plaque in faux-Victorian Gothic etching. There was no one to greet them. Clark was grateful, he could feel the sweat on his palms. Following Rod, he held a door open for Ron and with both men in front of him Clark moved his hands slowly into his chinos pockets and left them there, sweat soaking into the lining.

Rod led them past the sacristy into a long brightly-lit corridor with numerous rooms off of it, doors all shut tight and probably firmly locked. At the end of the corridor a door was ajar. Light bled out from it. Somewhere in the back of his mind he heard Rod say, 'He'll be in there,' and watched as his pace picked up. Clark knew on the other side of that door was a man who would either make or break his life. He slowed his breath down and pushed his hands deeper into his pockets.

Inside the room, hand outstretched and headed straight for Clark, was a short, trim man who looked no more than thirty. Clark set his face to full beam.

'You must be Clark Houseman. Welcome to our magnificent Faith library, Clark. And thank you for coming here at this hour. I'm Peter. Peter Gudsen.'

Clark already knew that. He had made it his business to know. Peter Gudsen. Thirty-six. Accountant. Married. Of course. Four young boys. The Faith's chief archivist. A man with a penchant for Faith history and a care for its words. Clark knew that such a responsible position must be chosen from within the Church's circle of trust and so, as the Faith's rising star, Peter Gudsen was the perfect conduit for Clark's ambitions.

'Thank you for inviting me, Mr Gudsen.'

'Peter, please.'

'I hope we haven't ruined your evening, Peter.'

'On the contrary, from what Rod tells me you and he might be about to make my century.' He beckoned for the others to follow him and then he walked quickly back towards the center of the room. 'While I was waiting for you, I took a little time to gather together some copies of our existing Testament of Faith. Which, as you know, is just a copy of the original. No one alive has ever seen the original. We just have these.' He talked fast. Excited. He wouldn't be good at poker.

Gudsen guided them over to where he now stood, at a tall table in the middle of the room. What looked like a large jigsaw made up of three huge pieces was already laid out on it. Clark would have recognized the document immediately, even without Peter's preamble. He could see the oversized Xeroxes of the extant copies of the Testament of Faith – the original of which had been transcribed by Rebecca Bright. The original was believed lost, and only these three copies had ever been found, possibly taken from a copy salvaged from Robert Bright's person before or after death. Days after capture Bright had been slain by his captors, who grew impatient waiting for the Federal Government forces to arrive and take him away. He was wanted Dead or Alive, so they'd get their money anyhow. Now he just didn't need feeding.

Clark's guess was that the Federal Government, who considered Bright and his flock heretics, had already caught up with the safe-keeper of the original Testament and dispatched him to an early rendezvous with his maker. That was why, for the past 150 years, no credible stories were told of where the original had gotten to, and why there was no evidence it had survived beyond the life of its bearer. Rebecca Bright made no mention of it in subsequent correspondence either before or after she reached the sanctuary of Reno.

Rod, who had been clutching the Bible on the ride over, passed it to Gudsen, who laid it on a book cradle in front of him. 'They're in the front?'

'Yes,' said Rod, 'and some entries at the back also.'

Peter turned the page slowly, as if fearing a disappointment in what Rod had briefed him was there, one that might physically wound him. To his side, he had some pages that Clark could see were samples of Rebecca and the other wives' handwriting. Researching Gudsen, Clark had discovered that he didn't have any academic credentials in manuscript verification. He certainly wasn't letting it show. He was well organized. He felt Peter's gaze land on him: 'Were you looking for a buyer for this Bible, Clark?'

'A buyer? Oh. I hadn't thought that far in advance. I was just keen to see if it was all for real,' said Clark.

'Well, thus far, despite the unorthodox nature of our Prophet's since outlawed domestic arrangements, or maybe because of them, it does seem genuine. From very basic perusal, it certainly looks like Rebecca Hardy-Bright's handwriting. You'll easily find a good buyer for this. I just don't know if it will be the Faith or not. It's not generally something they would wish to have reminders of.'

Peter closed up the Bible and pushed it back towards the three of them. 'Where's the document you think might be the Testament?'

Clark thought Peter was doing better now, playing it much cooler. But, judging by the amount of stuff he'd had time to pull out of the archives, he had left his wife and kids at home the minute he got the call and headed out into the freezing night. Clark knew Peter really wanted to see the Testament. Clark could tell by the way he busied himself folding up pieces of paper, not wanting to look nor make eye contact, not wishing to overly anticipate the unveiling.

Rod, smiling now, pushed the Bible back towards Peter. 'Where we found it.'

'In here, still?' Peter looked incredulous.

'We thought it would be safer there,' said Rod. 'After all, it's probably been in there, undiscovered, for a hundred and fifty years or more. And it doesn't seem to have come to any harm.' Rod prised the outer cover open for him to reveal the manuscript page hidden inside. Rod then passed Peter his tweezers and with the manuscript on the table in front of them, Peter took up a magnifying glass and began to pore over the document. Clark watched as his distorted lens eye feasted faster and faster on every word.

Clark made sure to stand silently as, next to him, Rod and Ron oozed excitement. It was better that way: if his plan didn't work, the focus of failure would be on the Rooks, Rod in particular, and not on Clark. That way he'd get to try again, another time, another document, but maybe with different companions.

Clark watched as Peter silently picked up the Xeroxed pages and his magnifying glass and began comparing them against one another and then with Clark's version.

'I've never been here before,' said Ron. 'Not back here. The Mission for service, of course, every Sunday without fail. But never beyond that.'

Be quiet, Ron, Clark wanted to say. But didn't. Instead, he gently took Ron's elbow and guided him silently away from the table, not wishing to distract the want part of Peter's brain, or risk bringing it back to the reality of reason.

'It's kind of ethereal, isn't it?' said Ron, looking skyward.

Clark figured Ron must mean the random beams of fake light streaked across the ceiling and the fact there were stained-glass windows up about forty feet in the air – not so much windows but huge panes of backlit painted glass featuring illustrated highlights of the Good Book.

'You see here, and here?' said Peter.

Clark and Ron stepped back to the table where Peter was now holding up Clark's document.

'This triangle? Sometimes it's Phoenician and sometimes it's Greek. It's not consistent. It symbolizes the planet Lumina and the gateway to the Faith. So, it may not have been someone from the Faith who transcribed or copied it. There's a few other examples. But, from what we already know, versions two and three we believe were orally transcribed from memory by someone who had seen version one,' said Peter.

'But not seen the original?' said Rod.

'That's correct. Two and three have a lot of the same inconsistencies. Version one hasn't.'

'Also,' Rod was looking at the documents now, 'it looks as if the hand that drew version one is the same hand that drew this version we discovered.'

He was right, of course. Well, almost. Clark had spent months copying those movements, getting that perfected.

Peter held up their version and his Xerox of version one, as he referred to it.

'But, and this is where it gets really interesting.' He put them down on the table and laid version one on top of their copy. He used an upended pencil to indicate a line of symbols at the very bottom of their version. His pencil then hovered over version one. 'Where version one is torn, all the way across, can you see here?' They all leaned forward, nodded assent. 'We can see little hints of a missing line from the bottom. A line that until now we have never seen the original of. But look how the small drawn parts of the symbols, ghosts if you will, from version one are here at the bottom of yours, fully formed.'

'Amazing,' said Ron and Rod at precisely the same moment.

'It is amazing, isn't it?' said Peter.

'Miraculous,' said Clark as he clasped his hands together, closed his eyes, a gesture the others all copied.

To exactly match those symbols to ones that were used in Phoenician, Egyptian and Greek alphabets, and to which he knew Robert and Rebecca Bright must have had access, had led Clark away from Abraham City and the surrounding state, a thousand-mile round trip to one of Colorado's most prestigious university libraries, where he had pretended to be a novelist's re-search assistant, in search of the secrets of the past. He felt bad when they asked when the book would be coming out. Next winter, he said, and almost believed it himself.

'Well, looks like you found yourself some treasure, Clark,' said Ron.

'But first we need you to get the Bible verified, even if it's ob-viously not for us. Once that's done we can begin verifying the Testament,' said Peter.

'Do you do that, Peter, the verifying?' said Clark.

'I do, with the help of some Faith scholars here at the library.'

So, no proper forensic testing. Just a few academics and Peter. Clark looked at the others. They all seemed to be sharing the same wide smile. Clark tried not to make his too wide.

21

November 2nd 1983, 9 am

Houseman Residence

Marty waited outside the nondescript house for Al to catch him up on the snowy path. 'Surprise is the best form of attack. Car on the drive. Lights on downstairs. One upstairs. Told you she'd be here, didn't I?'

'We should have called first,' said Al. 'What if it's not her? I got mountains of so-called evidence to wade through back on my desk. You too. And this place ain't exactly on our doorstep.'

'It's her.'

'Maybe it's a burglar.'

'Then this isn't his lucky day. C'mon.'

Marty knew they'd be there. About now: breakfast time. Knew that Edie Houseman would want to have some kind of normalcy for the kids. She probably hadn't even told them that their daddy was injured and in the hospital. Might not have wanted to worry them or answer endless questions they didn't have the ability to comprehend the answers to. Just keep it quiet, all bottled up inside. Then, if you didn't say it aloud too much, it couldn't be true, could it?

At the door they rang the doorbell so discreet it dared to be found. Marty, badge in hand, nudged Al. 'You not a cop today?'

'Not if it's a burglar: can't face the paperwork.'

'Yeah, and after all those tacos, don't think you could face the chase.'

Al was just about to reply when the door inched open. A petite, mousy blonde woman, looked about sixteen, except for the dark shadows underneath her eyes which told another story.

'Miss, we're here to see Mrs Houseman,' said Al. He had obviously bet on sixteen, or was hoping to score some brownie points.

'I'm Mrs Houseman.'

'Edie Houseman?' said Al.

'That's correct, Officer.'

Detective, Marty wanted to say, but didn't. 'We're here about what happened to your husband, Mrs Houseman.'

'Mommy! Mommy!'

Edie turned her face away from them and yelled into the back of the room. 'Sssh Jack, Mommy's busy.'

'Would it help if we came in?' offered Al.

'Oh, yes, I'm sorry.' The door swung open into the living room. She moved fast across the room and scooped up a young boy, maybe four or so, from out behind the sofa.

'That's his den, he likes it back there. Always hiding from Mommy. He's a little devil. Aren't you?'

'Little devil,' the kid repeated.

'Cute kid,' said Al.

Parents always liked that.

'Thanks. May I offer you some orange juice?'

Winter. Snow on the ground. Cold soft drink for the guests. She was definitely a Follower.

'That would be lovely, thank you, Mrs Houseman,' said Marty.

'Ice with that?'

'No thanks, ma'am,' said Al as she turned her back on them and headed out to the kitchen.

Marty nodded for Al to follow her. Al shot him a look, but got up silently and followed her out. Marty could feel Jack's eyes burning through his back. He'd have to stick to a surface search, no drawers or cupboards. In case the 'little devil' had a big mouth. There were a few framed photographs: a wedding picture, some baby pictures and a collage on the wall. He started with the collage, peering close to see if there might be anything of interest. There wasn't. The baby pictures were pretty standard, but he picked up the frames just to check the backs. They were cheap plastic jobs, from some Taiwanese factory. There was a picture of Edie and Clark. He assumed it was Clark. He'd looked kind of different the times Marty had seen him, all bloodied on the street, and all scratched and bruised up, that air thing on his face over at the hospital. And his driver's license had been different, he'd had facial hair. Clark obviously hadn't changed that picture for a few years because in this one he was clean-shaven. Marty held it up. Edie and Clark's faces were in close-up. It was dark. Except for in the darkness there was an unnatural glow, not just from the light of the flash, but from what looked like a neon sign in the corner of the shot. It was so close to Edie's face it looked as if it was sticking out her left ear. Marty smiled. Nice picture. They were having fun. Not Mission, obviously. She had make-up on. Her hair tonged and flicked. The Faith did not appreciate that kind of preening.

'Mommy.'

Marty looked around. There was no one in the room but him and the kid who was stood right next to him now, staring up at him. Good thing he didn't go through the drawers. 'Mommy. That's right. And Daddy?'

'Daddy,' the kid said, reaching up for the picture.

'Let's put it back, keep it safe, hey?' Marty placed the photo back on the shelf. It was devoid of books or whatever else it was Houseman was selling. Instead, the shelves were filled with little china nick-nacks. There was a small artist's sketch of Robert Bright, in a more upmarket-looking frame. Marty picked it up. Silver. A good weight. For some strange reason, Robert Bright was wearing a shepherd's outfit, carrying a crook, and was surrounded by animals up on a desolate hillside. It looked exactly like a picture Marty had seen of St Francis of Assisi when he and Sherri had been on their honeymoon in Italy. A wedding gift from her dad. They had argued the whole time. Marty hated Italy. But maybe it was just the company.

Marty wanted everything to be normal for Drew. He was eight then. So Sherri had tried to keep his routine going, but everything had been falling in on them, collapsing like the walls around a condemned house. Two days after Liss disappeared Sherri had collected Drew from his grandfather's and taken him to school. She had to collect him at lunchtime, his face streaked with tears, with what all the kids were saying about what had happened to Liss. Those kids didn't know anything, but Drew was too young to understand that. Marty and Sherri had sat him down, said to him that nobody knew where Liss was, particularly those kids at school. But one day she might be back, walk back in the door just like she'd walked out of it. Marty didn't know if they were trying to convince themselves or Drew. 'What about them?' Drew had asked as he looked outside where what looked like a delegation from every law enforcement agency stood out on the lawn.

'Do they know where Liss is?' Sherri had taken the boy straight back to his grandfather's house. This time the trunk of her car was filled with suitcases.

'I'm sorry. We had to make fresh. Your friend is good in the kitchen. He cut up all the oranges.'

'Sorry to put you to any trouble, ma'am,' said Marty as he picked a glass up off the tray.

'It's no trouble. It keeps my mind off —'

'It can't be easy,' said Al.

'It's awful. Just awful. My sister's coming over soon. I'm going back up to the hospital.' She looked at her watch.

'We won't keep you long,' said Marty. He was still standing by the shelf. 'Nice photograph. You and Mr Houseman?'

'Yes, we were in Vay . . .' she stopped herself. Was she going to say Vegas? That large C, Caesar's Palace, of course. He knew it looked familiar.

'Oh, Vegas. Were you staying at Caesar's?'

'No, no. No. Sorry. That's not Vegas. I don't remember where that was taken.'

Very interesting. Why lie about that? Something to do with having no books, no TV, and serving OJ when it's minus eight outside. Where would Vegas fit into that life? Maybe she and Houseman weren't so devout after all.

Al took his cue from the silence that followed: got out his notepad and pencil. 'On the day of the bombing, ma'am, did you see your husband?'

'Yes.'

'What time was that?'

'He woke me with breakfast in bed.'

'Do you remember what time?'

145

'Oh, about six am. I was surprised, it's usually just weekends he does that.'

'Was there a special occasion?'

'No. Clark just said he'd done a good deal on something and wanted to celebrate. We had pancakes. And syrup.'

'Do you know what this deal was?'

'He'd been out late, working on it.'

'Where was that?'

'Oh, I don't know. Probably far. He didn't say. He woke me up, coming in.'

'And what time was that?'

'Two am.'

'He didn't say who he was meeting?'

'No. Clark wouldn't discuss his business with me. The clients would expect privacy.'

'And he didn't say where?'

She shook her head.

Marty saw a handful of invitations on the small desk to the side of Robert Bright as Francis of Assisi.

'Going to a wedding?'

'Oh, no. I write those, for couples. It's called calligraphy.'

Marty held them up, so Al could see.

'Very pretty. You do all that? By hand?' said Al.

'Yes.' She looked proud now. 'Fifty cents each.'

Marty moved slowly around, checking what else the room might give up. He moved at a snail's pace so it didn't distract her from Al's questions.

'That's a nice little sideline.'

'It's great with the kids. It means I can stay at home part-time. Work from in here. It's fun. Clark and I took the class together.'

'And your husband, Clark, where's his office?'

'Clark's always on the road. Traveling here and there, with his coins, collector's items and all that stuff.'

'Do you have a number, for the office?'

'Oh, I never call him when he's at work.'

'Wish my wife thought like that,' said Al and they both laughed.

'I beep him sometimes but only if it's a real emergency. Like when little Jack broke his arm last summer. I called Clark from the emergency room.'

Marty jumped in: 'Called him? So, there is a number?'

'I'm sorry, Officer. I meant paged him. I paged him and he called back the number, the nurses' station in the ER. They let me use their phone.'

'That was nice of them,' said Al.

'It was. I was so upset. Stupid really. Only a broken arm. "Soon mended," Clark said when he arrived. Brought Jack some sweets and he soon forgot the arm. Although he got half the neighborhood to sign the cast and cried when they had to take it off.'

'Could we have your husband's pager number, Mrs Houseman?'

'Do you think it'll help find whoever did this?'

'Yes, ma'am. We do. We think he might have been going to meet someone.'

'Maybe the person who planted the bomb?'

'Maybe. No one's called here, saying they were due to meet your husband that day?'

'No. Clark doesn't get business calls here. His work is really very confidential.'

Marty figured that was Clark's way of getting out of the house, someplace.

Edie started foraging deep in her bag.

'Clark was lucky, really. He's still alive. That poor girl, Bobbi, wasn't it?' They nodded. 'And Brother Gudsen.'

She pulled out a whole bunch of stuff, keys, a tissue, a pen.

'It's in here somewhere, my address book, always buried.'

From the depths of her bag, she pulled out a couple of books. Small ones. One slimmer than the other. She opened up the tiny address book, with barely visible tabs.

'Clark. Clark. Pager. Here.'

She pointed the number out to Al and handed the book to him to copy it out. Marty was looking at the other book she still had in the clutch of stuff in her other hand. He put his hand on the book in his own pocket.

'That's a cute little book you have there, Mrs Houseman. Is that a Bible?'

Al looked up. He hadn't realised 'cute' was in Marty's vocab.

She smiled. 'Yes, it is. The Old Testament. My husband gave it to me.' She flicked it open so they could see. 'It's in Hebrew.'

'That's a lovely gift. Was that for an anniversary?' said Marty.

He could feel Al still looking at him, intrigued where this was going.

'Yes. It was. Last month. It was our fifth wedding anniversary.'

'Isn't that traditionally wood, for the gift?' said Al.

Trust him to know that.

'That's what Clark said. I wouldn't have known. But he said wood became paper. He said it had once belonged to Edgar Allan Poe.'

'Poe. That must be worth something.'

'Oh, I'd never sell it. It was a gift.'

Was it just a coincidence? Houseman had the identical Bible to Gudsen. Did they know the same dealer? Or was Houseman the dealer? If so, why did the widow Gudsen not know Houseman's name if the gift to Marion Rose was from her and her husband? Wouldn't her husband have at least mentioned it? And if not, why not? Something was not adding up about Houseman and Gudsen. And where did Bobbi Lomax fit into all this? Marty didn't know. But what he did know was that there's no such thing as coincidence.

'Did your husband know Brother Gudsen?'

'I don't think so.'

'Not a client of your husband's?'

'Oh, I wouldn't know that. Like I said, it's a very confidential business. Clark knows a lot of people. He's always very busy.'

'Thank you, Mrs Houseman. Keep it safe. Thank you for your time,' said Marty, nodding in her direction.

He tapped Al on the shoulder. Their cue to leave.

'Good day, ma'am. We'll let ourselves out.'

'Good day, Officers.'

Jack echoed her. 'Good day. Good day.'

'Wave goodbye, Jack.'

Jack waved. So did Al.

*

Stood out on the snowy path they looked at one another. Al spoke first: 'What was all the *cute* Bible stuff? You going all Hallmark on me?'

Marty took Marion's Bible out of his jacket pocket.

149

'You took that out of her handbag? You're good.'

'It was a present. From Marion Rose.'

'That neighbor lady. Of the Gudsens? The looker?'

'One and the same.'

'You don't waste any time.'

'Do you know where she got it?'

Al shrugged. 'I give up.'

'From Peter Gudsen. Supposedly from him and Mrs Gudsen.'

'And you believed her?'

'I believe that's what she believes.'

'Just a trinket from Mr Gudsen?'

'Hardly a trinket, but yes from Peter Gudsen. Question is: where'd Gudsen get it? Because if he got it from Houseman, we have our first link.'

'Ha, so me and Big Tex might be right about Houseman?'

'It's a bit of a leap. But maybe.'

'I knew I should have taken the odds.'

'Maybe it's a possibility. *Maybe*.'

Marty felt his beeper go off and then saw Al pull his off his waistband, his taco-filled belly too big to read it.

Marty got to his first.

CALLING ALL UNITS STOP SUSPECTED BOMB BLAST STOP MAIN STREET DOWNTOWN ABRAHAM CITY STOP ALL AVAILABLE UNITS RESPOND STOP

22

New Year's Eve, 1982

Reno, Nevada

They had driven. Passed on both sides of the highway by cars packed full of families or high-school kids; almost every car had ski-gear strapped to the roof. Ski and party. It was the day for it. He was hoping to do a little partying himself later. Clark loved skiing but he couldn't risk injuring his fingers, his hands, even an elbow or a shoulder. They were his means to everything. He had read that in the war Betty Grable had insured her legs for a million bucks. He had thought of insuring his hands, but figured if he needed to claim it would be tough explaining why his career was so dependent on them.

In the rear mirror he could see Edie as she breastfed Lori, staring out the window. Not that there was much to see, hundreds of miles of unbroken desert and mountains. Clark knew from his regular buying trips out to Reno and beyond that it would take ten hours driving, with a couple of stops scheduled in. It was a long way, especially with the baby. Flying would have been a lot faster and easier. But they had a new way of booking everything, on a computer. And Clark didn't trust those computers. Who knew where your information ended up? Often you'd have to quote your credit card number over the phone, even just as a deposit.

Clark hardly ever used credit, he thought it was an ingenious way of keeping track of you. Where you went, what you did and with whom. It would take a lot of collating all those little greaseproof carbon receipts, but where there's a will there's a way. It was just the kind of information the Faith would kill for. They loved information, especially if they were acquiring it, not providing it. It was just like the cable company, all the Faith needed was one insider in the bank or credit companies with access to the head office computer and you wouldn't even need to collate anything.

Sure, you could pay cash at the desk, out at the airport, give a false name and then disappear into the skies. But when you were trying to convince people you were a devoted Follower, being discovered by one of the Faithful buying a plane ticket for an illicit gambling den like Reno wasn't the smartest move.

Clark knew that if this trip to Reno didn't elicit the response he needed, there would have to be another mark, another destination and so on and so forth until he got it. He knew somebody, somewhere, would give it to him, eventually. He just had to ensure he left no paper trail in the process.

Clark had located Rebecca Bright's descendants easily enough. Back in November, long before the Rooks or Peter Gudsen clapped eyes on his Testament of Faith. But he had waited until they had before he made contact. Rebecca's great-granddaughter was living in the house she had bought with her share of the cash she and Robert had made from their followers. So, after a light nap and a freshen-up at the Riverside Hotel, both parents and baby found themselves sat as a family unit, on a small couch in a modest living room on the outer reaches of Reno with Clark's mark, the eighty-one-year-old Mrs Ruth Davidson.

They had made small talk over the apple and rhubarb pie and

English tea she'd prepared for them, mostly about the baby, family and life in the Faith. She wasn't a Follower. Her husband had died of an undiagnosed heart murmur aged just twenty-two, a few months after their wedding, and her belief in the Faith had died with him. She had never remarried. She showed them her wedding picture. They all agreed he was handsome and, gently, she put the picture back on the mantelshelf where it took pride of place.

'I have a surprise for you,' said Mrs Davidson.

'You do? How kind.' Clark hated surprises. One person's surprise is another's heart attack.

'Yes, but first let me see that Bible that's brought you all the way to Reno.'

Clark wanted to say, well, that depends on what the surprise is. But instead he took the Bible wrapped round with layer after layer of muslin out of his attaché case and started unfurling it.

'It's like Christmas all over again, and so soon.'

'Yes, isn't it,' said Edie. 'I've always loved Christmas, do you?'

Clark guessed from the delay in her response that Mrs Davidson didn't much love Christmas.

'I had my cousin Bertha staying here. We went to Cutler's restaurant down by the river. We couldn't be doing with all that plucking and fixings.'

Cousin Bertha. Who was she? Clark hadn't seen a cousin Bertha when he'd researched the Bright family tree. He stood, passed Mrs Davidson the Bible. He sat back down, hand in hand with Edie now, as Mrs Davidson opened it. That way if Edie spoke he could squeeze her hand and impose silence. If the baby started playing up, he would beckon Edie out of the room. Not out onto the snowy verandah, but just to a back room. He didn't want Mrs Davidson thinking he was a cruel, mean husband. He wasn't his father.

'Oh, my. Here they all are. It wasn't commonly spoken of in my day.'

Clark knew that. It was barely spoken of today.

'But you knew?'

'Yes. I overheard an argument once. My mother and father. It was what she had on him. The only thing, really.'

Clark could sympathize with that predicament.

'But it was never discussed in company. Ours or strangers.'

'Robert Bright. Our Prophet. Your great-grandfather. It must be like being related to Jesus!' said Edie.

Clark squeezed Edie's hand. She looked questioningly back at him, blissfully unaware of any social misdemeanor.

'If Jesus had three wives,' said Mrs Davidson, smiling politely. She stood up and passed the Bible back to Clark. 'I have something for you. It may help you in verifying the provenance, isn't that what they call it?'

'It is, ma'am, yes.'

Peter Gudsen had told Clark under no circumstances to even hint to anyone who might verify the Bible what they had discovered secreted inside it. Peter didn't want to influence their opinion either way: Faithful or not. Clark had absolutely no intention of telling anyone, particularly Rebecca Bright's family in case they laid legal claim to the Bible and its contents. He had worked long and hard to get this far and he wasn't about to do anything that would jeopardize this deal and his plans.

She was over at a bureau now. Reproduction. A nice copy though, in the French style. She took out a handful of what looked like envelopes, handed them to him. He saw the stamps, immediately recognized them. He also recognized the writing on the top envelope.

Rebecca Bright's.

'The writing on the Bible would seem to match this, Mr Houseman. Even with my bad eyesight. Some of these are Rebecca's. My cousin found them when her father passed.'

'Cousin Bertha?' Not such a bad surprise after all.

'No, my cousin Lily, over the other side of Lake Tahoe. Her father, Rebecca's grandchild, had been the family's unofficial archivist until he passed a decade or so ago. She passed herself last year, left me those in her will.'

'How kind of her,' said Edie.

This time Clark didn't squeeze her hand. Instead he nodded in agreement.

'We don't like publicity, Mr Houseman. We are a family of bastards, born of a man and woman with dubious morals.'

Clark tried not to look shocked at her use of language, or her unexpected honesty.

'So, please. You may take these, use them for your research, but please don't attach this generation's family name to the discovery should you be able to prove that this Bible did indeed belong to my great-grandmother. For myself, I hope it never sees the light of day again. Sometimes truth isn't a desirable commodity.'

Before Clark could second that, there was a ring at the doorbell and Mrs Davidson was wriggling up and out of her chair, mumbling about how her cousin never remembered her spare key.

He heard Bertha before he saw her. She appeared in the doorway all bundled up like an Eskimo, all that was missing were the huskies. She marched over and shook their hands, Edie's first. She didn't coo over the baby, just looked at it a bit quizzically before grabbing Clark's hand and almost shaking it off its joint.

'I'm Ruth's cousin. Bertha. Glad you folks made it, in this.'

'Bertha's from Florida,' said Mrs Davidson by way of explanation.

God's waiting room, thought Clark.

'Next year, Ruth, you'll come to me: it's not called the Sunshine State for nothing. I hate the darn cold. Did you tell 'em about the surprise, Ruthie?'

'About the letters?' Clark held up the letters. 'Thank you.'

'No, not those,' said Bertha, throwing the letters the same look she'd given the baby.

'No, Bertha, I hadn't gotten around to it yet.'

'Oh, Mr Houseman, we've got a treat for you. Oh, you haven't seen it either, have you, Ruthie?'

'No. Not that I recall. Maybe when I was a baby.'

'Well, Mr Houseman. I just trekked over to cousin Erica's. She got it from cousin Lily when she passed, with a few other little trinkets. But this one's the only photograph we have of Rebecca. And she's got a Bible on her knee. A family Bible. The picture must be ninety years old. Right before she passed.'

Picture. What picture?

Pinpricks of sweat popped on Clark's hands. He stared at the corner of the table, trying to focus on a fixed point in an attempt to ward off the nausea that was creeping around the back of his throat. He had been so close. So. Close. Signatures were one thing and easily forged. But the physical dimensions of a book were solid, intransigent. What would its cover be like? Black leather like this one, or lighter? Perhaps tan, which was very popular with ladies of the era. Would the cover be embossed or plain? Perhaps it was smaller, taller, thicker, thinner. Perhaps the page ends weren't as rough-cut as these? The possibilities made him almost vomit.

'Here it is. It's not a great picture. Not bad for a Victorian box Brownie or whatever they were using, with those old plates and a ten-second exposure. See how it's all blurred here and here.' She had taken the photo out of her oversized handbag and was holding it out for Clark to take. He didn't. Cousin Bertha shoved it closer still. 'What do you think of that, young man?' He took it from her.

The picture had been taken in this room. Right there the table had been, drawn much nearer to the fireplace than now. The fire must have burned all day then, thought Clark. In the winters that is. In the summer the heat up here would have been suffocating.

'Is this it, then? Our family Bible? Can't say as I ever recall seeing it in person before,' said Bertha, picking the Bible up off the table.

'Me neither,' said Mrs Davidson.

'Not a great shot,' he heard Bertha say.

Reluctantly, frightened of what he might find there, Clark focused his eyes on the blurry seated woman in the picture. Her hands clasped as if in prayer on top of a book.

Clark stared in disbelief at the photograph.

There it was. The Bible. Or one that looked just like it.

Clark couldn't have done any better unless he'd stepped back through time and put it there himself.

It wasn't a great shot, but it was a great picture. A really, really great picture.

23

November 2nd 1983, 10.07 am

Abraham City

Marty looked down at the already clotting pool of blood. A dog lay next to it, bled out. The falling snow formed a white crust on its body. Al crouched over it. 'I'm really starting to hate this son of a bitch.'

'Beagle. Good dog,' said Marty.

'Loyal.'

'Damn good dog.' It was Tex. 'Had one of those back in the army. Great detection dog.'

'Do you think the dog could have sniffed out the bomb, got too close? Set it off?'

'Sure. Although it would have probably taken a lot more damage. It looks pretty intact. It's got all of its limbs. But yeah, it's a possibility, depends where the bomb was in relation to the dog's height, and proximity, of course. Your guy Whittaker will be able to give you more on that. But maybe there was another dog? There's a couple of shredded leads just over there.' Their eyes followed his finger to outside a men's outfitters, its front window blown out, male mannequins strewn onto the pavement, suits ripped and charred.

'The other dogs got taken by a vet and a couple of the guys, down the block. To his practice.' Hobbs was beside them now. He'd been the first on the scene with Carvell. By the time Marty

158

and Al had hauled ass across town it was all over bar the shouting.

'So there were other dogs?' said Tex, puffing his chest up.

'Yeah, three,' said Hobbs.

'What other dogs?'

'The dogs the guy had.'

'What guy?'

'They dead or alive, the dogs?' said Tex.

'Alive, sir,' said Hobbs. He looked down at his notes. 'Sorry, Marty, Trevor Angel, a dog walker.'

'Angel?'

'Trevor Angel. Angelic Dog Walking Service.'

Marty exhaled loudly. 'Is Angel alive?'

'Dog walker? Where are we, the Upper East Side?' said Big Tex.

'There's a lot of expensive houses up there at the top of the canyon, Tex,' said Marty.

'Yeah, higher up they get, the pricier they are,' said Al.

'Closer to heaven,' said Marty and felt Hobbs bristle at the hint of blasphemy.

'Amazes me how they cling to the side of the cliff, like they're gonna fall off if the breeze hits.'

'I guess a lot of rich folks figure they got too much money to be picking up dog shit.' Marty wouldn't want to clean up steaming piles of crap either. Rich or poor.

'Can't be bothered to even walk their own dog. What's with that?' said Al.

'Where's Angel?' said Marty.

'County. His arm's a mess. Shrapnel in his face. Third-degree burns. He might lose his eye. They got him out of here about ten minutes ago.'

'He a suspect, you reckon, Hobbs?' said Al.

'Everyone's a suspect in this case, Al, remember? What are we now? Still three thousand plus? And now our guy's a dog killer.'

'Poor dog.'

'I got more . . .' said Hobbs.

'From Mr Angel?'

'No, from that guy over there.' Hobbs pointed over to where, behind a cordon, a huddle of what Marty assumed were local business owners watched anxiously as uniform, forensics and the fire guys went from store to store. Some of the locals were bleeding, their clothes ripped, faces and exposed bodies looking singed. Behind them a clutch of paramedics were dealing with them a few at a time. 'He owns that deli a few stores down. Trevor Angel is here every day. Same time. Like clockwork. Owner says he loves those dogs, treats them as if they were his own, parks opposite in the free hour slots, grabs himself a coffee from the deli, then gets the dogs out of his car, walks them up the hill a few blocks to the small park and back down here again. Been doing that for years.'

'Always at the same time?'

'Always.'

'What you thinking, Mart?' said Al.

'If Trevor Angel had any investments or was somehow connected to Gudsen or Lomax, or Houseman.'

'Like through the dogs?' said Al.

'Their wealthy owners.' Marty turned to Hobbs. 'Go on.'

'Near the usual hour, Angel comes back. Gets himself a smoothie.'

'From the same place?'

'Yeah. Starts putting the dogs in the back of the car to drive them back up to their houses. All totally as per. Then, boom! This is his car, right here. He has keys to most of the houses.

Someone found them along the street, covered in blood. I gave them to the vet. Figured the owners would be directed there.'

Marty looked at the brown Cherokee, half its front blown off, all the windows blown out. 'So, he was getting them in the jeep?'

'Yeah. Home time.'

'What was this doing here?' Marty looked at the tow truck, pushed halfway into the road, the back of it askew, almost as mangled as Angel's jeep.

'That car, next to Angel's, the Nissan, it was in the way of the road crew, they were getting it towed to the pound.'

'The tow driver OK?'

'Yeah, his door was open and he was behind it, outside, he had started to crank it up onto the truck, but had to stop, adjust something or other. His open door took the force of the blast, blew back on top of him, protected him from the fireball. All he's got is suspected concussion. Apart from that and a few scratches, nothing.'

'His lucky day,' said Al.

'Him and Angel went in the same ambulance. I sent Harris to the hospital with him.'

'In case one of them's the bomber?' said Marty.

'Well, that, and in case they aren't and remember something.'

'Good call, Hobbs.'

'Thanks.'

Tex was right next to what was left of the Nissan.

'The bomb was in this car.'

'You sure it wasn't in this one, Tex? In Angel's?'

'No way. The seat of the explosion was in the trunk of the Nissan. Hit the fuel tank. Boom. This is why this is all such a mess. I don't think the actual bomb was even that big. The fuel tank's done most of the damage, set off the recovery truck's tank also. Fireball.'

'Any chance of fingerprints?'

'Never say never.'

'You think this is another tilt, Tex?'

'Could well be. Whole thing's blown to crap, it's going to take a while to track all of it down. Let alone find what's left of the bomb.'

'So you think maybe when the truck picked it up . . .'

'Boom,' said Al.

'Boom. Yeah,' said Tex, gloves on now, picking his way through the carnage.

'Whose is it, the Nissan?'

'We got the tag off the engine, Marty. We're trying to trace the registered owner. A Mrs Eleanor Miller up in Dalewood County.'

'Dalewood? That's three hundred miles upstate.'

'Carvell called the local guys up there. There's no phone on record, they're sending a cruiser out to go see her.'

'Mrs Eleanor Miller hanging out with the wrong kind of people?' said Al.

'Maybe she *is* the wrong kind of people,' said Marty.

'According to the DMV, she's eighty-four.'

'She got any kids, grandkids . . . a father, even, that might be our guy?'

'Not living with her, Al. Not according to the DMV,' said Hobbs.

'Stolen?' said Al.

'I wouldn't take the odds on it not being,' said Marty.

'What is it with this case, Mart?'

'It's the devil's work,' said Hobbs.

'Well, the son of a bitch devil is giving us a run for our money,' said Al.

'Maybe God forgot we're the good guys?' said Marty. 'Or maybe he just doesn't give a rat's ass? Hobbs, you get Carvell to tell the Dalewood Sheriff if there's no response from the house, to track down Mrs Miller as if his life depends on it. Let's try and get ahead of the game here.'

'If that's possible at this stage,' said Al.

'Tell me about it.'

'A couple of the other store owners, they said the Nissan's been parked here at least a couple of days. A few others were saying maybe four days.'

'The thirtieth? The first day of the bombings?'

'That's what they think.'

'Any fix on a time?'

'Morning, but they don't know before or after breakfast. Well, the three of them can't agree a time.'

'Who are the witnesses?'

'Two guys from the jeweler's and one of those workmen. They're doing emergency repairs on the sewers. People have been complaining water keeps backing up in them ever since they blasted a hole through the canyon for the freeway. They were working their way along the street the past couple of days, little tranches at a time. The road crew kept asking if anyone owned the car, but no one did. They needed it out of the way. They were going to bump it, but saw it had tickets. So, the foreman called the City pound.'

'And they were only too happy to oblige?'

'Yeah.'

'Bet they're regretting that decision,' said Al.

'No one saw anyone park it here?'

'No. Sorry, it was mayhem. I just spoke to a small group.'

'Grab some uniforms. Get them on it. Get them to report to Al. I want you and Carvell back on our AWOL investors.'

'Talking of which,' said Al. 'Just in case there's any investors amongst that bunch of wounded and the gawkers over there, I'll check the IDs of all them and the store owners. Check them against the list of the disgruntled three thousand when I get back.'

'Great idea,' said Marty.

'I'm full of them.'

'Full of something, anyhow, Al . . . Find out if any of them been upstate, recently.'

'Dalewood?'

'You got it.'

Al moved away, reaching into his pocket for his notepad and pen. Hobbs moved with him.

Marty looked up and down the street. It was easy to see there were fancy houses nearby, the stores were all pretty upmarket: the deli, jeweler's, a gift store, a ladies' boutique, the gentleman's outfitters, and a few buildings down, one store, its oddly out-of-place Dickensian bay windows partially blown out either side.

The workmen's progress as they'd chased the sewer blockage was easy enough to trace, as they'd made such a bad job of re-sealing the road. Marty doubted Angel was the target. Bobbi Lomax fitted only because of Arnold, her slippery husband. Gudsen fitted because of the Faith's ambitions for him – and because of his business relationship with Mr Slippery. No one could find Hartman. And the man accusing him, Houseman, was in a coma he might never wake up from. How the hell did Houseman fit? Through a miniature version of the New Testament? Marty could already hear the judge's laughter if he tried to get warrants with that as the evidence for probable cause.

And Angel? Looked like he might just have been in the wrong place at the wrong time. The tow truck probably moved the tilt. But if the car had been parked there a few days, and someone had put a bomb in it – either before or after it was parked – who had they thought was going to drive it away and activate the tilt?

His feet on bumpy tarmac scars, Marty reached the point where the workmen had started digging. He was right in front of the Dickensian store. He noticed its sign, held by only one of its metal chains, hanging precariously over the street. Next to it dangled the store's awning, ripped and battered by the blast and the icy winter breeze, its name rippling almost in defiance: Rooks Coins & Books.

24

January 3rd 1983

Abraham City

Squeezed into a small booth in the overcrowded diner, the four
of them had feasted on pancakes – blueberry and maple syrup.
Ransome's treat. A rare occasion, so Clark had asked their server
for an order of bacon strips served on top of his stack. Edie
and Phyllis's warnings of death by cholesterol just made the
crispy rinds taste even sweeter. Clark had been so hungry. And
now he really needed a drink. The clock on the wall said fourteen minutes before ten. He hadn't meant to be this early. But
Ransome insisted he take twenty minutes to cross the street
from the diner opposite the Faith's offices. Just in case. At least
he wouldn't be seen breaking a sweat. 'Is that the men's room
along the hall, miss?'

'Yes, Mr Houseman. Last door on your left.'

Clark nodded thank you to the young receptionist and moved
along the corridor. It was a one-stall unit. Thankfully. He was the
only one waiting in the lobby. So he should have it to himself
for the duration. He locked the door behind him and moved
toward the sink. He stared at his reflection. Told himself that
today he had to be a better version of himself. Slicker, smoother,
cleverer. Quicker on his feet than he had ever been before. Charm
personified.

He was starting to sweat a little.

He threw water on his face and on his pulse points. Wrist and neck. Took a deep breath and reached inside his jacket pocket. He had found the almost impossibly slim flask in an antique store down in Scottsdale. Inside his suit jacket, his best, it was invisible. And now it was light, half empty. Clark had downed the other half right when they got to the diner. While the others waited in line for a seat, he had blamed nerves and nipped to the john. He couldn't remember another time when he'd knocked back the booze before breakfast. Not even as a student.

He put the cold silver nozzle to his lips, flicked his head back and downed what Kenny had told him was the finest Russian vodka. It was certainly priced like it, but it didn't taste too fine. It was what Clark needed to be: strong, potent, unstoppable. He would have preferred JD, but he couldn't risk its cloying odor. His body absorbed the vodka's essence as he leant up against the basin and stared at himself in the small square mirror.

Clark was a witness to history. His. Story. History. His story and that of Robert Bright. But if the meeting went smoothly, he would be history's writer. Literally. A new history. A new story. Different to the one Robert Bright had spun for himself and so very different to the one the Faith wanted Bright to have. They had airbrushed his three wives from history. Unsure which one of them to select, they had deselected them all. Rebecca was the vessel through which Robert Bright's visions from God had reached the world, she was his transcriber, for he was barely literate. Without her, Robert Bright's visions and his channeling of the word of God would probably never have carried as far as today. But Rebecca, his bride, was fourteen, or younger. And, therefore, it was best not to mention her too often. Especially not in the late twentieth century. Hopefully, that way, she would be eroded by time, if not by fact. The Faith would focus on his story. His. Story. Robert Bright's story. Not the *real* story. Clark would rewrite that story. Rewrite it until they no longer recognized it. Today would be the beginning of that. If he could just hold his nerve.

He ran the cold tap, picked up the soap, and turned it over and over in his hands until he couldn't see it for suds. His right index finger ran over his left hand and with it he traced a soapy vortex on the mirror. He stared into the centre of it as its lines came together, pulling him inside it.

Testament of Faith.

The find of a *lifetime*.

Testament of Faith. Our *Faith*.

Our Faith.

He stared as the vortex began to drip down from the mirror and down the white tiles towards the sink.

Testament of Faith. Our Faith.

He felt himself going under. He quickly closed his eyes, shook his head, he didn't want to be under, not today, not here. He just wanted to be inured to his own weakness. He wanted to be strong. And he really wanted to be unstoppable.

Clark's pager buzzed on his waistband.

> WE STILL ON FOR LATER?

Kenny.

How long had he been in here? If felt like hours. He couldn't have missed the meeting. Shit. What the hell time was it? He'd left his watch on the den workbench. Clark checked the pager's time.

9.56. Not even ten minutes. He wet a raft of toilet tissue, rubbed the mirror clean and then dry. He flicked open a box of tic-tacs and rattled out the last of its mints straight into his mouth. He threw the empty box in the trash, flushed the toilet he hadn't used, started up the air-dryer, let it run over nothing for thirty seconds and then stepped back out into the hallway. The receptionist smiled when he came back into view.

Around the lobby were framed official portraits of each of the Twelve Disciples. He moved between them. Each accompanied by a short biography and a motto filched from the Faith Bible. He was meeting with Alan Laidlaw, motto: 'That which does not kill you makes you stronger.' Or irritated, thought Clark. Dennis Browne: 'Before you sup from the bowl, ensure your neighbor is not hungry.' Mr Browne looked like he'd supped from his bowl and everyone else's. The last one on the end, Eric Jeffries: 'Live with the Lord's love in your heart. And you shall enter the Kingdom of Heaven.'

'Mr Houseman?' The receptionist was opening the door next to him. 'They will see you now.'

They?

He thought his appointment was just with Alan Laidlaw. Wasn't that what the secretary had said when she'd called him?

Alan Laidlaw came from a family who had converted in the early 1940s. Converted and donated a large part of their family's ranching fortune to the Faith. Clark had heard it was $10 million. Back in '48, that was quite the donation. Needless to say, a Laidlaw had featured in the Twelve Disciples since pretty soon after. Laidlaw was the eldest son of an eldest son. His father one of six boys who had seen action in Europe and Korea, none of whom had been killed, or even injured. Their parents' gratitude for this miracle was reflected in the establishing of Abraham City's first private college, reserved for members of the Faith. That was an additional $25 million, but it was rumored that they could more than afford it, for during the war the family had moved into the lucrative munitions market. Unlike farming, it was an industry not susceptible to the fickleness of the American weather, just to the fickle allegiances and dangerous ambitions of its politicians.

They.

The Order of the Twelve Disciples were ranged against the wall at a long, thin table directly facing the door and at their center was the Supreme Leader. It was Leonardo's *Last Supper*. And Judas had just arrived. A fact he hoped they would always remain oblivious to. It was either go forward, now, right now, or back out the door. 'Mr Clark Houseman,' the receptionist announced. As she left, she closed the door behind her.

It was not possible to go back.

'Good morning, gentlemen.' No one got up to shake his hand. By way of greeting there was a low group murmur, 'Good morning', at the far end of the table, 'Live with the Lord's love in your heart', still seated, opened his right arm, as if to guide Clark to the center of the room where sat a solitary chair.

Clark's seat was some ten feet in front of the table, directly opposite the Supreme Leader, to whose right sat Alan Laidlaw. To his left: 'Only the Lord knows what we do not know'. Arbuthnot. David Arbuthnot. They each had a clutch of stapled papers in front of them, on the top of which Clark could clearly see was a Xerox copy of his version of the Testament of Faith.

'Only the Lord knows what we do not know' spoke first.

'Thank you for coming today, Mr Houseman. And thank you also for offering us the Testament of Faith before approaching the open market with it. We are very grateful for your discretion and consideration in this matter.'

Murmurs of agreement.

'Your father was Thomas Houseman, was he not?' asked 'What doesn't kill you.'

'Yes, Mr Laidlaw, he was.'

'And your mother Helen Storey of Reno?' Clark could tell the man could barely utter the word Reno, couldn't brook what it stood for. It was only a very slight movement, but Laidlaw's eyes wandered to Clark's Bible, which sat on the table in front of him. Closed. As if to open it would somehow bring forth the shame of the past, bring it into this hallowed room. Multiple wives, underage brides, the murder of the Prophet, his missing will and the ensuing deadly power struggles as Rebecca's son Jeremiah, barely sixteen, waged a war of succession against his eighteen-year-old half-brother Abraham. A struggle that raged from Reno to Abraham City and in every desert canyon that separated them. Hundreds of the Faith's followers died violent deaths as the Faith was cleaved in two. Jeremiah's followers, who described themselves as the Real Faith, signed a compact to stay in Reno, and the Faith, now headed by Abraham, remained in what soon became Abraham City.

Jeremiah and Rebecca had claimed that in the hours after he was mortally wounded Robert Bright had written a will, rumored to be signed in his blood, that anointed Jeremiah, his first son with Rebecca, as his successor and tasked him with carrying the Faith to the outside world. A task he was happy to fulfil. But Abraham had other plans. As the first-born son of Elizabeth, the first and conventionally legal wife, he believed himself to be his father's true heir, despite the fact father and son were widely thought to loathe one another.

Clark figured that the Faith, still sore 150 years later about their tawdry, violent history, wouldn't be opening the Pandora's box of Bright's Bible anytime soon. Even the word Reno could barely cross their lips. 'My mother, Helen, was indeed from Reno, sir.'

'She has passed?'

Clark could almost feel them all hold their breath, waiting for confirmation of what they already knew. He nodded. 'Yes, sir.'

No, sir. Three bags full, sir.

'May the Lord Prophet take pity upon her soul.'

'Amen.'

'And your father lives in Phoenix now?'

Shame it's not further south. Say, hell.

'Yes, sir. That's correct. He remarried. A widow. Her late husband was in charge of a Mission down there.'

They all nodded. Obviously, that was also in the briefing papers.

'You've recently joined the Canyon Road Mission?'

'That's correct.'

As he'd expected they had done their homework. Sure, Gudsen and the Rooks had helped get him in the door, but he knew he had to be the real deal. His version of it.

'Where did you worship before?'

'Where my parents worshipped their entire married lives.'

'The Lumina Mission?'

'Yes, sir. Since my marriage a few years back, I've been working hard, out on the road, trying to build my business, take care of my family. I worship where I can – in any town where there's a Mission. Sometimes, when I know attending's not going to be possible, I give thanks in my car.' Thanks for what, Clark didn't say. But mostly thanks to K-ZLV for pushing their radio signal across the desert.

'It's hard to keep bread on the table.' That was Browne. Hard to keep food on their table and out of his belly.

'Yes, sir, it is. But we still want to have a large family. I was an only child. I don't want my son to be.'

Approving smiles all around. The bigger the family the better. Every one a tribe of instant believers. Just add water.

They soon moved on, asking Clark all about how he discovered the Bible and how he felt on discovery of the Testament of Faith hidden within it. So he told them the story, and was sure to punctuate his words at least several times with his punchy little soundbites:

Testament of Faith.

The find of a lifetime.

Testament of Faith. Our faith.

Our Faith.

At various points in his monologue Clark noticed that along the length of the table, most of the Disciples were leant forward in anticipation of the next part, although he knew that they would have already received a blow-by-blow account from either Peter Gudsen or Rod Rook. Or both. Did the Disciples fear Clark's narrative might have a different outcome? Clark knew that their obvious investment in the story meant that either the Bible or the Testament itself – or even both – had been verified by Peter and his academic collective at the Faith library. Unless, of course, the Order of the Twelve Disciples were toying with him like a vengeful cat plays with a mouse right before it eats it alive.

He was right not to relax. They wanted to ask more questions.

Unsurprisingly, no one mentioned the Bible. Obviously the note written on lilac letterhead by Dora and Bertha had sufficed to verify that and they didn't want to dwell on its existence. 'What doesn't kill you' was holding up the Testament and looking directly at Clark. 'It's an interesting artefact.' He made it sound like something they'd dug up in a temple in Luxor.

'Yes, it is,' said Clark.

'My Brother Disciples have requested I ask you how much you'd want for it. Would twenty thousand suffice?'

'Twenty thousand. Oh no.'

The Disciples' faces set harder.

'I couldn't take money from the Church.'

Their faces relaxed again. And he saw what must pass for a smile on the Supreme Leader's face.

'Before you sup from the bowl' spoke again. 'Mr Houseman, that's mighty generous of you.'

Clark spoke quickly, he didn't want his 'generosity' mistaken for charity. 'No, no money. Instead, I thought we could trade the Testament for documents from your library collection? I took the liberty of checking with Mr Gudsen and you have a couple of copies of each of the documents I'm interested in, so it wouldn't deplete the Faith's collection.'

'And what would be their value?'

'No more than twenty-five thousand. Retail.'

Laidlaw looked at the Supreme Leader. He silently nodded and almost simultaneously the Disciples were up, swarming Clark – no handshakes, but lots of back claps and warm thank yous.

And then they parted, almost instinctively, and the Supreme Leader stepped forward and kept moving forward until the great lump of a man had clutched Clark in a papal embrace, squeezing the life out of him, before he planted a kiss on each cheek. The words 'Bless you' in one ear, and 'for you are a true Brother' in the other. He clasped Clark's hands in his own and said the Blessing of the Light. As he did, the other Disciples and Clark joined in.

'In the beginning was the Lord
And the Light
The Lord and the Light
Who we could not see
Because we were blind.
We were blind.
Until our Prophet Robert Bright
Opened our eyes unto the Light
Unto the Light.'

'Father,' said Clark with his hands still firmly clasped inside the Leader's.

'Yes, my son.'

'I have been approached by the Real Faith.' All murmuring in the room stopped dead at the mention of the Faith's rival church. 'Somehow the Bright family Bible has come to their attention. They want to buy it.'

'What doesn't kill you' stepped forward now. Still at the Supreme Leader's right side. 'Did they say how much they would pay?'

'A figure of ten thousand was touted.'

Indignant murmurings from the Disciples.

Clark continued, best to ratchet up the tension as soon as possible, go for the jugular: 'They want to display it in their museum, back in Reno.' Clark could almost feel the entire room turn back to look at the Bible, which was still sat in front of their leader's empty place at the table. The Supreme Leader squeezed Clark's hands tighter.

'Whatever they have offered, our offer will be greater and truer. *We* are the one true Faith.'

'Thank you, Father. If it's possible I would very much like to have occasional access to the Faith library? It would prove useful for my private study – and, after this find, I'm hoping people will begin to offer me other Faith documents to buy. It would be useful to help assess those documents in their proper context.'

'Indeed. I'll let Brother Peter know to arrange it and, also, collection of the documents you desire.'

'Thank you, Father.'

'I'll have a check cut for you this afternoon, Brother Clark, for the Bible. Stop by anytime,' said 'What doesn't kill you.'

'Make it for fifteen thousand, Brother Alan, as an acknowledgment of our Brother's loyalty,' said the Supreme Leader.

'Thank you, Father,' said Clark, bowing his head like a true supplicant.

Almost like a vapor, they vanished through a side door, leaving Clark alone in the vast room.

Clark looked up at the elaborately painted ceiling depicting man's flight through the stormy, starry heavens from the planet Lumina to planet Earth. Clark thought of the most popular Faith sermon, the one where the Supreme Leader is God's representative on earth – how this gave him God's sight to see man's lies and deceit and how God had given his permission to destroy those who would deceive.

Clark threw out his arms in surrender and awaited the fate of the deceiver.

Nothing happened. Just like he knew it wouldn't.

He picked up his attaché case and made his way towards the exit.

25

November 2nd 1983, noon

Faith HQ

They have their own questions, he could tell. But he bet they wouldn't answer until he had asked them whatever questions he had. They could wait. But so could he. And he wasn't in the mood to take any of their bull.

It was just supposed to be a meeting with Laidlaw, but there they all were – lined up like the defense at the Superbowl. And he was going to have to run the line. Dodge their blocks, like the cop version of Joe Montana.

He took out his notebook. If they wanted to present an official front, well, he could match them. Good job they couldn't see it was page after blank page.

They all looked pretty settled. He figured they had met before he arrived. Talked amongst themselves, briefed the Supreme Leader, and taken a vote on how best to proceed. There were a few options how that might go:

a) They'd provide no information, just questions;

b) Some information, some questions; and, more likely,

c) Nothing but a thick wall of silence.

They'd already given away their main game plan: that it was important to them, *really* important, or they wouldn't have fielded their best team, let alone their star player. 'Marty, we're glad you could come.' Was Laidlaw trying to make out like they'd invited him, rather than inviting himself?

'I'm glad you could see me.'

'We were just discussing how concerning it is that no one's been apprehended in this matter and barely a couple of hours ago, another bombing.'

So that's how they wanted to play it.

'Well, Mr Laidlaw, gentlemen, that means we have something in common. In fact, I'm of the belief that the Faith might be able to assist the investigation.'

Silence.

Marty looked along the line at each and every one of them. Stone. Cold. Silence.

Laidlaw leaned forward. 'And why, may I ask, do you think that?'

'Because Peter Gudsen, a man who no one has a bad word to say about, is lying in the morgue.'

'Brother Peter.'

'May his soul be brought into the light.'

'Amen' all along the table.

A delay and then a somber, baritone 'Amen' from the Supreme Leader.

'From what I gather, from speaking to folks, Mr Gudsen was a high-flyer? Maybe, even a future leader.'

'He was well-regarded. Yes.'

'Anything else would be improper speculation.' Marty recognized the speaker, David Arbuthnot.

'I'm told that Mr Gudsen might have been in the habit of conducting business late at night, here, at your offices.'

'We couldn't possibly discuss Faith business.'

'I didn't say it was *Faith* business.'

179

Touchdown.

'But you may have a point, Mr Laidlaw – it was *very* late. Our witness saw him, a little after ten pm. I doubt the Faith have need to conduct their usual business that late. He appeared to be meeting a young man outside here – a couple of weeks back.'

'It may well have been library business.'

'The library open that late?'

'No. But Brother Gudsen was one of those responsible for it. Sometimes he worked late.'

'Did he have a key?'

'No. We have twenty-four-hour security out front.'

Did they now? That was new.

'And the young man? Any idea who he might be?'

'One of the Faith's PhD scholars, perhaps? They come from all over the world. Many like to assist in the library, cross-checking indices, that kind of thing.'

Sounds a hoot.

'Care to give me some names?'

No one spoke.

'Specifically the name of the young man who met Mr Gudsen after ten pm on Wednesday,' Marty feigned looking at the pages. Luckily his memory wasn't as blank. 'Wednesday, October 19.'

Silence.

As game plans go, silence was pretty lame. He had his own game plan. One which should unseal their lips. If it didn't, he might find himself on permanent suspension from the department.

'I'd like to tell you gentlemen a story.' They looked surprised. He didn't wait for permission to continue. 'When I was a rookie, in LA, back when my dad was still alive, I worked the beat down in Chinatown. One night there was a bombing at an illegal gambling den above a long row of restaurants, hugely popular places with locals and tourists, everyone. Three people dead including a pregnant cocktail waitress. When we did the door-to-door of all the restaurants, no one was saying anything and looked like they'd rather we tore out their tongue. What could we do? We couldn't even speak the language. So, I went to our Captain and told him, "It's a wall of silence." And you know what he said to me? "Money talks, son. Money talks." I think, he's gonna bribe them. Maybe the little guys, the waiters, the chefs. Someone might take our dime, spill and run. But no. He's got other ideas. Within an hour, he had fifty guys pulled off every other case in town: day shift and night shift. Everyone with a day off? It's cancelled. Report for duty. He closed down the entire block around Chinatown. No one could get in, no customers, no deliveries, and all the restaurant owners had for company was the smell of rotting trash. Turns out the Triads don't much like losing money, their cut of thousands of covers a day. Plus booze, plus gambling, plus drugs and hookers. The silence lasted less than eighteen hours before we got an anonymous tip which collared us our bombers and their paymaster.'

'What are you saying, Marty?'

'I'm not saying anything, Alan.' Forget that Mr Laidlaw crap. 'It's just a story. Told for the interest of those here present.'

Alan, arms folded, leaned forward on the table. He looked like he was going to say, 'Don't you come in here, to our House, and threaten us, you son of a . . .' but he didn't speak.

'I'm just saying. We might find, in the not too distant future, that the safety of the brethren of this good city is in a great deal of jeopardy. Bombs going off all over town and not even one confirmed suspect in our sights. All I'm asking of you gen-tlemen is that you do what you can to assist me in keeping all our brethren safe. Or we might find it of vital necessity to close down our fair city. Particularly downtown. Starting with a five-block radius of where we're currently sat.'

'You don't have any authority to do that,' Browne chimed in.

'You're right. I don't.'

'So how are you going to make that happen? We won't allow it,' said Laidlaw.

They wouldn't allow it. Of course. They owned the city. Or thought they did. 'I was hoping for your co-operation. I obviously made a mistake.' Marty started up out of his chair and began a slow move to the door. 'I don't think you gentlemen have quite gauged the mood out there. People are scared to send their kids to school. What's going to be next? One of your Followers' kids? A school bus? The public of Abraham City don't like to be scared, looking over their shoulder. That's other cities, not this one. That's why they left other cities, sought sanctuary here. And what people *really* hate is when those who profess to protect them turn away from them in their hour of need. They look to you to set an example.' He wanted to finish with 'A good one,' but thought that might be overdoing it. Instead, he stood facing back into the room, his hand on the door handle. 'We've already got the public asking when we're going to get Federal help. And when the Feds come riding over the mountain a five-block lockdown will be the least of your problems.'

There was no answer. He watched them looking up and down the line at one another. He knew that he had hit a nerve. Even the threat of closing downtown, or any part of it, would make their Followers think that those who were supposed to be watching over them had lost control of their own city and with it the safety of their flock. And that might make their Followers have doubts about the Faith and its regard for them. A fidgety, newly questioning flock and the Feds on the doorstep were not what anyone at that table wanted.

Marty watched as the Supreme Leader wrote a note on a piece of paper and then another one. He passed one along the table to his right, the other to his left. Each Disciple would read it.

Marty tilted his head to the ceiling. He'd only been in this room once before. A lifetime ago. He had never forgotten the clouds on the ceiling and how he wanted to pull one of the cotton candy shapes down and climb onto it and float back up to its stars and away to another galaxy. His father had been furious when, finally, they'd found him in here just as a Disciples' meeting was about to start. Marty could see he was mad inside, but he wouldn't have got mad in front of the other Disciples. Wouldn't have wanted to jeopardize his chances of ever becoming Supreme Leader. A dream Edward Sinclair had had since a little boy. But God had other plans. After an almost slavish devotion to the Faith for almost fifty adult years, Edward Sinclair had died a long slow death of pancreatic cancer. Whatever God was looking down on him had obviously wanted him to endure pain, right up until the closing second of his life. Marty didn't know why God was so vengeful: for apart from his consistent, but fleeting outbursts of anger, Edward Sinclair had mostly been a benign father and husband. He had saved all of his passions for the Faith.

Several times over the course of his father's illness Marty had been called back the thousand miles from college at UCLA as the Disciples held Last Prayers at Edward's bedside, downstairs in the family's living room, where what passed for a hospital room-cum-hospice had been mocked up, his father insisting he wanted to die at home. Marty thought Edward was having the last laugh at his colleagues' expense. 'See, you idiots, I didn't make it to Supreme Leader, but I got you at my beck and call anyhow.' Marty wondered how many times the Disciples would get woken from their beds to shuffle silently out in the middle of the night to administer the Last Prayer, and then another and another, before one of them slipped Edward a morphine overdose. They must have been relieved when, in a twist of medical fate – or was it divine intervention – he had died of a heart attack alone at day-break one cold October morning as everyone else in Abraham City was preparing for Sunday Service.

Just a few hours later, a temporary – and eventually permanent – successor from the Supreme Chamber was chosen to replace him. Alan Laidlaw, Sherri's father. By that time, Marty was at po-lice college and had to get special permission to take forty-eight hours off to attend the funeral and listen to the reading of a will that left everything Edward Sinclair owned to the Faith, with the exception of the house, which was to be held in some kind of Faith-held trust, and which his mother was allowed to live in until her death. The Faith didn't have to wait long to stake their claim on the Sinclair family home. Joyce Sinclair died a few months later from kidney failure.

Murmurs went along the line from either side and the two pieces of paper returned to the Supreme Leader, scribbles over both. He read them quickly. Nodded.

Alan Laidlaw stared at Marty. 'What is it that you want to know?'

Marty could have sworn he said *Judas*.

But maybe it was *Detective*.

*

Later, as they all followed the Supreme Leader out of the side door, Alan Laidlaw hung back, looking at Marty, willing him to leave, perhaps. Marty wasn't expecting an apology or even a question about Liss. And then, he realized, Laidlaw was waiting for him to say something. But what? He would know about the progress of his granddaughter's investigation, the Captain and he played golf together over at that swanky club in Silver Canyon. And then he realized. Sherri.

'You hear from Sherri lately, Alan?'

Laidlaw didn't answer. Couldn't admit it to himself.

'At least that's one thing we got in common, Alan.'

'What's that?'

'She hates us both.'

26

February 4th 1983

Abraham City

Time was running out. He needed to find somewhere. And fast. Had to make the call. The last place he'd stopped he had just got through to her when a shrill sound somewhere off in the distance made him stop and turn. Over on the other side of the parking lot, near the road, a woman in a bright blue uniform, one that had probably last fit a decade ago, was calling his name and waving like she was drowning. Mary-Beth, Edie's best friend, after her sister of course. 'Hey, Clark. You going in?' He looked to where she was pointing, to the diner the other side of the dry cleaner where he stood, still holding the handset. 'I got thirty minutes, I gotta run to the bank, but I'll be back if you wait.'

Why hadn't he remembered Mary-Beth worked there? He didn't want to yell back over, draw attention, not more attention anyhow. A couple of people peered out from their window booths to see who their disappearing server was yelling and waving at so frantically. He shook his head. Held the handset up. 'Just got an urgent page. I already ate. Thanks.' Whatever kind of urgent pages coin dealers get. She looked confused.

'Not Edie, I hope? Baby Lori?' She was still yelling.

'No. Work. A meeting. I'm late.' He pointed at his watch.

She didn't yell. Instead, she was just stood staring at him, half in half out of her car blocking the exit.

'I better go,' he spoke as if she was next to him and pointed over the lot to his car. A kind of mime. She waved at him. Hopefully, that was a goodbye, the end of it. He didn't want her coming over. Standing by him. He hung up the phone. He would try somewhere else. She was back in her car. Before she could drive over to him he began walking, weaving in and out of parked cars towards his own. Behind her another driver had just pulled out from the dry cleaner's. She couldn't stop any longer on the narrow exit, thank goodness. But just in case she turned around, or looked in the mirror, Clark forced a wave back in her direction and a kind of sad face with a shame-we-couldn't-catch-up half-smile. He would try somewhere else. They had said the morning. It was now almost midday.

*

He had headed out over surface streets towards the mostly undeveloped area just a few miles away on the edge of the city. Here was good. He looked at the strip mall, a diner behind it, just a handful of cars in the car park. Quiet. And the wrong side of town for any of his or Edie's friends. Hopefully. He could see a couple of payphones next to the diner. At least one of them might be in service. It was ten after twelve, there was no time to start again.

Ring, ring; ring, ring. Eleven times. Pick up. Pick. Up. 'Newsdesk, Debra Franklin.' He shoved a dime in. An impatient voice. Denver. He had guessed she was an out-of-towner from the slant of her articles.

'Hi, Debra.'

'Did you just call, earlier?'

'Technical problems.'

'What can I do for you . . . ?'

'Cliff. Cliff Hartman. How interested are you in the Faith, Debra?'

'Are you recruiting me, Mr Hartman?'

'Not quite.'

'Glad to hear it.'

'I've got something that might interest you.'

'What?'

'Information.'

'What kind of information?'

'The cover-up kind.'

'Keep talking.'

And so they'd talked. Or at least Clark had, while she scribbled notes and asked a ton of questions. He hoped he had disguised his voice enough. He had spoken low. Not exactly Deep Throat, but something that hopefully didn't sound like Clark Houseman or his close associate Clifford Hartman or anything in between. She had been invited to Monday's press conference. The Faith were going to present the Testament of Faith to the world. He told her that there was something far more important, and it definitely wouldn't be on display. He called it the Bright Bible. Reporters love that kind of shit. He told her that the Faith had bought it, beaten the Real Faith out of the deal. When she sounded surprised they would buy it with its polygamous details writ large, he laughed and told her they hadn't bought it to sit on display in their museum next to the Testament. For all he knew, they would probably burn it. She really liked that. Book burning always made for great copy, especially if you wanted your articles syndicated across the globe.

She was impressed he didn't want money for the tip. He said he would call again, he was sure of that. And wished her good luck for the press conference. He could almost hear her planning Monday's ambush as he replaced the handset.

As he moved away from the phone, he stopped for a minute outside the diner. It was lunchtime and excitement always made him thirsty but his flask was empty. Maybe he could get some lunch instead. A man, his skin crisped by long exposure to the desert sun, lines burnt deep into his face, shuffled past him. A paperback book clutched in one hand. He nodded towards Clark. Clark nodded back, smiled, and watched as the man moved to the back of the diner and disappeared inside a tiny low-built hut, just a few yards behind the payphone. Clark had been so busy concentrating on his call, he hadn't even noticed it. He looked at the hut, at the phone, back at the diner. He smiled. It might just work. It was certainly worth a shot. He moved towards the hut. 'Hey, sir? Excuse me?' There was a piece of dark fabric over the entrance. You would have to duck down and push it aside for the person inside to see you. Clark didn't want to stick his head in there. Silently, the man opened the fabric. Clark noticed he was sat cross-legged on the floor like a skinny version of Buddha. He didn't say anything, just stared out at Clark. Clark crouched down a little. Not too far. But near enough so he didn't have to raise his voice any.

'You always here, sir?'

'Me?'

'Yes. You here all the time?'

'Between here and my suite at the Waldorf.'

Funny.

Clark smiled. The guy smiled back. Something caught the

corner of Clark's eye. Writing. Printed writing. Rows and rows of names. Titles. And then he noticed. The hut was constructed entirely of paperback books, all laid like bricks, so the spines faced outwards. A paper igloo.

'This is pretty neat. You do this yourself?'

'Yeah. But now people bring me the books. I don't have to go digging in the garbage outside the Mission any more.'

'Banned books, hey?'

'They're the free ones.'

'You like books?'

'They keep me warm. And dry. And it's pretty soundproof in here. So the breakfast folks don't wake me up. In winter, I put that tarp over the top. The extra layer of books on the floor and around the base. That way the snow and rain don't seep in.'

'That works?'

'Still alive, ain't I?'

'Do you want to make some money?'

'That would kinda depend how.'

'Answering the phone.'

'The phone?'

'Yeah, that one. The payphone. Politely.'

'I can do polite.'

Clark looked at him. Eyebrows raised. 'You sure about that?'

'What's your name?'

'Clark. Clark Houseman.'

'Clark Houseman's . . . office.'

'Great. You're a natural.'

A surge of chatter and laughter behind them. Clark turned around as a large group vanished into the diner. Another group of smartly dressed people were jaywalking on the opposite side of the road, towards them, from what looked like a newly built retro building.

'What's that building?'

'You not from around here? That's the new synagogue.'

'What happened to the one over on Providence?'

'Sold it to the Faith. Built that one. It's bigger.'

'What's it like? The diner?'

'You ask a lot of questions. You a cop, mister?'

'Not today. Seriously, what's it like?'

'Great schnitzel,' he smiled. 'That's the newest thing on the menu. Gloria, she usually gives me her dinner. You know they get a free dinner?' Clark guessed Gloria was a waitress. 'And sometimes half the dessert. She likes dessert. I like the pie best. Apple.' Clark took that as a hint. 'She doesn't mind I don't tip. I always offer her a book. She likes books. Thrillers, mostly.' Clark liked thrillers, a lot. Schnitzel was good too, but had to be cut razor thin. And the fat at just the right temperature before the breaded chicken hit it. Otherwise it became a soggy rubbery mess.

'Here's my pager number.' Clark took out a pen and an old receipt and wrote on the back of it. He didn't want to give him his card. If something happened to the guy, he didn't want people finding his business card in amongst the possessions crammed inside the igloo. 'I'll give you a dollar for every call you take for me. Get the caller's name, number and what they're looking for: books...'

'Books, huh?'

'Yeah, first editions, manuscripts, that kind of stuff. That's what we sell. And then you page me as soon as you can. My associate's name is Clifford Hartman...'

'Oh, yeah. Where's he at, then?'

'I don't let him out much. He's a little unpredictable. We only sell. And don't get either of us mixed up. I'm Clark. He's Cliff. It's all highly confidential. Think you can handle it?'

'I can handle anything.'

'I don't doubt it.'

'Sell, sell, sell. Make it two bucks a pop and you and your unpredictable friend Cliff Hartman, you got yourselves a deal.'

'Alright. Two bucks – every time you send through all the correct info. Here's a pen – and a bunch of dimes for the pager calls. And here's five bucks, get yourself some of those Post-It notes and extra dimes for spare. I saw a stationer's right along the street. You can stick them up on the walls, inside. That way, in case I can't understand the page, you won't have lost the original note.'

'That's good with me.'

Clark handed him the dimes and the pen and fished another twenty out of his pocket. 'That's an advance. I'll stop by every couple of days, eat schnitzel and pay you. There'll probably be a lot of calls, starting Monday, you OK with that?'

'Not going anywhere.'

Clark started to move towards the phone.

'Where you going?'

'To get the number.'

'Six, thirty-three, forty-six, fifty-five.'

Clark turned and looked at him.

'Check if you like. But I know it by heart. My mom calls me on that. I don't want her to know I'm . . .' He looked at the book-gloo surrounding him. 'Y'know.'

Clark nodded. 'Yeah. I know. Six, thirty-three, forty-six, fifty-five.'

'You got it.' He held the money up. 'Thanks, man.'

Clark begin to walk towards the diner.

'Hey, Mr Houseman! What are my hours?'

Clark looked back over his shoulder. 'Nine to five. Monday to Friday. Start Monday.'

'Dress casual?'

'Yeah.' Clark smiled back at him.

'My name's Ziggy!'

Clark, one hand on the diner door, looked back over his shoulder. 'Ziggy . . . Bookman. Thanks.'

Ziggy smiled, waved the cash at Clark and let the cloth door drop back down.

27

November 2nd 1983, 4.13 pm

Marty watched from across the room as the Captain got up, his phone cradled to his ear, its cord overstretched, and closed his office door, casting a glance in Marty's direction as he did. The Faith – Laidlaw – probably calling to complain about him. About his tactics. Too bad. He had got what he wanted. Correction. What he knew they had to give him in terms of information, if they wanted him to go away and not cause them any immediate problems. They had more. He knew it. And they knew he knew it. He had meant it about closing down the city. It was easily done. A few roadblocks, searching for evidence – or bombs – in vehicles, at each of the three freeway exits serving the various parts of the city. Traffic would be backed up for miles. Their Followers would lose money: their tenants in the offices, hotels and retail outlets downtown would lose the most. And when they were losing money, the Faith was losing their ten per cent of all that, not to mention fielding a deluge of calls from pissed-off tenants and business owners wanting to know what the hell was going on.

'Still alive, huh?' It was Al. He was smiling. Wider than the Cheshire Cat. And walking fast toward him, not his usual meander.

'Looks that way.'

'Man, I thought I'd see your head on a stake above the Mission.'

'You might get that wish before you know it.'

Al flung himself down into his chair and spun around to face Marty. 'How did it go?'

'The usual.'

'That good?' He smiled. 'Screw them, we got a break.'

'Oh yeah?'

'Yeah. For sure. We got ourselves a witness.'

'To what?'

'To the parking of the car, and the parker.'

'The parker?'

'Yeah.'

'Who's your witness?'

'The dog walker.'

'Our eye-witness is a guy that's about to lose an eye.'

'Yeah, but he hadn't lost it before he saw the guy.'

'So, it's a guy then? Not old Mrs Miller?'

'They're still looking for her. And Angel's not gonna lose the eye. I was there when the doc was looking him over. He's gonna have an op. Later today. But it's all looking good for the eye.'

'That's a relief.'

'For him too, I guess.'

'Yeah. But for us, it's good not to have a blind guy as the only eye-witness.'

'Better than no witness.'

'I guess. Funny how none of the so-called sighted have seen a damn thing. No one's even phoned in with any credible suspects, not for even one of the bombings. It's like this guy's a ghost.'

Al flipped open his notepad. 'Maybe he was, until now. But by tomorrow we might have a picture of him, courtesy of the dog walker. Some kind of likeness we can circulate.'

'Did he recognize him?'

'No, never seen him before. There or around. I just got the basics. The doc was pretty keen on getting me out of the way. But Angel saw him, our guy that first morning.'

'Or who we hope is our guy.'

'Yeah. That day Angel's got an appointment to get to. A potential new client. A lawyer lady. One of his current clients, a Mrs Nickalls, she recommended him. It's at ten fifteen downtown, her offices. She wants to buy a dog she can keep in the office. Something small, but that likes kids. She works with traumatized kids. Thinks the dog might put them at ease. But she doesn't want it barking all day when she's trying to work, or biting the kids' hands off. So, she wants some advice on picking a good breed – and also to see if Angel can come over and walk the thing a couple of times a day. Anyway, so he tells his other clients he has to do the poo-walk earlier than usual. Thirty minutes. So he can get home, showered and back downtown as it's the only time lawyer lady can do. When he gets to the space opposite the deli, it's mayhem. His usual space has some kind of machinery parked in it, there's a road gang already going at it with a digger. And the last space in that hour row just gets snaffled by some guy.'

'In the Nissan?'

'You got it. Anyway, Angel doesn't sweat losing his spot too much because he thinks the road gang don't look too bright, they're working right next to his spot and he's thinking they might drop some bit of machinery on his precious jeep. So he goes and parks further up, nearer the park.'

'So the deli guy was wrong.'

'You know witnesses. Memory and trauma don't work too

good together. But it's virtually the only time Angel's not parked in that exact spot. So, actually, it's an easy mistake to make. He still gets his coffee, but he brings his dogs with him as he wants to save a bit of time and is starting to worry he'll be late for the meeting. When he comes out of the deli, the car guy is still there, he's putting something in the trunk, or getting something out. Anyway, the beagle starts barking at the car guy.'

'The beagle? Interesting. I wonder if he could smell something on him.'

'Possible. And then all the dogs start. Angel almost scalds himself with the coffee trying to yank the dogs away from the edge of the road. Car guy looks over at him, "as if looks could kill". And then another dog coming down their side of the road distracts Angel's dogs, and he yanks them all off towards the park.'

'So he didn't get much of a look?'

'Not a long look, no. I said I'd send the sketch artist over tomorrow morning. But I got a description.'

'Go on.'

'Thick glasses, green jacket, slim. My height. So five ten. White.'

'Hair colour?'

'He thinks dark.'

'Thinks.'

'The dogs were distracting him.'

'Age?'

'Thirty-five maybe.'

'How old's Houseman?'

'Twenty-eight.'

'Shame. You think this is Hartman?'

'Time will tell.'

'Maybe the sketch artist and Angel will flush him out.'

'Let's hope.'

'I called the artist already. She's going over there at ten. The doc said they're operating tonight. But the sketch might get delayed if Angel is groggy or still in recovery. I told the sketch girl to wait at the hospital, no matter what. And I put a uniform on the door 24/7.'

'Good call. Where's Hobbs?'

'Didn't you send him after the AWOL guys?'

'Yeah. Haven't heard from him. Thought you might? Radio him or page him for me? Give him the description of the suspect and the time and all that. See if it tallies with anyone he's seen so far – or any of the AWOL guys. And circulate it, but make sure you tell them it's just interim. We'll have something better tomorrow.'

Al got up off his chair. 'Hopefully. What did Laidlaw have to say?'

'It wasn't so much Laidlaw. Although he did most of the talking. It was all twelve of them, lined up like a firing squad.'

'All twelve . . .'

'Yeah, but I wasn't leaving there without some kind of answers. Even their versions. But they're still holding back. Something. And it must be big because they'd even rolled out the Supreme Leader.'

'Trying to intimidate you?'

'I guess. I told them the Chinatown tale.'

Al smiled. 'Works every time.'

'Lifted the veil of silence, that's for sure. But not enough. They seemed pretty focused on Lomax and the missing money from his property investment scheme. They mentioned him a lot,

Bobbi Lomax, Linda Lomax. They even suggested Bobbi Lomax's high-school fiancé. Neither Bobbi nor him were Faith, needless to say. So they *really* thought he should be in the frame.'

'Yeah. Weird that.'

'For they can do no wrong.'

'Unless it's lose a million, like Lomax.'

'Every flock has its black sheep.'

'What about Angel and the beagle? What's Bobbi Lomax's ex got to do with them. He a dog hater?'

'I don't think the Faith's figured out a connection yet.'

'Give 'em time.'

'But they as good as admitted that Peter Gudsen was tipped for the top job. His main focus though, until he ascended to world domination, was looking after the Faith library, which occupied much of his spare time when he was working, plus a lot of his time when he left Lomax in the summer.'

'Worth getting Bobbi Lomax's ex in here?'

'I don't think so. Get Hobbs and Carvell out to his place though, just in case. We can't be seen to be ignoring tip-offs.'

'Even the ones that seem like they're giving us the runaround?'

'Depends on the source. What interested me was what they weren't saying. There were no helpful suggestions of a connection between Gudsen, Lomax – Bobbi or Arnold – and Houseman.'

'No one else seems to know about one, either.'

'But what about that miniature Bible?'

'The one Gudsen gave Marion Rose?'

'And which Gudsen might have got off Houseman.'

'He didn't have a store, did he?'

'No. So he must have had some kind of client–dealer network going, selling to regulars.'

'He might have an address book at his place. Might have the names in.'

'He might. But we're not going to get any kind of warrants unless we can put pretty overwhelming evidence on the table.' Marty picked a folded newspaper off a pile of them on his desk, and pushed it towards Al.

'Check this out.'

'What?'

'That story. The one with the picture. On the way back from the Faith, I stopped off at the *Desert Times*. I thought I'd try and find some other connection with Houseman and Gudsen or Lomax. Even the dog guy. Anything, no matter how left-field.'

'This entire case is left-field.'

'The archivist helped me track down some stuff. There's a few entries for Clark Houseman and a whole bunch for Gudsen, his mostly to do with the library, some exhibitions of religious books they ran over there, a bunch of mentions to do with the financial meltdown, Gudsen, Lomax. Even a picture of Bobbi Lomax. Prom Queen.'

Al held up the paper. 'Is that him, in the center? Houseman?'

'Yeah. This is the first Houseman article in the paper.' Marty patted the pile on his desk. 'I got back copies, a bunch of them and some copies the librarian made for me off microfilm.'

'Houseman looks different here.'

'He looks different in every picture. Guy's a chameleon.'

'This the Supreme Leader? Laidlaw?'

'The full line-up.'

'I think I saw this on TV. They found some old document. An original or something?'

'The Testament of Faith. And guess who found it?'

'Houseman?'

'Yep.'

'Where?'

'In an old English Bible. Tucked right inside. Imagine that. After all those years, it just shows up like that. The paper said it's worth fifty K.'

'Fifty K? How come nothing like that ever happens to me?'

'I have a feeling it just did.'

'What do you mean?'

'Look at the picture again. See Houseman sat there, looking like the cat that got the cream, and all the rest of them, looking even more smug.'

'I'm looking.'

'See that hand on Houseman's shoulder? The person's been cut out of the shot. The fingers, long, slender. Almost like a woman's?'

'Yeah.'

'And the varsity ring on the finger?'

'Yeah.'

'That's Peter Gudsen.'

'How do you know that, from just a hand?'

'I saw him, after the bombing, remember? I noticed the ring. And his fingers. It's him, but just to help that ID along a bit, here.' Marty gave Al the next paper from the pile. It was a page-size ad in the *Desert Times*. Lomax and Gudsen were standing amongst the painted backdrop of a new development, out at the top of the canyons, appealing for investors. 'See the suit jacket?'

'Yeah.'

'Notice how it's only got the two buttons. Usually there'd be three on the cuff.'

'Yeah. But how does that help?'

'Because in this other picture the arm with the missing person only has two buttons. And if you look close enough you can see a little thread from the jacket, where the missing button was.' He handed Al a small magnifying glass.

Al looked sceptically at it. 'The department's gone hi-tech, huh?'

'Just look.'

Marty looked at the top of Al's head as he peered down at the photos. He had a few flecks of grey pushing through the dark mop. Probably not a good time to tell him.

'Yeah. OK. I'll give you that it's the same jacket. And it might be the same hand. But what does it prove? They were in the same room together. Once.'

'I think it proves more than that. Look at the press conference picture. The way Gudsen's hand is kind of clasping Houseman's shoulder. A "well done, man" hand on his shoulder. A tad familiar for two guys no one seems even able to put together in the same sentence.'

Al looked at the picture. 'Looks like he's giving his shoulder a good old squeeze.'

'Like I said.'

'Strange how none of the wives mentioned them knowing one another.'

'You mean the live wives?'

'Yeah.'

'Question is, as only one of them is dead: what did Bobbi Lomax know?'

'Pillow talk, maybe?'

'More pillow talk than a wife of forty years, I'd bet.'

'You and me both.'

'You thinking that Houseman might be some kind of accomplice to Gudsen and Lomax and whatever was going on in that property investment firm?'

'Yeah, because I'm thinking, why are the faith so keen on deflecting me away from Houseman?'

'Maybe they suspect him?'

'Or maybe they're protecting him.'

'He'd have to be of value to them to be risking that.'

'Maybe it's damage limitation? By protecting him, they protect his accomplice.'

'Why would they protect Lomax? He's the one center-frame for all that money going missing.'

'No. Gudsen.'

'They're protecting Gudsen?'

'He who shall inherit the Faith crown.'

'But then why in the hell is Gudsen dead? And Bobbi Lomax? And Houseman and the Dog Angel in the hospital?'

'Maybe someone, or something, decided to protect the Faith from the growing investment scandal. And an urgent, growing need to disassociate themselves from it, whatever the cost.'

'Are you saying what I think you're saying, Mart?'

'That the Faith had them all killed? Or tried to?'

'Yeah.'

'That's exactly what I'm saying.'

28

February 7th 1983, 10 am

Faith HQ

'Overwhelming'. 'Awesome'. 'Privileged'. Clark didn't know how many times he'd repeated those words in the past ten minutes or so, but it was way less than the word 'blessed'. He'd used 'blessed' a lot. Usually with his hand pressed close to his chest, somewhere near his heart, peppered with occasional flourishes of clasped hands, closed eyes and an almost imperceptible bow of the head. He was the humble Follower. The blessed humble Follower who had rejoiced when it was attested by the Faith's own historical archivists that he had discovered the Prophet's original Testament of Faith.

Clark had rehearsed his responses earlier in the half hour after Laidlaw had shown him the pre-approved list of questions selected for the morning's press conference by the Faith's PR department. There were TV cameras present and rolling. The Faith considered it reckless to allow uncensored questions. Particularly when your leaders' responses would be recorded and beamed out of context into living rooms around the world via the evening news. The journalists, the Faith's usual favorites, were dotted around the room, to give the appearance of democracy and spontaneity. Their questions bland, congratulatory. They sounded more like members of the Faith's PR team than journalists. Clark doubted they even knew the meaning of the word 'journalism'.

His jaw was starting to tire from smiling when, after the barrage of blandness and suffocating congratulations, an almost forgotten question, the one Clark would have asked first, was asked. 'Excuse me, sir, could you repeat that?' said Clark. He wanted to draw focus to it, so everyone could hear it.

'Oh, I'm sorry, Mr Houseman.' The young man, whom one could easily have mistaken for an overgrown Boy Scout, stood up, and this time took care to enunciate his every word. 'How exactly did you find it? The Prophet's Testament of Faith?'

'Exactly?' Clark wondered how long he could delay his response for as he felt the tension levels rise, as the Disciples all seated alongside him silently wondered exactly how much detail he would reveal of his find. God is in the detail. But detail will kill you too. He knew they feared him mentioning the Bible. The Bright Bible, which they'd probably already locked away in their secret vaults. Or burnt.

'The Testament of Faith was discovered . . .' Clark thought back to his discovery, thought back to how something so contrived, so manufactured, could appear so natural, so spontaneous, so organic. He thought about his long trip hundreds of miles upstate. He looked down at the Testament. The almost tobacco-coloured page unrecognizable from its original incarnation as a far less yellow page of a large State Land tract that Clark had stolen wholesale from the State Land Records and Deed Office. He had only needed a quarter of it, but there were a few scattered researchers in the library, so rather than noisily ripping off the piece he needed, it had been far easier to just fold it up and slide it down the back of his trousers, covering it over with first his shirt, then his flyer's jacket. He had needed a piece of 1836 paper, or one produced before that time. Very helpfully, in the public spirit, the

Deeds office had arranged their box files in chronological order. Finding a piece of paper that had been partially used had been quicker than he thought. Several of the Deeds and Tracts had been written on much larger pieces of paper and then the whole folded in on itself so the blank parts of the page acted as a kind of envelope. He could have been out in less than ten minutes, but instead, he made sure to take a couple of boxes back to the desks near the librarian and pretend to take notes whilst mulling over dull tracts selling off one piece of barren land after another. The paper dug into him, but he could live with the pain. That which does not kill you.

Later, back in his den, he'd used a clean quill from his turkey stash dipped into a freshly made pot of 1836 ink. A lot of Germans had made it to Abraham City at the time, and Bright had a German lieutenant, so it was only reasonable that his techniques may have filtered down to Bright and Rebecca. When Clark had returned the boxes to the shelf, he took down a box marked '1838' and took out another large-paged tract and shoved that also down the back of his pants. He didn't want to have to come back too often. Some places it was best to stay under the radar. Thankfully he had a great memory for faces. If he had to go back and there was a different assistant on, he would sign in under Clifford Hartman, in a different hand, and not as Clark Houseman. If anyone ever read the library visitors' book, he didn't want to be noticed as a regular.

Exactly.

Clark smiled along the line of Disciples. They seemed to be holding their breath. Clark looked over the heads of the journos to the back of the room. 'Exactly . . . well, it was discovered by Mr Rook over there, in an antique volume I brought him for appraisal.'

All eyes followed Clark's gaze toward Rod Rook. He was sat next to Ron, crowded into the back row. Rod acknowledged the curious stares with his customary clasped hands. Ron reciprocated, beaming a wide, proud smile. No doubt thinking, by association, he'd sell a lot more coins this week.

'How much did they pay for it?'

It was her.

She stood up.

Amongst the sea of men in black suits, she was an angel, in a white trouser suit, her hair and face so white Clark thought they shimmered under the lights. Her crystal-clear voice made everyone in the room sit up and pay attention, including the Disciples, who were just beginning to relax. From somewhere along the podium Clark heard someone say, before she'd barely got a sentence out, 'No more questions. Thank you, ladies and gentlemen.' They had started to shift back in their seats, as if about to move away.

'Oh, I think you'll find it's a priceless document for our Faith, Mrs...?'

'Ms, Ms Franklin.'

Ms Debra Franklin. In the flesh.

Laidlaw leaned in towards the mic. 'As Mr Houseman says, it is indeed a priceless document. A miraculous document. Thank you, Miss Franklin.'

She was undeterred. 'I didn't mean that one.'

She nodded towards where, on the table at Clark's fingertips, sat the Testament safely tucked into a see-through plastic folder.

'We've taken all the questions for today. Thank you for attending, gentlemen.' Laidlaw looked at her. 'Miss Franklin.'

Around her, the other journalists were packing away their dictaphones and notepads. She didn't move. 'Could you tell me, gentlemen, what is the purpose of the Faith buying the so-called "Bright Bible"? Which I understand you considerably outbid the Real Faith in order to secure.'

'As you know, Miss Franklin, we don't discuss our collections. So we can neither confirm or deny what you say.'

'But surely if you hadn't bought it, you could say that?' She leaned forward now, her hand-held recorder pushed out as far as her arm could stretch, over the heads of the other journos.

Laidlaw stood up. His lips pursed. Clark could see him trying to smile through them, aware the cameras might still be rolling. He bent down towards his microphone. 'Thank you for your question, Miss Franklin, but we are done for the day.'

'So, are you denying you bought the so-called Bright Bible?'

Clark leant back in his seat, looked along the row at the Disciples' faces: their jaws were set, silently urging Laidlaw to close this down and fast. Clark could see that some of the other journos had sat back down now, shifting in their seats, scribbling her questions and Laidlaw's answers. None of the other Disciples around him dared to intervene.

'But if you had purchased it, what would you do with such a historical document, detailing as it does Robert Bright's three wives? Wives the Faith seems to have conveniently forgotten?'

'Today is a celebration of the miracle that has brought the Testament of Faith back to where it belongs. We should focus on that, Miss Franklin,' said Laidlaw through gritted teeth.

'Surely it would be a double miracle if this Bible exists? Genuine, as it sounds from the description I've heard.'

A miracle. Yes, but not for the Faith. For the Real Faith. She was goading him and Laidlaw, reeling onto the ropes now, struggled to get away from her without taking any more blows.

Before she could get out another question he said: 'We are only answering submitted questions. But your biased agenda is clear, as always, *Miss* Franklin.' He was sounding more aggressive; next he might actually tell her to shut the hell up. Clark could not have envisioned the opportunity Laidlaw was affording him. A chance to show his true allegiance to the Faith and its leaders. Clark stood up, holding the Testament. He put his hand gently but firmly on Laidlaw's arm, and pushed him softly down, back towards his seat next to the other Disciples. Clark bent towards the media mic in front of him, and smiled his megawatt smile. 'Thank you all for coming, Ms Franklin, gentlemen. Refreshments are now being served in the library, where I would be happy to show you the original Testament of Faith. We have prepared Xerox copies for you all.' At the mention of refreshments most of the journalists were noisily on their feet and headed towards the library. Clark looked back at Laidlaw and the disciples. They all nodded gratefully at Clark as the room broke up – and the red light on the camera switched off. 'Blasted woman,' said Laidlaw, his hand over the table mic. 'She's always scratching around for some scandal or other.'

'I guess Reno put her up to it.' Clark couldn't call them the Real Faith, not here. He looked out at the press pit, as the remaining journos, obviously from more liberal news organisations, made a beeline for Debra Franklin. Closely followed by two dark-suited members of the Faith's PR team. The journos and the PR boys would be keen to have a clue to her source, albeit for very different reasons.

'I guess they're hoping you'll sell them the Bible now.'

'They can hope all they want,' said Laidlaw. 'It's not for sale.'

'If I could ask you to wait there a moment, gentlemen, I'll just get a couple of shots for official release.' Clark noticed the guy didn't have a press pass. He must be the Faith's go-to photographer. They didn't want unflattering or undignified pictures of their leaders peering out from the morning's newspapers.

As the photographer settled them all into the frame, Clark looked up, directly into the camera. He felt the others shuffle into position around him. He watched the photographer's hands, one hovering near the button, the other clutching the large flashbulb and ushering them all closer. Clark pushed the Testament of Faith closer towards the camera. Everybody set. A hand on the shoulder. Peter's. Squeezed him. A whisper. Well done. The Supreme Leader, sat to his right, put his hand forward onto the top corner of the Testament next to Clark's.

'Quite a find, son. Truly marvellous.'

Clark didn't take his eyes from the camera. 'I think I'm getting a nose for it.'

As he waited for the photographer to click the shutter Clark knew he would have two lives. His life before this moment. And his life after it.

29

November 2nd 1983, 4.24 pm

They made their way out of the precinct, around the side of the lot, towards the far end of it, where what passed for the state's first, and only, forensics lab sat like some kind of shiny mirage amongst the clutch of rusting cop cars long ago abandoned to the extremes of the desert temperatures.

Marty, the code forgotten, stepped aside as Al punched it in. 'What is it?' said Marty.

Al tapped the side of his nose, that would be telling, and pushed the door open for Marty, following him in, the wooden door slamming behind them. Whittaker turned to them.

'Don't touch anything. Yet. Gloves.' Whittaker indicated a large box of latex gloves next to the door. They each grabbed a pair. 'Come on. I'll give you the nickel tour.'

They looked around at all the tables groaning under the weight of thousands of transparent baggies, most of which seemed to contain nothing but unrecognizable fragments.

'Looks a mess,' said Al.

'Nature of the beast,' said Whittaker, leading them to the far side of the room. 'Hopefully, even the ultimate chaos yields order.'

'Here's hoping,' said Marty. 'Because right now we could do with a little.'

'And maybe even a few clues.'

'We got a couple of tables going for each bombing. The cars are out back in the shed. We're still going over those. But this is Mrs Lomax's evidence. Right behind you is Gudsen. Next to him, Houseman, and lastly, over by the door, today's: Mr Angel. We've prioritised certain elements of each for fingerprints. But we're striking out. Nothing on the boxes, on the ribbons, or on any of the bomb housings.'

'He wore gloves?'

'Not necessarily. It just means the explosions and/or fires wiped out what was there.'

'So we might luck out?'

'Sure. I've sent my guys back out to each of the sites again, in case we missed anything,' said Whittaker.

'Like what?'

'For starters: this.'

Whittaker moved back across to the table by the door. Dog Angel. He held up a baggie with a small dented clump of what looked like lead.

'What's that?'

'It's a blast cap. The bombs were all pipe bombs. You stuff each end with a lead cap. We only found one at this scene.'

'Was that why it was a smaller explosion?'

'Possibly, Marty. Although perhaps it was a smaller device. You'd have to ask Tex about that. It's possible that it's there and we just didn't find it first time around.'

'Perhaps it got blown to smithereens, huh?'

'We don't think so, Al. We got all the others.'

'Maybe he ran out, used something else?'

'Possibly. I'll let you know how my guys get on. We're searching for whatever we can find.'

Footsteps from out the back, from the car shed. Marty looked up as Big Tex emerged from the open doorway. He was wearing gloves, but his hands were smeared with oil and grease. 'Hey, Mart. I bet you're wondering how Mr Houseman managed to blow up two others and then himself, plus another one while he was laid up in County?'

Marty smiled. 'It had crossed my mind. Your theory taking a knock?'

'Like hell it is.' Tex had taken off his dirty gloves and was replacing them with a fresh pair as he moved fast across the room towards where they still stood at the Angel table. 'And this proves it.' He picked up a baggie. Mangled metal inside it.

'What's that?'

Big Tex grinned like all his numbers just came up in the lottery. 'A timer. That's what.'

Marty and Al peered closer. 'We'll take your word for that,' said Marty.

'Do. The cunning son of a bitch used three tilts . . . and, today's, a timer. So much for a bomber's signature.'

'That's some planning,' said Al.

'So, you still think he blew himself up. Maybe on purpose?'

'That I don't know, Mart. I just do facts.'

'Sure,' said Marty. 'Well, four bombs is a fact. No matter what was used. But Houseman as the bomber, that's not fact, just supposition. In fact, if the timer was set to go off *after* all the others, but set before the first bomb, then that throws suspicion not just on Houseman but all the victims, including the dead ones.'

'I hear ya, Marty,' said Tex.

'Yeah. And who's to say Houseman or one of the others didn't have an accomplice? Either one of the other victims, or some other SOB who's still running around town, planning who knows what?'

'Al's right, Tex. We got nothing else here. No fingerprints. Nothing. Any of these guys could be the accomplice of the other. Or none. Who would Houseman's accomplice be?'

'The wife maybe?' said Al.

'Not unless she's got Stockholm Syndrome,' said Marty. 'And I don't think she has. She's a loyal Faith wife, but I don't think it stretches to murder.'

'Maybe the timer's his only accomplice.'

'It might be the only one, Tex. Sure. For any of them. What was all that stuff in Houseman's trunk, Whittaker? Did you dry it all out?'

'Looks like a lot of old paper.'

'What you hoping for, Mart, a scrawled confession?'

'That'd be nice.'

'Wouldn't it? Then maybe we could go home,' said Al.

'Show me where it is.'

'Sure, Mart. Back over here.'

They moved as a unit, following Whittaker back over to the far corner of the room. 'It's all here,' he pulled out a huge cardboard box out from under the table. It was stuffed with small baggies. Marty pulled out one. A tiny piece of browned paper, so small it only contained the merest hint of a pen mark, not even a letter. He pulled out another. 'They're all like that, Marty. Each piece in a separate bag. There's over forty-eight hundred pieces in there. Four boxes full.'

Marty looked under the table at the other boxes. 'Any idea what it is?'

'None,' said Whittaker.

'The longest confession in history,' said Al.

'And we just don't have time to find out now. Like I said, we're…'

'Prioritising. I know.' Marty turned to Tex and Al. 'What's Houseman's motivation?'

Al shrugged his shoulders. 'Anger. If he's invested with Lomax and Gudsen and lost his money.'

'Is he on the List?'

'What list?'

'Jesus, Al. The List. The disgruntled three thousand.'

'I didn't see his name.'

'Check again for any of his family: wife, parents, sister-in-law, the lot.'

'How about Angel? He wasn't an investor?'

'No, he said not.'

'Check him again. But if Angel wasn't an investor and it turns out he isn't connected to Lomax and Gudsen, even through his clients, and judging by the fact he most likely wasn't parked in his usual spot, he probably wasn't the target.'

'No? Then who?'

'I don't know. But whoever they were, they got business somewhere along that strip.'

'The deli and all that?'

'Yeah. 'Cos even if the timer was supposed to go off the same day as any of the other bombs, that car was parked there deliberately. Whoever Angel saw, they weren't in any hurry, not panicked in any way, and a few days later the car is still there. And then, boom. Looks like that beagle was right, they were worthy of barking at.'

'Don't forget, Mart. The first bomb. The nail bomb. Someone hated Gudsen more than they hated the rest of 'em.'

'Or wanted us to think they did, Tex.'

Bang.

Bang. Bang. Bang.

'Looks like you're not the only one forgot the code.' Al moved across to open the door. It was barely open before someone was pushing their way through. The Captain.

'So this is where you all are.'

No one answered, they just stared at him. Probably wondering why he was wearing a tux to visit the forensics shed. Another back-slapping function, no doubt. Tough at the top.

Whittaker broke the silence. 'Good to see you, Captain. You haven't been over here since you helped the Sheriff cut the ribbon.'

The Captain mumbled something inaudible back at him, then turned to Marty.

'You do realise I'm on the board of the Mission.'

What he should have said was: You do realise I'm trying to ingratiate myself a place in the Supreme Chamber. Marty looked him square in the eyes. 'You realise I'm a cop, sir?'

'Yeah, one with a grudge against the Faith.'

'I'm not the one with the grudge, sir.'

'Against Laidlaw and who knows who else. What's all this got to do with the Faith, anyhow?'

'Haven't you noticed, Captain, everything in this town has something to do with the Faith?'

'Keep it in check, Detective, or I'll have you directing traffic on the freeway . . . or was it closing down the exits?'

So it had been Laidlaw on the phone.

The Captain looked over Marty's shoulder and his eyes fell on table after table of bagged evidence. He looked as if he'd woken up from a sleepwalk to find himself on an alien planet. 'In the name of our Lord Prophet: what's all this mess?'

'Our case, sir.'

'This is it?'

'Pretty much.'

'Get someone in the frame for this, Marty. No one wants the Feds down here, sticking their nose in everything, and I'm not going to be able to keep them out much longer if we don't close this case.'

Marty wanted to ask if it mattered whether they were guilty or innocent, but knew it didn't. What the Captain meant was the Faith didn't want the Feds here. Marty didn't much either. They'd lost opportunity after opportunity to find Liss. Although the Faith hadn't exactly facilitated their presence in the Canyon, Marty believed the Feds when they said the Faith had hampered them at every turn.

'We need warrants.'

'Warrants? For what?'

'Searches. Homes. Businesses. Gudsen. Lomax. Houseman. Angel.'

'The *victims'* homes, businesses? Have you gone crazy? You got probable cause?'

'We're working on it.'

'No probable cause and you want warrants? Are you trying to get me fired?'

No. But it was an idea.

'Nobody stops until we find this guy. Nobody.'

Marty guessed he meant everyone in the room not wearing a tux. He watched as the door banged shut.

A collective smile. Shakes of the head. A whistle from Tex. 'Someone's got their panties in a bunch.'

'Glad he's not my boss,' said Whittaker.

'I'll second that,' said Tex.

'Count yourselves lucky,' said Marty.

'What now?' said Al.

'I'm going to get us our warrants.'

Al raised his eyebrows. 'From on high?'

'Pretty close.'

'You want an assist?'

'Better I go on my own. Can you get a couple of uniforms to take those boxes over to the evidence room for when I get back? That OK, Whittaker?'

'Sure, if you use their side room. I'll give you some sheeting also. I'll seal the boxes. Give you a pack of gloves.'

'Thanks.'

'What are you going to do with it all, Mart?' said Al.

'Put the shit together, of course.'

'All that?' said Al.

'Every last piece.'

'Hell,' said Tex. 'The Captain's right: you are crazy.'

30

February 8th 1983

Nate's Diner

Clark, his empty plate in front of him, was staring at the newspaper. He couldn't believe that he had done it. He looked to where, behind the ketchup and menus, he'd tucked the large envelope to give to Kenny. He hadn't told him anything on the phone. Just that it was a courier job. And it was urgent. And to pack his overnight kit.

Behind that envelope was an identical one, inside which were three lists. Wish lists. One for the Faith, one for the Real Faith and one for the more literary-minded collectors and booksellers and their clients. Clark would get them copied up later. On the lists were individual lost gems. And many gems that had never even existed. Clark thought that was the ideal scenario. That way you could create the ultimate document for each client. Bespoke forgeries. Clark hated that word, 'forgery'. 'Creation' was far less unpleasant. 'Forgery' was such a negative word. He was an artist, not a forger. A creative artist.

'Good?' Clark looked up from his newspaper. Gloria, a forty-something career waitress, was stood over him. 'The schnitzel?'

'It came highly recommended.'

'Looks like it sure lived up to the recommendation. Room for dessert?'

'I shouldn't.'

She leaned down toward him.

'See that line by the door?'

Clark looked up. While he'd been lost in thought, the diner had filled up, not a spare seat in the house. By the entrance a gaggle of seniors were stood, menus in hand, primed to shuffle at a pace towards the first table that looked like it might be ready to expel its diners.

'If they see you just sipping on coffee, gazing out the window, they're gonna turn you to stone with their stares.'

Clark looked back over to the seniors. They caught his stare and heads tilted almost in unison, seemed to be waiting for him to get the hell out of Dodge and relinquish the four-person booth he was hogging all to himself.

'Look what they did to those two.'

She indicated out to the thin green strip of what passed for lawn outside the diner, where, planted in the lawn, were two stone grotesques. 'I obviously missed the warning. Maybe in a few minutes. I'm waiting on a friend,' Clark told her.

Gloria looked down at Clark's open newspaper. 'He as famous as you, this friend?'

Clark's eyes followed her gaze to where in the center of the page sat the Faith's official group photo from yesterday, all of them grinning out at the world as they gathered way too proudly around the Testament. 'It's not me.' Gloria picked up the newspaper, held it up to her face, peered over the top of it at Clark, then back to the newspaper.

'Not you? Your twin then?'

'You could say that.'

'Says here that old bit of paper was worth fifty grand, that's more than my house!'

'Everything's only worth what people will pay for it,' he looked at her name badge, 'Gloria – and you gotta take into account a whole bunch of criteria. How much would you pay for your house today?'

'With my old man in it? Nothing!'

'And with Harrison Ford in it?'

'Well, I'd sell my soul for that – and throw in the house 'n' all.'

'I rest my case.'

She took up his plate. 'Well, Mr Houseman, if you or your twin ever bump into Harrison, be sure and send him to 1321 South Beacon.'

'Sure will.'

Clark had just turned back to his newspaper when he heard a commotion over by the door. He looked up to see a blond man in biker's leathers squeezing past the diners. Kenny. Now everyone had a reason to stare. 'Sorry! Sorry! I had a drop-off downtown. Jeez, this place is out of the way.'

'That's kind of the point.'

Kenny threw himself down into the booth, made a grab for the envelope. 'This it?'

'Careful.' Clark grabbed Kenny's wrist, moved the envelope out of his reach. 'It's fragile.'

'Can I have a look?'

'Not here, no. When you get it to its destination.'

'LA?'

'Yeah.'

'That's why I brought the Harley.'

Technically, it wasn't a Harley. Not an official one, off the production line. Kenny had spent the past decade cobbling original Harley used spare parts together to create his very own dream machine. Discount version. 'Sweet ride.'

'The Harley? Where you gonna put this?'

'I got a studded calf-leather side satchel. Beautiful detail. I'm gonna pop it in there.'

'Isn't that near the exhaust?'

'It's *above* the *side* of the exhaust.'

Why was Kenny talking to him as if *he* was the idiot?

'It's paper.'

'It's padded, this envelope, isn't it?'

'Yeah.'

'Don't sweat it, it'll be fine. I've got a T-shirt in there, for my overnight kit. I'll wrap it in that also.'

'You got insurance?'

''Course. Some of those big rig guys out on the highway, they don't even see us. Wipe you out just like that.'

Clark did not want his document wiped out, just like that or any other how. 'This envelope is worth twenty K to the dealer and I don't want it getting lost or burned up by the exhaust.'

'Twenty K!? The envelope?'

Now he was a comedian.

'What's inside.'

'Another document? Where'd you find this one? You're better than those guys, y'know, the ones with the sticks that find water out in the desert.'

'Diviners?'

'Yeah. Them. So, where'd you get it?'

'A collector.'

Kenny waited for him to tell him the collector's name or details. Instead, Clark just smiled at him. 'Anonymity – a God-given gift.'

'And one I'd happily forgo for ten million greenbacks or a roll in the hay with Kathleen Turner.' Gloria was clearing the booth behind them. Kenny turned to her, 'Can I get the special and a Coke float, miss? Thanks.' He turned back to Clark. 'You not eating?'

'Apparently, I'm having dessert. Whatever pie you got today, Gloria. Thanks.'

'Vanilla float?'

'That'd be great. Thanks, Gloria.' Kenny smiled, winked at Clark.

'Coke float. How old are you?'

'Old enough, dude.' Kenny laughed to himself.

Clark leaned forward in his seat. Kenny copied him.

'OK, listen up, here's the details.'

Kenny moved even closer. Maybe it was because Kenny was pissing him off, but Clark wrapped his right hand gently around Kenny's wrist, pressed his fingers into the inside of the wrist and dropped his voice down into a muted hum. Kenny didn't say anything, he just stared curiously at him. Thought it might be part of the details. *Idiot.* Kenny leaned forward a little. Clark placed the fingers of his left hand on Kenny's left temple.

'Close your eyes.' Kenny closed his eyes. 'Now imagine you're in California. By the ocean. Maybe Redondo, Laguna, Malibu. Wherever the girls are more beautiful. The surf's up.'

'I'm liking this trip already,' said Kenny.

Not under yet. Keep trying. 'Sssssssh. You need to be quiet. Really, really quiet.'

Clark took a quick look around, everyone had their nose in their food or their menus. Clark dropped his voice even lower, moved closer to Kenny. 'There are bikini-clad women everywhere and as much weed as you can smoke in a lifetime.' Clark noticed that Kenny's stooped head was looking a bit heavier. Clark glanced to the side. Kenny's eyes were firmly shut.

'You're going to take off all your clothes and swim in the surf, the sea is amazingly warm and soothing, like the best hot tub ever. You forget about your long journey and all your aches and pains, life's disappointments just ebb from you. But first, before you can do any of that, you're going to drive very, very carefully with this package to the Harris Salesroom, 415 Rodeo Drive, Beverly Hills. They're expecting it. Tell them your name is Dave and that Cliff sent you. Clifford Hartman. He's the dealer.'

Kenny could so easily have been a Dave. Or a Neanderthal.

'And if you look inside the package, or get sight of the document, you are going to instantly forget what is in there.' Kenny's head looked super-heavy now. Clark's head was bent down next to his, they looked like they were in prayer so no one in the diner batted an eyelid. Clark had forgotten something. 'Ensure you get a receipt. And when I click my fingers in a minute, you will open your eyes and remember that you're in a hurry and have to leave so you can get most of the way there before nightfall. When you come back from Cali, you better come see me right away before you do anything else.'

Clark sat back in his seat. Clicked his fingers loudly. Kenny sat back in his seat, startled. 'What happened?'

'I think you nodded off. Something I said?'

Kenny didn't answer him, instead he looked at his watch.

'What's up?' said Clark.

'I gotta get on the road, man.'

'What's the rush?'

'It's getting late.'

'One special: bacon, mac 'n' cheese, and a coke float. Vanilla.'
Gloria had appeared beside the booth, hands full of bounty.

Kenny looked at the food. Back at Clark. 'I don't have time to
eat this.'

Gloria looked at Clark. 'He's kidding, right?'

'Something tells me no.'

Kenny was up now, out of the booth. Taking a twenty out of
his pocket.

'Forget it, I got the check,' said Clark, passing him the padded
envelope.

'OK, man, that's great. Thanks. I'll keep it real safe.' He headed
for the exit.

'What am I gonna do with this?' Gloria pushed the plate
towards Clark.

'Why not give it to Ziggy?'

'That's kind of you, Mr Houseman. What about the Coke
float?'

'I'll take that.'

Clark took the Coke from her and she made back towards the
kitchen.

Clark could hear the roar of the Harley as Kenny rode out of
the lot. He dug his spoon into the ice cream, took a few bites. Not
bad. He finished it and went back to reading his newspaper.

31

November 2nd 1983, 8 pm

The Other Mr Laidlaw

The '69 Mustang twisted high up into the canyon, its lights picking out half-lit entrances to driveways which grew less frequent the higher it climbed. It was a full minute since he'd passed the last house when the heavy wrought-iron gates of 6700 Jericho Drive reared into view. Robert must have been watching him wind his way up the canyon, for the gates swung wide open before he'd even stopped the car, let alone thought about reaching out to ring the buzzer at the side of them.

His headlights lit up the house, a palace of wood and glass. The snow fell deeper up here, but it was neatly piled in white walls on either side of the drive. Robert stood at the open front door.

Handshakes and Marty was inside.

Robert took his coat from him, hung it on a hanger and tucked it away into a discreet cupboard to the side of the vast entrance hall, a glass cathedral at the center of the house, reaching out to the stars and beyond.

'Where's Cerise?'

'Gone to her sister's in Palm Springs for the week. Back Tuesday. Her case finished early. Your call broke the silence.'

'Some winter sun? I could do with getting out of town.'

'I heard.'

'The Mission? Alan?'

Robert held up his hands. 'I am not my Brother's keeper. And he sure as hell isn't mine. But, in my job, it pays to keep abreast of local news.'

'And gossip?'

'Always gossip. Although usually that comes via Cerise's circle of real nosey friends.'

Marty smiled, shook his head. 'Shame no one can tell me who the bomber is.'

'Come on, it's through this way now. Cerise had the whole place remodeled in the spring. Colonial style. All this, it's Canadian maple.'

They were inside a vast study which led off the hall. Through the floor-to-ceiling window that formed the outside walls of the room, the entire city was at their feet, marked out by a carpet of white lights.

'The view hasn't changed.'

'Yeah. I'm still not sure whether that's a good thing or a bad thing.'

'I'll second that.'

Robert moved across to the drinks cabinet. 'Not going well, your case?'

'Too many suspects, not enough evidence.'

'You remind me why I quit the DA's office.'

'I got to find this guy.'

'Can't help you much on that one, gossip or no gossip. But I might have something better.'

'Yeah?'

'A fantastic Calvados, I got it last time we were at Amanda's in LA. Remember, Cerise's sister?'

He remembered. She was too beautiful to forget.

Robert slowly poured two fingers into each cut-crystal tumbler. 'She's on her third multimillionaire husband now. Each time the cellar gets better. I should tell her to divorce this one and trade up again. Ernest, that's the latest one, he gave me a couple of bottles when we were leaving. He's a good guy, straight up. You'd like him.' He handed the drink off to Marty. 'I'm hoping Cerise will bring a case of it back this time.'

Both men sat down in the large leather armchairs. Robert took out a large cigar from a box of Cubans on the side table and offered it to Marty. Marty waved his hand, no. 'May I?' He took out one of his roll-ups.

'If you must. It'll insult the Calvados, but why spoil the habits of a lifetime?'

'Cheers.' They leaned forward and clinked glasses.

'To Ernest,' said Robert.

'Ernest.' They took their first sips.

'Delicious, isn't it?'

'You're right about that. That new too, the drinks cabinet?'

'I got it in Scottsdale. Antique store. It's on wheels. I'm too old for lifting heavy crap. Makes it easier to slip out of sight when I have more, how can I say, *particular* guests.'

'Playing with fire.'

'No fun not to. I keep reminding myself I've a lifetime appointment. They have to pay me off to get rid of me. And you know how the Faith hates to part with its money.'

'And its information.'

Robert smiled. They took another sip. Fell into silence. Only the crackle of the logs on the fire filled the room. 'What can I help you with, Marty, I know you're not here to chew the rag.'

Marty took another drag of his roll-up. Exhaled. 'I need

some warrants.'

'Warrants? For murder? I can issue warrants, but not for murder.'

'I don't want you to issue it for murder.'

'What then?'

'Fraud, financial misdemeanor. I've no idea. I just need to get inside some houses and a couple of business addresses.'

'Not a fishing expedition, is it?'

'No. But I'm going in with my eyes open.'

'What is it you're looking for?'

'A ledger, details of secret bank accounts, illicit payments in or out. All that jazz. Oh, and not forgetting the bomb factory.'

'You think that's it, fraud, the motive for the bombings?'

'I think it might be. And right now I'd really like to rule it either in or out. We got a list of three thousand investors and I don't want to have to interview every damn one of 'em, not if there's another way.'

'Three thousand potential complainants. I can see your problem. You got probable cause?'

'Not much. But I got two victims on the slab and two in the hospital. And a dead dog. And who knows how many victims tomorrow and if that's not cause I don't know what is.'

'Death and injury's not enough. Tell me what else you got.'

Marty told him about the ledger and about Linda Lomax's divorce, the investment company's vanishing money and Peter Gudsen's concerns, ending with a brief overview of Houseman and Angel. When he'd finished they were on their second tumbler. Robert Laidlaw exhaled deeply, shook his head. 'You know what I'm going to say?'

'That it's not enough.'

Robert nodded. 'It's not enough, Marty. Besides, isn't this a Federal case already?'

'No. Not yet. Nothing filed.'

'The fraud will be filed soon enough. After the Sheriff's little stunt on TV the other day.'

'But, in the meantime, while the Feds are snoozing, can you do anything . . . ?'

'I can't get you warrants for them all. But . . .'

Marty sat up in his seat. 'But?'

'It's not going to be easy – and you probably won't be much ahead of the Feds – but I can grant you warrants for searches for Gudsen and Lomax. House and business addresses.'

'The others?'

'There's no link. Nothing. But. And this is down to you now. I need you to get complainants.'

'Complainants?'

'For the fraud. If it's not a Federal case. We have to file a case into the Chancery court records. It's an antiquated system. Which has its benefits. And in a case like this I need ten per cent of the total potential complainants before we can put it on record.'

'That's three hundred people, Rob.'

'Thanks, Einstein. I already did the math. And that's the minimum. Without it, you can't file and I can't issue the warrants.'

'Signing up three hundred people. That's going to take forever.'

'Not if they think they can get back their lost money and that without the warrants, every minute that ticks by their case is probably being destroyed.'

'How are they going to get their money back? Linda Lomax said there wasn't enough money to settle her divorce case.'

'The money's there. At least, it usually is in this kind of case. They're just not finding it. Even if it's only assets left which they could liquidate. Who lost the most, perhaps they should be your first three hundred calls?'

'It can't be them.'

'Why not?'

'It just can't.'

'Marty.'

'Because they're the ones with the most likely motive.'

'They're your suspects?'

'I didn't say that.'

'Of course not.'

'Do they all have to make depositions?'

'No depositions, not yet. They just have to agree to make a joint complaint.'

'How am I gonna get three hundred of them?'

'Maybe the folks who invested the least? I'm assuming they're lower down on your suspect list? Even though their loss might have hurt them the most.'

Marty nodded. 'You're right. My guys said those who lost tens of thousands seemed to mostly shrug it off.'

'Professional investors.'

'Seems that way.'

'They take the rough with the smooth. Find those whose investment seems smallest – that way you'll get your ten per cent soon enough.'

'I guess it'd bite the small investors more. Do they have to have a lawyer?'

'Of course.'

'Not a different one for each of them?'

'No. They just need one lawyer to rep them as a whole. It's a formality. They sign a very simple form of engagement with the lawyer. And, collectively, they can change the lawyer at any time.'

'No fees up front?'

'None.'

'Where do I get the form?'

'Do I have to do everything for you?'

'I'm criminal, not civil. That's your bag. Call me if you run a stop sign with a gut full of Calvados.'

'Thanks. Damien Jones. He seems to win everything that comes before Chancery. He'll give you the forms you need.'

'Not your golfing partner, is he?'

'No. Alan's.'

Marty scrutinized him.

'Relax. I'm kidding. He's the best. Works this state and Delaware.'

'Delaware?'

'Used to have our system. Helps if you know your way around it. Wins a lot of cases. He'll be able to help your investors.'

'You wanna give him a call for me?'

'Do I look like your secretary?'

'I dunno. She doesn't exist. The department can't afford one, especially not your pay grade. I'll buy you a pastrami on rye next time you're down at the Courthouse café.'

'Can't wait. Pass me that phone.'

'Now who's the secretary?'

Marty picked up the trim binatone dappled with leopard print and passed it, smiling quizzically, to Robert, who quickly began punching in the numbers, whispering, 'Cerise got it in London . . . Ssssh . . . It's ringing.'

'A good start.'

Robert smiled widely, pointed into the handset, 'Hey, Damien. Yeah, Robert. Judge Laidlaw to you.' He laughed. 'I got you a client. Scrub that. I got you three hundred new clients. Great case. You'll be on the front page of the *Wall Street Journal* again with this one, my friend. You interested?' Robert's smile got even wider, he gave the thumbs up to Marty. 'Great. I'll get their spokesman to call you in the morning. Yeah, at the office.'

Robert hung up and fished around in his Rolodex, pulled out a card. 'Here. Get their spokesman to call him in the morning.'

'Spokesman? We don't even have one claimant yet.'

'You'll get them. Just start spreading the word. Come on. You need to get dialing. Where you headed?'

'Back to my desk.'

'That's the spirit. Talking of which, better you don't have any more of this.' Robert took Marty's tumbler from his hand and downed the remaining Calvados.

*

Marty was shrugging his coat back on. Robert had his hand on the door. 'You know they'll find out pretty quickly, you won't be able to keep it quiet. Work fast.'

Marty nodded.

'If you think the Faith are embroiled in this somehow they won't let you get your warrants, won't want you finding things out, that's if there's still anything left for a warrant to find. You need to get to the complainants before they do. They probably have more leverage than you – unless you're offering a place in heaven.'

'Not today. But I've got a plan.' Marty shook Robert's hand, nodded farewell.

'A plan is good.'

'A good plan is even better,' said Marty, pulling up his collar.

32

Valentine's Day 1983

City of Angels

The last lots he'd sold at an auction house were a series of framed lobby cards signed by Monroe, Lemmon and Curtis. Signed just by Curtis back in the day, but Clark had spent a happy night in his den with round after round of Upper Berth Manhattans and soon Monroe and Lemmon, flourish perfect, appeared right alongside Curtis.

Clark had hoped there might be a movie buff out in the desert someplace, but there'd been two. Luckily. One in the room and one on the phone. Clark had bought them from a yard sale he'd passed on his way down to Scottsdale the previous month. Forty bucks the lot. A hundred fifty for new frames. On the day, they'd sold for five thousand.

Usually, when he was selling, if it was a coin, he'd take Kenny with him. Let him get out of the car first, go in and register. He'd hold back ten minutes. Kenny always registered under his mother's address in Santa Fe, that way no one noticed two lone guys, pretending to be strangers, arriving almost at the same time from the same place. Clark didn't want people marking out dots and joining them up. Once the auction was in full swing Kenny would bid on a few random things, come in low, bid a couple of times and then drop out early; then, when it came to Clark's lots, bid a few rounds, up the price, and drop out at the last minute.

Always stand at the back of the room. There you can read the backs of people's heads, how tight their hand is clamped on the paddle; what page the catalogue is open on, even where they've kindly marked out what they're after – multiple inked rings around something usually equalled very interested. Some even scribbled down next to the item the maximum price they were prepared to bid for it. At the back of the room, it was like a game of faceless poker. Kenny was good at poker. Some days he was almost as good as Clark. At auctions it's always good to have someone on your side in the room, bringing heat, buzz to the crowd for your lots. Just like a good game of craps. Money follows money. Everyone wants in the game when they watch someone else putting their coin on chance. You can't wait for the roll of the dice to decide, the dice fall faster than the gavel and then it's too late. Kenny had helped bid up Clark's coins to way more than they were worth on many an occasion. He didn't know they were counterfeits and Clark had no intention of telling him. Ever.

Today, in the unfamiliar room, the auction in full flow, there was no Kenny, so Clark was working a different plan. He'd already bid on a few items he wasn't remotely interested in, just so he could appear disappointed when he didn't get them. Next to him was Travis J. Winkleman the Third, who, according to the envelope for his catalogue, resided at 613 North Arden Drive, Beverly Hills. Clark had spied him during his earlier pre-sale tour of the items. He'd been lingering near Clark's lot, gazing curiously at it as he peered in to where it was laid out flat in the temperature-controlled glass cabinet. Clark had watched him as he read the blurb in the catalogue and then stood watching while a few other people approached it, almost like he wanted to ask them something but didn't dare. TJ had marked its entry in the catalogue with a question mark. And then another.

The auctioneer was barely through the first twenty lots and TJ had already spent almost twenty-seven thou, on a clutch of French furniture, an art deco diamond bracelet, and a gaudy golden filigree and enamelled confection that looked like the poor cousin of a Fabergé egg.

Going, going, gone.

The gavel came down again. The successful bidder's number was quickly jotted down and almost instantly the auctioneer's assistant was up again walking around the room, showing off Exhibit 21. Clark's. Up at his lectern the auctioneer was glossing its merits as TJ and some others leaned forward to hear anything of note that might help them determine how high to bid.

'Do I have eighteen thousand?'

A numbered paddle towards the front suddenly shot up. One of the staff manning the telephones also nodded and back and forth the trio went until the bid hit twenty-nine thousand. TJ hesitantly clutched his paddle as it hovered a few inches off his lap. Clark leaned towards him and whispered, 'You're not sure if you want to bid?'

'Not at all sure,' TJ whispered back.

'It's not my money – but I'd go for it.'

TJ was looking at Clark now. Clark switched his smile to megawatt. 'Religion never goes out of fashion. And the Faith's the fastest-growing religion in the world. You got a growing audience and not many historical documents or manuscripts: you'll always find someone to buy it from you.'

'Really?'

'Sure. And for a good price.'

'Forty-two thousand,' said the auctioneer's phone assistant.

TJ leaned in towards Clark. 'How much should I bid?'

'Oh, only what you can afford.'

'Thanks.' TJ's paddle shot up and with it the price. 'Forty-five.'

'Forty-five to our regular gentleman in the back there. Thank you, sir. Late to the party on this, but here all the same.'

On the phone. 'Forty-six.'

'Fifty,' shouted TJ, and with that, his phone rival was silenced.

He turned to Clark, smiling. 'Great. Thanks.' Shook his hand, before turning back to the auctioneer and yelling out 'One thirty-one.'

'Well, if you're ever looking for anything, coins, books, manuscripts – religious or otherwise – give me a call.' He handed TJ his card.

TJ took a quick look. 'Thanks, Cliff. I'll do that. I'm Travis, by the way. What you bidding on?'

Clark flicked open his catalogue. A double-page spread. '*Peter Pan*, first edition.'

'*Peter Pan*. Neat. That's all of us, isn't it? You know, the little boy that never grew up.'

Clark smiled back at him.

'How high you going to bid, Cliff?'

Clark casually shrugged his shoulders. 'Oh, no more than fifty thousand.'

TJ stood up, shook his hand again. 'That's what you say now. Wait until the auction devil gets inside you.' He laughed. 'Good luck. I need to get out of here. I'm way over my limit for the day.'

'Have a good day now, Travis.'

'You too, Cliff.'

'No doubt about it, Travis.' *Fifty thousand* for a non-unique piece of Faith history, just one of several Faith documents he'd traded for the Testament of Faith. Clark was going to have a very good day indeed.

*

His head full of his little game with Travis and his subsequent successful, but bank-breaking, bid on the *Peter Pan* of eighty thou, Clark had just started to move away from the cashier's desk toward the exit when he saw people near him turn back to stare toward someone who was yelling. Yelling for Cliff Hartman. It was a voice he vaguely recognized. He really hoped it wasn't Travis J. Winkleman the Third ready to confront him about why he had encouraged him to bid on his lot. And then the voice again: 'Hey, Hartman!' The voice was louder this time. And nearer. 'Cliff Hartman!'

He recognized the voice now, for sure. No need to even turn around, but he did. It was Dougie Wild, larding toward him, stogie in one hand, waving the sales catalogue in the other. Clark felt like somewhere in his head he'd pressed repeat. 'Hartman, you lost your hearing?'

'Sorry, I was miles away.'

'Great to see you, son.'

'You too, Mr Wild.'

He grabbed Clark's hand and shook it, hard. 'Dougie. Please. What brings you to town? *This* town?'

'I could ask you the same.'

'That you could. Staying the night?'

'Sure am.'

'Did you drive?'

'I got a cab, from the hotel.'

'A *cab* in LA? Your first time in town?'

Clark nodded.

'Figures. You ordered one to take you back?'

'I was going to ask the girl at the . . .'

'Don't. You'll be waiting an hour for it. At least. And they'll know you're a tourist. And rip you off. Crooks all of them. I bet you got ripped off on the way here.'

'Probably.'

'I got a ride outside. Where you staying?'

Staying.

Clark was going to drive his car to the beach and sleep in it. Just like last night. He liked to go to sleep listening to the back and forth of the ocean, it was like a lullaby, so he had cranked his front passenger window down a tad. Not too far. It was LA after all.

'The Beverly Hills Hotel.' He'd spotted the sign pointing off the road as he'd driven east up Sunset from the beach, not long before he'd parked his car six blocks away where it was quarter the price of the auction house's valet service. Besides, an Oldsmobile wasn't part of the impression Clark was trying to create, squeezed as he was into his wedding suit and silk tie and freshly shined shoes, trying to look like he belonged in Beverly Hills, not Nebraska.

'Beverly Hills Hotel? Business good, hey, Cliff?'

Clark smiled. Said nothing. A man like Wild respected discretion. They were by the valet now. But Wild wasn't handing the guy a ticket. Instead, he was waving at a chauffeur. 'Harry! Hey, Harry! Over here.' The driver stubbed out his cigarette, threw his cap back on and hopped back into the stretch. 'I'm up at a friend's house. Near Mulholland. I never stay in those hotels. Total rip-off, you can't breathe but you have to tip some schmuck. Worse than the Strip. Why don't you come over, later? Hit the hotel, freshen up and drive on over.'

'Sure. Why not?'

'Unless you got other plans?'

'No. No other plans.' Not unless you count chowing down a bargain bucket and watching the sun drop out of the sky.

*

They were in the back of the limo now as it turned onto Sunset. Dougie was scribbling on a strip of paper he'd ripped off the bottom of the *LA Times*. 'Here's the address, for later.' Clark looked down at it. '8448 Wonderland Avenue, in case you can't read my scrawl.'

'I can read it perfectly.' He smiled at Dougie. *I could copy it perfectly too.*

'You'd be the first.'

Don't tempt me. Clark held the ragged strip of paper up. 'Thanks for the invite.'

'No problem, Hartman. What are friends for, hey?'

33

November 3rd 1983, 8.47 am

Abraham City

It had started with Al's mechanic just after 9 pm. And ten hours later ended with Mrs Dreyfus the beekeeper's wife over in the Saints Valley. Three hundred and fourteen Claimants, most of whom knew someone who knew someone else that had invested with Lomax, and through that night the phones of Abraham City had never known so much chatter.

Who needed sleep anyhow?

Investor Number 1784. Eduardo Reynaldo, City Motors, a car shop Al had been taking the family's cars to for the couple of years since they'd moved from LA. Once Marty had explained to Al what they needed to do in order to get their warrants and that it could only include investors who weren't Faith, Al had found Eduardo, a devout Catholic, on the list. Eduardo was many things, said Al, but Faith he definitely wasn't. Marty hadn't understood what Al said in Spanish to Eduardo over the phone, but he knew what he'd briefed him in English. It was a lie. They both knew that, Al just had to sell it to Eduardo. Pump Eduardo up, so he would tell the next person and so on and so forth. There was no margin for error, the first pitch would have to work, without that there wouldn't be a second.

Maybe it wasn't so much of a lie as a distinct possibility that the Faith would likely cut or at least marginalize non-Faith investors out of any financial compensation deal they were planning with Lomax's insurers or the financial authorities. It'd be in their interests to get the most compensation for their Followers. They didn't get ten per cent of anyone else's income.

Hopefully, Al had told Eduardo that the trick was to ensure he and his fellow non-Faith investors got to the pot of gold at the end of the rainbow before it vanished into the ether. But they had to work fast, for if news of their plan got back to the Faith then it would fail. Marty's advice, delivered via Al, was to tell no one and to meet in the Hilton's ballroom at nine the next morning. The final request was for the names and numbers of any other non-Faith investors Eduardo might know. He had given them five names. Customers and also a couple of friends. Some Hispanic. Some American. Al and Marty split up the list and got dialing. Mostly one name led to several others and so on and so forth. Until Marty and Al's phones were seared into their ears. Everyone agreed on discretion and to their 9 am appointment at the Hilton. Eduardo had been happy to be counted as the spokesman. It was vital to get an Everyman. Someone you could put up in front of a judge as Mr Average who had lost money he couldn't afford. Money from a legitimate business that employed locals. Not some professional investor trying to recoup the stake on one of his failed gambles.

Before they'd started the ring-around Marty had called the Hilton and booked the ballroom. There was a lunch in there at 1 pm, they could use the room until 11 am. Pastries and OJ, sales tax, city tax and room hire was a grand, all in. Marty charged it to his Visa and breathed a sigh of relief when they hit over three hundred claimants. Judge Laidlaw was right, they were motivated. He'd probably never see the money back, but if he could get to the bottom of this case it'd be worth every cent to wipe that holier-than-thou smirk off Alan Laidlaw's face.

The claimants couldn't wait to sign. Some were out in the Hilton's lot and hanging out in the lobby an hour or so before, formed into hushed groups, frightened someone from the Faith might overhear and scupper Marty's great plan. So when Damien Jones rolled up fifteen minutes early, with a couple of paralegals in tow, Marty had to head him off at the pass and take him in a side exit in case he got mobbed before the main event.

*

A couple of hours later, Damien's rousing speech on due process resulted in 314 new clients and a drafted, signed and sealed Notice to the Court, together with a bunch of requests including the issuing of urgent warrants in case vital documents in the case were destroyed by certain parties.

After a short recess in the Chancery case of *Burtleson's Metals vs Ridgeway Construction*, presided over by Judge Laidlaw – and without informing the Captain – Marty, Al, Whittaker and two of his guys were inside the Gudsen home effecting the first of the four warrants they'd been granted by the good judge. Marty knew they were deluded to even think that they'd be able to effect all four warrants before the Faith or the Captain found out, but he had a plan for that eventuality and she should be here in less than an hour.

'Marty, where you want us to start?'

'Show us where you saw the keys.'

'Keys? What keys?' It was Mrs Gudsen. Marty had informed her either she or a proxy had to be present throughout. She was the only one in the house. Besides, she offered, perhaps she could help them find things. Things that might catch her husband's killer. Or implicate Gudsen in events leading to his own death and even beyond it. Depending which side of the fence you were standing.

'Back through here,' said Al, leading the group of them along the corridor to the back of the house and into the dark panelled study, a large captain's desk at its edge overlooking the garden.

'What keys?'

'My colleague saw some keys in here, ma'am. They could be important. To a safe.'

'We don't have a safe.'

'Nothing? Not even a secure place to put jewelry, documents. Stuff like that?' He knew what the keys were for, but it was worth checking to see if she did.

'We don't possess material things, Detective. For papers and the like, I have an old shoe-box I use. It's upstairs at the back of the wardrobe. Would you like me to bring it down?'

'That won't be necessary, ma'am. We'll make our way upstairs in due course.' Marty stood by the entrance to the study with her. The others had followed Al toward the desk, watched as he went right to the drawer. Marty could see him almost hold his breath, and then snatch up something out of the drawer, holding it up with his latex fingers. Two keys. Red ribbon. The Lomax keys.

'Bag it,' said Marty, smiling. Whittaker stepped forward and did just that. 'But don't take it anywhere. I'm going to try it out someplace first. Here,' Marty held out his hand for it. Whittaker sealed the baggie and passed it to him. Marty looked down at it as the others carried on, emptying out drawer after drawer. 'Do you recognize these keys, ma'am?'

'No, no I don't, Detective. What are they for?'

'Did you ever see your husband with a ledger?'

'A ledger? Peter was an accountant. He was rarely without a ledger.'

'This would have been recently. Very recently.'

'Recently? You mean, just before he . . .'

'Yes.'

'I don't remember anything in particular. He mostly worked in here. When he wasn't at the office. The kids kept me too busy to even visit with him in here.' Her voice began to break, falter. 'He was in here, the night bef . . . the night before . . .' Oh no, another one. She began to cry. When Marty looked over to the others for help, they all seemed suddenly engrossed in searching desk drawers.

'I'm sorry,' she sniffed.

'Please don't apologize.' Marty looked around for tissues.

Al, without even looking, held out his arm, a large box of tissues in it, swept down off the bookshelf. Marty passed her one and she slumped down onto the chaise and blew her nose louder than a trucker.

If this was going to go on all afternoon, they were going to need back-up or they'd never make it to the Lomax house or Houseman's.

*

Marty rang the doorbell. He listened this time for her heels on the parquet, but heard nothing and then the door swung open. He took a step back.

'Mrs Rose.'

'Detective Sinclair.'

'Marty, please. We're just over at Mrs Gudsen's today.'

'Oh?'

Marty had the miniature Old Testament in his hand. 'We've been so busy with the case. I wanted to thank you. It's a kind gift. I was going to call . . .'

'It's better in person.' She smiled.

Beautiful smile.

He had no idea what to say next.

She watched as he slipped the Bible back inside his jacket pocket.

'I'm glad you appreciate it. Peter said it was very special, wished he could have kept it for his collection.'

Marty looked at her. Green eyes. 'What collection?'

She shrugged her shoulders. 'He had a collection, I guess.'

'A collection of Bibles, Mrs Rose?'

'Marion. I guess so. He didn't say.'

'Do you think Mrs Gudsen knows about this collection?'

'I don't know, she never mentioned it.'

'You sure about that, Marion?'

'Positive.' She opened the door wider now. 'Would you like to come in? I was thinking of making some tea.'

Marty shook his head. 'It would be great if you could come over to Mrs Gudsen's. We've got a search going on.'

'A search?'

'Execution of a warrant, ma'am . . . Marion. We need people – not our people – in the rooms with us. We can't search otherwise. And Mrs Gudsen, she's a tad . . .'

'Fragile?'

He smiled. Rather she said it than him. 'And we really need to get this search done. We're under some time pressure.'

'With the boys away, I'm free all day. I could come over now.' She looked at him. Smiled. 'If that's what you're asking, Marty?'

'That's what I'm asking.'

She smiled like that was a good thing. 'I'll just fetch my shoes.'

As they moved across the street back towards the Gudsen house he stopped her, his hand in the crook of her arm: 'Don't say you mentioned that to me. About the collection. I'll ask Mrs Gudsen about it when we go back in.'

'I don't mind if you say anything to Betty.'

'It's best not to. Sometimes knowledge complicates friendships.'

'Oh.' He could feel her looking at him, waiting for him to explain.

He didn't.

But he would bet his life Peter Gudsen hadn't mentioned anything to wife Betty about a gift to their divorced neighbor. Their absolute knock-out of a neighbor. Bible or no Bible.

34

8448 Wonderland Avenue

Outside on the front lawn, three finely formed girls in skimpy bikinis ran in and out of the sprinklers' spray. Nearby a forty-something wild-haired guy filmed them on a Super 8. He shouted out instructions which they seemed to only half-listen to, the main one being to run towards the camera.

Clark looked up at the door of the mansion, and at the piece of paper Dougie had given him. This was 8448 alright, just like the cabbie said when he'd dropped him at the curb. Inside a party was in full swing. It was just after 4 pm. He could see clear through the house, along the corridor, through the vast living space and out onto the deck and beyond that the pool where people were diving off the board, one, two, three at a time. He should have brought his bathing suit. The city sat below it all, a mass of grey and white buildings, huddled where the V ended between the towering canyons. He walked through toward the pool, scanning for Dougie as people darted in and out of rooms along the corridor. A butler. In full white-tailed livery. His hand under a silver salver filled with crystal goblets. He pushed the tray toward Clark. Clark took one. 'Thanks, man.'

The butler nodded and was about to move away.

'Do you know where Dougie's at?'

'Sorry, sir. I don't know who that is.'

'But you work here?'

'Just for tonight.'

'Oh.' Waiter not butler. What was with the outfit? 'You know who owns this place? The name of the guy? Maybe he knows where Dougie is.'

'No. Sorry. My supervisor's around here someplace. He'll have the name of the client, unless it's all organized through a party organizer.'

'Thanks.' Maybe Dougie wrote the address down wrong. Great. Clark looked over to the pool. A buffet along one entire side. He was pretty hungry. Maybe he'd stay a while.

Lobster tail and filet mignon. Clark slipped off his tie and unbuttoned his shirt. He was eyeing a spare seat he could grab at the tables laid out where the pool met the landscaped garden when, into his vision, came a stunning blonde in a long white evening dress, her hair crimped into a '30s style. She smiled at him. At least he hoped it was him. He smiled back. She smiled wider. 'So glad I'm not the only one overdressed.' She put her finger on his chest where the open buttons on his shirt ended. 'You must be hot in that jacket.'

'Baked.'

'Well, I'm parched.' She held out her empty glass. 'Where did that waiter go?'

'Inside. I just saw him.'

'There must be more than one.'

'Didn't see any. You can have this.'

He handed her his half-full glass.

'And what about you?'

'I'll wait until he comes back.'

'He might never come back. Say, why don't you go find him

and I'll find us a table. Here, let me take that for you.'

She took the plate off him, handed him her empty glass and walked away toward where a table was freeing up. 'I'll be over there. Hurry back. If you find the bar, I'll have a White Russian.'

He knew that. Clark watched as she picked her way through the revellers. He had been her, not so long ago. Large K, a whole selection of vowels in the surname and amongst it all a g that seemed to be detached from the rest of it. She had been a challenge. It was important to ensure that the gaps between the g and the letter preceding and after it were precise to a fraction of a millimeter. He had churned out twenty of her signed photos after that film she did with De Niro broke box-office records. Once the signature had been mastered it had taken less than ten minutes to sign the photos in her favorite red Sharpie. Hopefully, soon, she'd be an even bigger star and instead of five hundred dollars for ten minutes of his time, it'd be five thousand. There was that waiter guy, his tray full again. 'Hey, sir, can I get one of those from you?'

The waiter didn't even turn around before he disappeared into the house and made his way toward a door at the end of the hall. Clark followed him quickly, stepped through the door after him. The door led into another hallway. The waiter was nowhere to be seen. Off the hall was door after identical door. All shut tight. There was no one through here and he couldn't hear the disco music or any of the guests. Weird. He turned around, but where the door had been now there was nothing but a wall. 'What the hell?' He looked back down the hall. 'Hey! Hey, waiter!?' he tried one door after another: all locked. He banged on one after the other. No one behind them, or if there was they sure as hell weren't answering. And then he saw him again. The waiter. At the far end of the hallway, coming out of a room, the door closing behind him. 'Hey! Hey you!' He ran after him, the hall was sliding downwards, round and around and around.

Down, down, down into the bowels of the earth.

Clark turned a bend to chase him but there was nothing there at all. Nothing but a long winding corridor and the waiter nowhere to be seen. Clark turned around, tried the handle of the door the waiter had emerged from, amazed when it swung wide open. He stepped inside.

A vast double-level library. Books pushing up to the skies of the windowless room. And no one in there but him. What heaven this was. He was feeling a bit tired, but he had to get back upstairs, find a drink and deliver it. To a very beautiful woman. Maybe if he just sat down for a second. There was a leather chaise in the corner almost calling to him. He kicked off his shoes and lay down and before his eyes could even close, sleep overtook him.

*

Muffled voices out in the corridor. Laughter. He was still lying down when the door opened and two middle-aged men appeared through it.

'Speak of the devil and he appears. Hey, Hartman, I've been looking for you all over, didn't realise you'd turned into Goldilocks. Come and meet Sanford T. Winkleman.'

'Winkleman?'

'That's right, son.' His voice was even deeper than Dougie's, his handshake firmer, and his stogie twice the size.

'Sanford here's in the movie biz.'

'I AM the movie biz, don't you mean?' The two men laughed loud.

Clark smiled. Sanford still clutched his hand. 'Good to meet you, sir. I'm Cliff. Cliff Hartman. Are you related to a Travis J.?'

'Yes I am. That's my errant brother. Hasn't been causing you problems, has he?' He looked around them. Towards the door. 'He's not here, is he? He could sour anyone's party.'

'I didn't see him, sir. I met him earlier.'

'At the pink palace? That's what they call it, isn't it, Sanford?'

'That it is.'

'Not at the hotel. He was over at the auction house.'

'Was he?'

'He was sat next to me.'

'I didn't see him,' said Dougie.

'Nice guy.'

'Ha. Some say that and some say the truth,' said Sanford.

'Is this your library, Mr Winkleman?'

'All mine. And, please, call me Sanford.'

'It's awesome, Sanford. Absolutely awesome.'

'You had a look around?'

'No, just admiring from afar.'

'What's your favorite kind of book, Cliff?'

'For reading or collecting?'

'Collecting. Don't think I read all this shit, do you?'

'More lifetimes than a cat, you couldn't read all this,' said Dougie, sucking on his stogie.

'Children's, for collecting.'

'Good choice, Cliff. I like this guy, Dougie.'

'He's a good kid. I told you.'

'Telling and seeing are not the same. Come over here, Cliff. Let me show *you* something that'll blow your mind.'

Over in a darkened recess was a tall glass cabinet and inside it, on a raised glass slope inside yet more glass, was a manuscript with a scruffy edge. Aged yellow long before Sanford had put it in there. Clark strained to see what it was as Sanford took a set of keys off his belt and unlocked the cabinet. 'Come on, Cliff, follow me.' Sanford put the manuscript in the crook of his arm, lightly pinching the corner to keep it in place, and took Clark to a side table and laid it out for him.

Alice's Adventures Under Ground.

'How do you like them apples, Cliff?'

'A million bucks of apples,' said Dougie.

Clark leaned in towards it.

'Here.' Sanford passed him a pair of white gloves.

Clark almost ripped them in his rush to put them on.

'This one's Alice's own copy.'

'I thought that was in that library. In England?'

'That's right, Cliff. They have one. I have the other. And mine is far superior. Mine is signed from Carroll to Alice. See.'

Clark was turning the page, looking at Carroll's reasonably accomplished illustrations and his strange, childlike, fastidiously neat feminine hand. The illustrations were simple pen sketches, but the chapters had flourishes of angry red ink in their headings. All was not as it seemed in the life of Alice's creator.

A hand on his shoulder.

'So, Cliff. Dougie and I have a proposition for you.'

'For me?'

Sanford was behind him now, sweeping up Alice Under Ground and ushering her back into her glass cage.

'You might not be interested. You might like it way out there in Abraham City too much.'

'What Dougie's trying to say.' It was Sanford, speaking from beside the cabinet, as he locked it up and placed the key back onto his belt. 'Is that we'd like to offer you an opportunity.'

'An opportunity?'

'If you're interested. We're gonna open up a store, over on Hollywood Boulevard.'

'Hollywood Boulevard?'

'Yeah, I know it's a flea-pit, but it won't always be like that.'

'He's right. Look at Vegas. Sixty years ago it was a dustbowl.'

'What kind of store?'

'Like my store. The one you came to. In the hotel. All that stuff for the tourists, signed this, signed that. Memorabilia. Film, music, sports, you name it – we'll sell it. Everyone wants a little sprinkle of gold dust in their life.'

'And we'll give them that, Cliff. Franchise the whole outfit, send it around the world. Just like my movies.'

'You interested, Cliff? We could make you richer than your wildest dreams. You may get to own *Alice* one day, if you play your cards right.'

'So, Cliff, how about it?'

He thought he might still be asleep. Dreaming. But this was a dream: the best offer he'd ever had. Perfect. He could 'get a store' like Dougie had told him last year and provide it with its finest stock. His creations. 'On one condition.'

'Stand by for the haggle, Sanford.'

'You answer me one question.'

'Sure, Cliff. What is it?'

'Where in the hell's your bar?'

When he woke up he could feel his back damp, cold. He opened his eyes. His hand felt wet, he followed the sensation of liquid to his fingers where his hand was splayed in the pool. He tried to lift it but couldn't. At the opposite end of the pool was the pool boy. Clark looked at him. He had the deepest of tans, bluest of shorts and a smooth naked torso. The early morning smog burnt behind him and then Clark realized who it was. It was Robert Bright. Bright spotted him staring at him, smiled and waved, began calling to him. Around Bright three naked women danced and sang. Clark could see their faces clearer as each woman moved slowly to the end of the diving board and slipped silently into the water before they completely disappeared under it. Bright's three Graces: Elizabeth, Rebecca and Ellen. Robert moved onto the dive board, put his staff into the water and moved it back and forth, very very slowly before pulling a clump of something out. With the other hand he waved again at Clark, beckoning him over to the light. Clark wanted to move towards him, but for some reason he couldn't get up, couldn't make his body move. That tab. The one she'd given him. It must have paralysed him. Oh no, not the hands. He couldn't feel them, nor his arms or his chest. The pressure inside his chest was intense, he could barely breathe. He looked down and realized there was a woman, in a gold lamé bikini, sprawled on top of him.

All that glitters isn't gold.

It was her.

His wedding tie was knotted around her waist. He shifted a little, trying to wake her. Suddenly, she woke up, moved quickly off the lounger and crawled over to the pool and vomited into it. Over and over again. Robert Bright quickly made his way over to her. Clark could see him now, out of the sun. 'I throw a damn good party, don't I, Cliff?' It was Sanford. He put down his cleaning net, shrouded her in a white towel. As they passed him Sanford dropped Clark's waterlogged jacket into his lap, turned and led her away as she groaned and sobbed, 'I'm sorry,' over and over again until they vanished back into the house, where, through the glass, Clark could see people dancing to an almost silent track.

35

November 3rd 1983, noon

Gudsen Residence

In the open-plan living space Betty Gudsen sat watching Whittaker and his lab assistants search her kitchen, silently guided by Al. Marty made his way over to where she sat. 'Ma'am, Mrs Rose has kindly agreed to help observe the search. That way, we'll get out of your hair a lot faster.' Marion bent down to where Betty sat on the sofa and silently embraced her as she looked up at her, broke out a small smile.

'Thanks, Marion. Thanks so much.'

'It's the least I could do.'

'Mrs Gudsen, do you know if your husband had any collections? Possibly a Bible collection?'

'Peter just had the one Bible. His Faith Bible. It was his mother's. It's still sat by our bed. He read it every night. Used it to prepare his sermons. Would you like me to fetch it?'

'No, ma'am. Thank you. Leave it where it is. We'll get to it as we go.'

'As for collections, Detective, we don't possess things of value. Not material value, anyhow.'

'Did Mr Gudsen use his study often, ma'am?'

'Peter lived in that room. Just last year he had some carpenter friends from Mission come over and fix up those shelves. They made him that desk from scratch.'

'It's a beauty, ma'am.'

'Peter loved it.'

Her tissue went back up to her face. 'Don't you upset yourself, Betty. They'll be finished soon enough. I can stay all afternoon,' said Marion.

Marty turned away. Al waved silently at him, held up a finger, mouthed, 'One minute,' and beckoned over toward the study.

'This way, Mrs Rose.' She turned and followed Marty into the study.

'Oh, I forgot my magazine. It's OK to read a magazine?'

'Sure, as long as you peer over it now and again, so I can tell the judge we had an independent observer at all times.'

'I'll ask Betty for a magazine.'

'There's some here.'

Marty was over at the shelves now, he picked up a couple of magazines. '*Accountants' Gazetteer* or *Faith Weekly*.'

'I think I'll pass, if it's all the same,' she smiled that smile, 'you don't want me to nod off, do you?'

'No, ma'am.'

'Marion.'

She made her way back down the corridor, past Al who was headed in Marty's direction.

Marty looked at the shelves. Five of them and a cupboard underneath to the floor. On the other side, in the same glossy mahogany, the alcove was covered up with a large fitted panel, intricate wooden beading all round the outside. In front of it sat a sculpted wooden plinth mounted with the statue of a golden angel. Marty would have counted that as material possessions – ethereal or not.

'I heard from her. The sketch artist.'

'Good. How's it going?'

'Do you want the bad news, or the randomly good news?'

'Bad news. But wait a sec, does that look odd to you?'

'What?'

'This. One side shelving, the other side that panel?'

'Maybe he didn't have anything to put on the shelves, except those magazines.'

'Why build shelves you got nothing to put on them? Did you guys take anything off this shelf?'

'Nothing much. A couple of client files, that's all,' said Al.

Marty crouched down to the floor, opened the cupboard, peered inside.

Al bent down towards him. 'She paged, gave me a number over at the hospital, no incoming calls. So, I got through to Grady's kid on the radio. There were complications in the surgery. Angel. Something to do with the anaesthetic. Bad reaction. He's in the ICU. Room next to Houseman. Last night and overnight again, at least, according to the docs.'

'He gonna make it?' Nothing in the cupboard they hadn't already checked. And, at the back, just the same coloured paint was on the walls. Marty tapped on the wall. Nothing hidden inside unless it had been bricked up and concreted over.

Al nodded. 'They think so.'

Marty looked up at Al. 'Well, that's something. We really need a sketch of this guy.'

'I told him to tell the artist girl to go home. No point her staying there, getting all tired. But to keep in touch with Grady and his shift replacement. You wanna hear the other news?'

Marty stood up now. 'Is it any worse?'

'I spoke to Hobbs.'

Marty tapped on the paneled-over alcove. 'Doesn't sound too hollow.'

Al tapped it. 'Maybe you're right.'

Marty tapped a few other parts of the panel. Same dull sound. 'Might be something behind there.'

'You might be right.'

'What's Hobbs doing at the hospital?'

'Grady put him on the line. He's the lead detective on the case.'

'What case?'

'The drugstore cowboys.'

'They found them?'

'They found us.'

'What do you mean?'

'I'll get to that. But they finally found *her*.'

'Who?'

'The old lady whose car went boom yesterday.'

'Mrs Miller. That's good. What did she say?'

'Nothing. She's in the morgue.'

'In the morgue?'

'Yep. Getting buried tomorrow.'

'Murdered?'

'No. Apparently people die of other stuff.'

'So I'd heard.'

'This one had a stroke. She's been in the hospital for ten days. Her son says the car was parked out front of her house, way out in the boondocks. She'd been housebound almost a year. When he went back to hers, after the ambulance got her to hospital, the car had gone.'

'He didn't report it stolen?'

'No, he thought his son might have *borrowed* it. Dopehead.

Didn't want to get him arrested. Again.'

'And?'

'That's where the drugstore cowboys come in. They called 911 this morning. Emergency ambulance. No police required, but Curtis from the traffic boys was nearer so they sent him first.'

'Curtis, the paramedic?'

'As was.'

'Well, he goes to this hotel. Where they're supposed to be staying, but they're out back hid near the laundry room amongst a pile of bloodied bed linen. And the receptionist says they never checked in. One guy's shredded real bad. He certainly didn't get those injuries in any hotel room. Not any normal one, anyhow. His buddy has somehow managed to stitch him up. Trouble is, the wound keeps erupting. Curtis says the kid looks like Frankenstein's monster.'

'Sounds a mess.'

'Curtis thinks it looks like he went through a windshield and figures these two might be the guys Hobbs is looking for.'

'Oh yeah?'

'So Curtis IDs the kids. They claim they don't have any. While the paramedics are working on the younger kid, he searches the older kid. Bingo. ID. Last name?'

'I give up.'

'Miller, same name as the old lady.'

'So where'd they get this other car? The one they put through the pharmacy?'

'Stole it, of course.'

'What happened to their Nissan?'

'Somebody stole it.'

Marty laughed. 'That's their story and they're sticking to it.'

'From what Hobbs could find out, they've never even been out of Dalewood County before.'

'Wow, some adventure, huh? Abraham City wouldn't have been my rebel destination.'

'Now or then?'

'Now or never.'

'Billy-Ray, that's the cousin, fifteen, he went through the windshield and then got dragged away by Dopehead before the whole place ignited . . . he'll have a pocketful of memories, that's for sure.'

'And the scars so he doesn't forget. So, our bomber's also a car thief. That's interesting. They leave the keys in the ignition?'

'No. They weren't carjacked neither. Curtis found the car key to Grandma's Nissan in the older one's pocket.'

'So our bomber knows how to hot-wire a car.'

'That's if it was him. Could be someone sold it to him?'

'Then we need to find *that* guy. How long the cowboys been in town?'

'Almost a week. They ran out of money fast, could only afford one night in some hotel the other side of town. That night the car got stolen.'

'When was that?'

'Night before the first bombing. Twenty-ninth. With no money and no shelter, they broke into an empty hotel room and put the Do Not Disturb sign on before the chambermaid yesterday called security. So they stole the Pontiac, to sleep in. Hit some black ice and skidded off the road.'

'Right into the pharmacy?'

'So they say.'

'They weren't trying to ram the place, and get some drugs, hey?'

'Of course not: that would be a felony.'

'Wouldn't it now,' said Marty. 'Damn it, how in the hell do I get inside this thing?'

'Maybe you don't. Stand aside, Shorty.'

'Go ahead. We can't all be children of the Amazon.' Al stood on tiptoe, reached up to the top of the panel, ran his hands along behind it. Nothing but dust. 'Hang on, Al. If Gudsen was the bomber – maybe this is where he hid his bombing paraphernalia?'

'Oh, man. Tilts, timers, what's this one: booby-trapped?'

'Could be. But maybe this is just where he stashed the ledger?'

'Sorry it took me so long. Betty didn't have any.' Marion was in the doorway now. She dropped her voice. 'I should have guessed. They're not allowed anything frivolous.' She held up a copy of *Harper's Bazaar*. 'I dashed home.'

'Got something, Mart. Now might be a good time for you both to step back.' Marty and Marion took a pointless step backwards. 'Gotcha, you awkward son of a . . .'. Al jerked something upwards and the alcove panel, rigged as a door, popped open a little. Al peered curiously around the partially opened door. Marty and Marion stepped forward. Al stepped back towards them, drawing the door open with him. Inside, on the back of the door, were rack after rack of brightly colored hardbacks, cellophane covers around each one. On the exposed shelving inside the covered alcove were beautiful leather-bound Bibles with word after word in gold engraving and at the center of it all a small green cast-iron safe. Marion was by Marty's side now, her arm brushed against his.

Marty took down one of the books, opened it. Looked up at the others. 'Well, if this isn't a collection, I don't know what is.'

'So this is what he meant. The one he wanted the Old Testament for.'

'Not that he'd have anywhere to put it, Marion. Not even a miniature.'

'Not enough room for another sheet of paper. Unless it's in the safe,' said Al.

'We need to get that safe open. Maybe that's where the ledger is.'

'Who's good with tumblers?' said Al.

'Bank robbers. And explosives experts. Call Tex, see if he can get a small charge in there. Before that, you better go fetch Whittaker. Discreetly. Get this safe dusted. And the door. I want to know who's been in and out of here.'

Al nodded silently, moved back over to the door. Marion turned to Marty. He could feel her breath on his face. 'I didn't like to say, it was such a kind gift, but what would Edgar Allan Poe be doing with a copy of the Old Testament in Hebrew?'

'What?'

She moved her head back a little. He hadn't meant to raise his voice. He checked himself. 'What did you say, Mrs Rose?'

'Marion.'

'Marion.'

She repeated her question, but there was no need. He'd heard. It was the same second time around. 'What would Edgar Allan Poe be doing with a copy of the Old Testament in Hebrew?'

What indeed.

Although the bigger question might be what Poe was doing with two copies.

Marty looked down at his watch. Patricia Kent should be here soon. She had promised to get the story on top of the local news. Not that he'd told her what the story was yet.

36

July 8th 1983

His blood had dripped into the makeshift pot he'd improvised from a miniature jam jar he'd lifted the previous week from the campus hotel breakfast bar. He'd already spent two hours practising the signature in pig's blood on similar density paper. He'd thought of Robert Bright, thought of his life, how puffed up and sinfully proud he must have felt after almost two decades of gathering a flock which numbered in the thousands. The Faith's increasing popularity and its Followers' lives, lived on the flipside of society's rules, had provoked Bright's frequent clashes with authority and made him a marked man.

Focused on Bright's rage against authority, Clark had dipped his quill into his freshly drawn blood-ink and scratched Robert Bright's angry oversized signature onto the page. Clark would say this was Bright's own blood – it wasn't as if they had anything to compare the blood to, just so long as it was human it would pass cursory tests. Clark stared at his creation. It was perfect. Just like Bright, Clark loved to seek perfection in artifice and, in so doing, make myth reality. Like Bright before him, Clark found it flattering when his creations spun him gold from air.

Clark studied Arnold Lomax's face, brow furrowed, mouth opened as if trying to drink it all in as he looked at Clark's Polaroids, the red blood signature just visible on the brown paper in the badly lit shot. Polaroids Clark had brought with him, ostensibly straight from the wealthy dealer's house in Fort Lauderdale where, he gleefully told Lomax, he had spent the Fourth of July weekend in a house on the intracoastal waterway, opposite where the Bee Gees and a legion of other stars lived and where the weather was warm and the people smiley. He hoped Lomax wouldn't ask why he hadn't taken a photo of the house or the eighty-foot yacht moored at the bottom of the garden and facing out to sea. Or, for that matter, a pictorial memento of his tête-à-tête with his most generous host.

The Polaroids also included a handful of the three aged, worn letters that Clark would use to form part of the package he was preparing in order to verify the provenance of the *pièce de résistance*, the Letter of Accession – as it had been called by the Faith for over 150 years. The Letter that no one had ever seen, or seemed to have owned, but which everyone in the Faith was absolutely certain had existed. In the Faith's telling of the story, Robert Bright had written this letter to Jeremiah, his son by Rebecca, passing the Prophet's mantle to him. But Clark had other plans.

He had spent weeks researching back in his old haunt of Colorado State Library at Boulder and running up a five-hundred-dollar hotel phone bill calling every major university library around the world, until he was convinced that nowhere in the American or European archives was there a document that would one day rear up its head and claim to be the original Letter of Accession written by the Faith's prophet and signed in his blood, not Clark's. In its absence, Clark's version would become *the* version.

'But I don't know the first damn thing about ancient stuff,

manuscripts and all that. How can I tell what it's worth?' Lomax said, brow still furrowed.

Antique, not ancient, Clark wanted to say. Instead, he turned on the megawatt smile, 'Well, that's what I'm for, Mr Lomax.' I'm your path to a quick buck and you're the $500K I need to pay Dougie before his and Sanford's deadline runs out and they pick another guy as co-investor for the Hollywood store and close me right out of the deal. Sometimes Clark tired of all the bullshit people told one another, instead of just coming straight out with the truth. But it was all a game, he guessed. People preferred games to truth. They always seemed so suspicious of the truth. Or frightened of it. 'That's just three of the letters. He wouldn't let me take pictures of the entire collection.' Clark knew there was no need to have created all eleven letters, not just yet. Not until his appointment with the Faith. They would most likely ask for details of them all and even to see the originals. Either way, Clark was already getting prepared.

'So, let's get to the nitty gritty, son. Nitty gritty I can do: you need five hundred K?'

'That's correct, sir, ideally the money would be in a lump sum.'

Clark needed the money paid into his account for two different reasons. The first, to pay Dougie for his share of the Hollywood store; the second, so that should the Faith get curious and task any of their spies with checking on Clark's financial health, with Lomax's money he could show he'd held and then paid the requisite deposit of $500K for the document, transferred to the account of Dougie Wild. The Faith wouldn't know who the hell Dougie Wild was from Adam. But if they chose to find out, he would be listed all over as a documents dealer.

'And my cut's twenty per cent?'

'Of net profit. I think it's going to be quite a healthy net. I might be able to push the sale price to the Faith north of two mil.'

'Two mil?' Lomax whistled. 'Well, how about this: I pay over a month or so?'

'As long as at least one hundred K is the first part of the payment.'

Ideally, Clark wanted all the money upfront, so he could pay Dougie and, also, go to the Faith quicker. Now he'd have to wait a month. But a hundred thou should keep Dougie and Sanford quiet a while.

'Twenty is no good to me. I want twenty-five percent.'

'Twenty-two point five.'

'You cut a hard bargain,' said Clark. And *you're* a greedy bastard.

'When you gonna pay my cut?'

'The faster I get the whole five hundred K, the faster I can get your money back to you. But you'll get your original investment back thirty days after cleared payment for the sale, to the Faith or whomsoever. I'll pay out your profit thirty days after that date.'

'Why don't I get it all the day the deal is done?'

'There's always a delay, gives the buyers – us and our eventual purchaser – a chance to pull out if they find anything amiss with the document.'

'What do you mean, amiss?'

'Sometimes things don't always work out. Legally, people have to be able to change their mind.'

'You been down there yourself, though, haven't you? Fort Lauderdale, checked it out? Because I could go back down with you this week. Show them we're serious and we're not going to stand for any bull.'

'I checked it out. I brought an independent assessor along with me.'

'You did?'

'Sure. Clifford Hartman. He's particularly skilled in Robert Bright's era.'

'And this Hartman guy was happy?'

'Very. This is his letter of authentication. And that of the dealer.' Clark took two separate letters out of his attaché case.

'You should have brought him today.'

'Believe me, I wish I could. But he's a very busy guy and he charges by the hour. Three hundred bucks. Five thou for the weekend in Florida, plus airfares.'

'Damn, I'm glad you *didn't* bring him. Don't want to cut into the net.'

'That's what I figured.'

'Five thou. Crazy. Who knew bits of paper could be worth so much. I followed my daddy into the property business. But if this pans out, I might switch to the paper business.'

'Well, if you're serious about that, we can do another deal after this one.'

'What's with the interest, the delay on that?'

'That ensures your discretion.'

'No flies on you, hey son?'

'The stakes are high.'

'Sure are. I should be able to get you the cash by Monday. I just got to find my shovel first.' He laughed. 'I got problems with my wife, we're divorcing. She knows I got some money stashed away someplace, damn shame she doesn't know where, but it's not for the want of looking.' He leaned back, laughing in his chair. He scanned the Polaroids, picked up one of the three letters Clark had created between Bright's first and second wives. Clark had stapled transcripts of the letters to the shots. Lomax silently read one. 'Three wives. And all at the same time? Bright must have been crazy.'

'Either that or he was on to something.'

That made Lomax laugh again, even louder.

Clark leaned toward him. 'This is a very delicate stage of the deal now, sir, so for the next couple of months or so, I'd be really grateful if we could keep this arrangement between you and me. I know that Peter's your business partner, but . . .'

'Colleague. Peter's not an equity partner or anything.'

'Good. Because I can't emphasize enough how we have to keep this arrangement and deal secret, because if the Real Faith get wind of this, they will come in with a much higher price direct to the dealer, just to get their hands on this document, and we'll lose it to them.'

'Don't worry. I can keep a secret. Do you really think Bright left everything to Rebecca's son, Jeremiah? That the Real Faith really are that, the real Faith – and ours is . . .'

'Nothing?'

Lomax nodded silently.

'I believe what it says there.'

'Then this document is going to stir up a hornet's nest.'

That was the plan. That and to make a ton of cash.

'Why would the Faith even want this old document, if that's the case?'

'Would you want your adversaries to own these? In effect to own you, probably hold you to ransom threatening to reveal the contents to the world?'

'I get it. So you're doing the Faith a favor?'

'Simply providing a service.'

'Why didn't you go direct to the Faith for the five hundred thou then?'

Megawatt.

'Because, as much as I'm a Follower and I love the Faith, I'm a businessman – just like you and those houses you're building: I want to make a profit. Need to make a profit. And so, I have to stop the Real Faith getting hold of this document. Even if our own Faith finds out who the dealer is, they'll cut us out of the deal. And we won't make a red cent.'

'And you're not running a charity, hey, son?'

'No, sir. I wish I could do it out of the kindness of my heart, but I have a wife and two babies to feed, and opportunities like this only come around once in a lifetime.'

'Well, I have the ex-wife to feed, so I feel your pain.'

'The high, almost instant, return for the investor is meant as a thank you. Without this money to buy the document I know I wouldn't be able to do the deal. I'm sure the Faith will be very appreciative.'

'Well, son, I rely on your discretion to ensure they don't ever know that information. They might worry I'm *gambling* their Followers' cash – a lot of their people invest with me. I'll keep your secret, you keep mine.'

'Speculating, not gambling,' said Clark. 'There's no risk here, no reliance on chance. And you'll have your money back within a few months. No one will even miss it.'

'Are you done yet, honey? I want to go to the mall.' Clark turned to see a glorious young girl in a dripping wet bikini, clutching a beach towel, standing in the doorway that led in from the garden. Clark had heard about Lomax's domestic troubles from

Peter Gudsen. Heard about the soon-to-be-former Mrs Lomax, and the newer, springier model now living for all intents and purposes as the second Mrs Lomax. Lomax's face had lit up instantly when she'd appeared behind them.

'This is my fiancée, Bobbi. Bobbi, this is Mr Clark Houseman.' Lomax looked at Clark.

Clark nodded, we're done.

Bobbi stood with her back against the aluminium doorframe, water still dropping off her bikini. She smiled at Clark. 'Hi.'

'Hi.'

'I've just been in the hot tub. It's so relaxing. You should come over and try it sometime, shouldn't he, Arnie?'

'I'm sure Mr Houseman's got better things to do than sit in hot tubs all day, Bobbi. Now, why don't you go get dressed, and I'll show Mr Houseman out.'

She didn't move. Instead, she just stared at them as Lomax gathered all the Polaroids up and handed them back to Clark. Clark put them in his attaché case, stood up to leave.

'Bye, Mr Houseman.' She stared at Clark, waited for him to say his first name, so she could repeat it. Over and over. Trip it off her tongue. Try and make Old Lomax a little bit more jealous. Clark had north of two mil and his entire future riding on not allowing himself to take the bait, as tempting as it was. Instead, he just smiled politely. Bobbi didn't smile again, just pulled the towel she was holding tight around her, tucked it into her bikini top and passed across the room. He guessed she knew they'd be watching so she cranked up her wiggle as she moved out and along the corridor. All she needed was heart-shaped sunglasses and she would be Lolita. A hundred and fifty years ago she would have made a great wife for Robert Bright.

Lomax swung the front door open for him. 'Just give me 'til Monday. We'll meet at one of the banks downtown. I'll let you know what one, nearer the time. Now go confirm our deal.'

'Thanks, Mr Lomax.'

'Arnold, son. Call me Arnold.' He clapped Clark on the back. 'We're friends now. Partners.'

'Thanks, Arnold.'

With the mercury pushing one hundred, Clark stepped out onto the driveway and followed the shade of the trees on Lomax's front lawn until he reached his car. Once, when he was a kid, he'd been given some advice by his mother's uncle, a wily old dog, and a rich one to boot. Clark had never forgotten it: 'There's no friends in business, son . . . and as for partners, if they'd been a good idea God would have had one.'

37

November 3rd 1983, 4 pm

Lomax Residence

The door opened. It was Audrey, the sister. Marty could see over her shoulder to the corner of the room where Lomax sat marooned on the couch, a crocheted blanket clutched around him, his head heavy, hair unwashed. The sister looked at them apologetically. 'Who is it, Aud?' said Lomax.

Marty held up the warrant, pushed it towards her. 'May we, ma'am? That's a warrant to search the premises.'

'Search here? What for? Arnold, did you hear what they're saying? They're gonna search. They got a warrant.'

Lomax was standing up now, staring in their direction. 'What do you mean, they got a warrant?'

'Miss Lomax is correct, sir. We have a warrant to search the house and your business premises downtown.'

'I already gave you a list of my investors that first day. The day Bobbi, Bobbi . . .' his breath caught, faltered. He coughed, continued. 'You wanna find Bobbi's killer, you need to be looking at that.'

'We are.'

Lomax was advancing on them. 'Then you should be out there, searching. Interviewing the people who might have reason to kill her. What do you want a warrant for? You think I killed Bobbi?'

'The warrant isn't about your wife's death, sir.'

'It's not? Then what in the hell are you doing here?'

'For search and seizure of any evidence relevant to the case of the Investors versus Lomax Enterprises.'

'The what!? Some kind of case I never heard of.'

'It's new,' said Marty.

'You need to be looking for Bobbi's killer, instead of searching for money that isn't here!'

Anger made Lomax seem more alive.

'Maybe it's two parts of the same whole,' said Marty.

'*That's* why I gave you the investors list. You should talk to the people on that. They all blame me for the property investment plan running into trouble.'

'What kind of trouble did it run into, sir?'

Lomax ignored him. 'Someone on there must have wanted to kill me.'

'What about your former associate Peter Gudsen, you think his death was linked to the collapse of that property company or do you think they were still trying to get just you?'

Lomax didn't say anything.

'He was no longer a part of the business – that's what confuses me. Why would anyone go after him? Mr Houseman? Mr Angel? Any of them connected to your company?'

Lomax shrugged his shoulders. 'Not that I know.'

'And Mr Gudsen was alone when he was targeted, you weren't with him, were you? It wasn't intended for you? An impromptu meeting perhaps?'

'No.'

'You were at the Hilton the morning your wife was killed. You'd had a row with her, the night before, taken off to the hotel, that's what Detective Alvarez said.'

'Don't remind me why I wasn't here, couldn't help her . . .'

'And there was no car in the drive?'

'Mine was in the shop. I'd taken Bobbi's with me.'

'Why do you think your wife was outside so early that morning?'

He shook his head. 'I don't know. Maybe she heard, thought she heard, my car in the drive. But it was him.'

'Who?'

'Whoever did this. Maybe she picked up that box and thought that it had a present in it from me to her. Maybe to say sorry. Oh, God.'

His entire body seemed to crumple in on itself.

Audrey stepped in, caught him, put her arm around him. 'It's not Arnold's fault the business failed. The land that they were sold up in the Old Canyons. It was no good. Something to do with the soil. Something wrong with it.' She whispered now, 'Somebody cheated him, the investors and a whole bunch of other buyers who bought tracts. Cheated them all and cleared out of town with their money.'

'Is that right, Mr Lomax?' said Marty.

'He's been warned not to say anything, who they are. Nothing. Haven't you, Arnold?'

'Don't listen to her. She doesn't know what the hell she's talking about.'

'I do so.'

'Are you protecting someone, sir?' said Marty.

Lomax didn't say anything.

'You can tell them, Arnold. They'll protect you. They're the police.'

Marty didn't know so much about 'protect'. 'Your sister's right, sir. You can tell us.'

Lomax looked up, doubtful. Marty saw Whittaker and his guys coming up the path. He thought he'd try a new tack. 'Can you tell us if you've been in contact with your insurers to pay out on your wife Bobbi's life insurance?' Marty could see Lomax didn't know how to answer. 'The policy you took out on her.'

'You never told me you had insurance on Bobbi, Arnold.'

'Two hundred and fifty thou,' said Al. Helpfully.

Audrey's hand went up to her mouth.

'You could see why we might consider that motive, Mr Lomax. That's a considerable sum of money. Could you show us into your study please, sir?' Audrey stood up with her brother. 'Ma'am, if you could just wait here. With Mr Whittaker and his team,' he beckoned them into the house, 'they'll begin to conduct a search out here. We need a witness to watch as we search each room.'

Audrey looked at her brother, he waved his hand at her. 'Sure, if we have to, might as well keep an eye on them, make sure they don't plant anything. Try and make me look guilty of something I'm not.'

Marty let the slight go. You're guilty of something though. Aren't you?

They followed Lomax into the study, Al tight on Lomax's heels, the bag rolled up in his hand.

In seconds they were at the safe. The ribbon untied. A key in each lock.

'Hey, where did you get those keys?'

Marty turned his head. 'You wanna tell us where you think we got them, Mr Lomax?'

Lomax didn't answer.

Marty nodded to Al, they turned their keys at the same time. The safe opened.

'Hey, what are you doing? You can't go in there.'

The safe was completely empty, except that flat on the floor of it was a piece of paper. Marty picked it up. A regular piece of paper folded over on itself. He opened it. Showed Al. A hastily scrawled IOU, and a tiny signature scrawled next to it in a different hand.

'What's this, sir? Must be pretty important as it's the only thing in here.'

Lomax didn't answer.

'What's this?' He peered closer at it. 'Six hundred and sixty-six thousand dollars, to include interest and other payments, inter alia. Whatever that means.'

Marty looked at Lomax. Lomax looked like a man deciding whether silence might be a good game plan.

'Are you a licensed lender, sir?'

'You know damn well I'm not.' Not silenced, yet.

'It's a licensed *property* investment company, is that it?'

'Yes.'

'Do you want to tell me who this is, who owes you this money?'

'It's not my money.'

'But it says at the top: "Payable to Mr Arnold Lomax". And it's got your address right here.'

'I said, it's not my . . .'

'I guess it was your investors', huh? This your writing, sir?' Lomax was sat huddled on the chair to the side of the desk, almost shrinking after each question. Marty doubted he was their bomber, but ruin could make a man do crazy things. 'It's kind of difficult to read this signature, sir, but maybe you just forgot the name. Looks like a toddler's scrawl. I mean, I could easily forget someone owing me almost three quarters of a mil. Hey, Al?'

'Easy to forget their name,' said Al as Marty passed the paper carefully to him. Marty watched as Al strained to read the handwriting, shook his head, handed the paper back to Marty. 'What happened, did he forget he owed it to you?'

There was a very small movement of Lomax's head towards Marty, maybe not even an inch, but Marty had noticed it. Knew he had to continue. 'Is that what happened with your company, sir? You lent money you shouldn't have to the wrong person, they couldn't pay it back, not even when you were charging pretty hefty interest by way of incentive? Is that why your wife and those other folk are dead? And we got two maimed people in the hospital?'

Arnold's silence condemned him. If it wasn't true you'd deny it, in an instant, unless the truth was even worse. Marty picked up a magnifying glass off the desk, moved the paper around trying to get a good look at the almost indecipherable signature. Looks like whoever signed this didn't want to. Arnold didn't speak. 'See that, Al, just there in the bottom corner.'

'The blood?'

'That blood, not much, just enough to catch what looks like a thumbprint. Al, get Whittaker in here.'

'Sure.'

Marty moved closer to where Lomax was still sat. 'Who's Cliff Hartman, sir?'

'Who?'

Was that a faint flicker of recognition in Lomax's eyes?

'Cliff Hartman.'

'Cliff Hartman? I don't know any Cliff Hartman.'

'That's not what it says here, sir.'

'Where?'

'Right here.'

'What? Cliff Hartman? That's impossible. *He* signed it, I saw him.'

'Who, sir?'

Lomax stood up, grabbed the paper off Marty, strained to look at the tiny signature. 'Hartman!? Hartman. The son of a bitch!' Lomax, like a man possessed, lunged for the page, started to rip it up, but Marty moved fast, grabbed it back off him. Marty shoved Lomax back down into the chair. Held his hand on him to keep him there.

'Would you like to tell us who this Mr Hartman is? And where we might find him.'

'Do I need a lawyer?' Lomax didn't look at Marty. Marty could feel his heaving sobs under his hand.

'I don't know, sir, do you?'

'Everything OK in here, Mart?'

'It is now.'

Marty turned to where Al was standing in the doorway with Whittaker.

'How long to search that card index for a thumbprint?'

'Depends how good the impression is. And if he's in the system.'

'Oh, this guy's on the system alright.'

'Let's hope he's on ours, Marty.'

'Let's hope.' Marty held out the card. 'I think this is Hartman's thumbprint.'

'The mysterious Mr Hartman? Really?'

'Yeah, him or the person who made him sign it. You on our

fingerprint system, Mr Lomax?' Marty looked at Lomax. Lomax head down, still sobbing, didn't answer. 'You got anything from the bomb sites you might match it to?'

'No, Marty. Nothing.'

'Let's count ourselves lucky if we can even find out who he is.'

Al looked at the card again, passed it to Whittaker, who moved it quickly into the light and out again. 'Not great, but not bad. If we got a few people, should maybe take a few hours. We're not New York.'

'Send one of your guys back with it. Al, radio in. Michaels should be down in Records, ensure you get him some help. If this guy's in our system, the three of them should find him soon enough. And, Al, tell them to keep it quiet.'

Al's pager buzzed. Marty watched as he took it off his belt, read it. 'Grady Jnr.'

'Oh yeah?'

'He's awake.'

'Who? Angel?'

'No. Houseman.'

38

October 20th 1983

Hollywood Boulevard

He had got there early, walked up and down the Boulevard. Not far, just back and forth a couple of times between LaBrea and Vine. Sanford was right, it was a flea-pit and it wasn't even dark but the tourists who'd come to stare at the stars' hand- and foot-prints were already being replaced by panhandlers, hookers and their pimps. As Clark had waited to cross the road, one guy walked past him and, under his breath but just loud enough to be heard, mumbled, 'Eight-ball for a ten-spot.' It had taken a few seconds for it to register and when Clark looked around the guy was still walking, but looking back towards him. Clark shook his head, the guy turned his head back and just kept walking.

Dougie was right though, that section had real potential and Clark was glad he had invested. He would make a great return on the building alone. Not that he wanted to sell. He was in for the long haul. A franchise in every city all over the world.

It had started to rain, so he'd gone into a mom and pop café across the street from where their store was being built. He could see hoardings surrounding their corner of the block and not much else. There was activity behind them. In the falling light, he could see a couple of arc lamps throwing down light onto who-ever was working underneath them. He couldn't see in. Not from outside the site, or from across here. Or get in, it was all locked up.

At least it was well protected. Dougie had sent the plans through, and it was certainly a good spot. That and the influx of tourists year-round, there couldn't be a better spot in all of LA. Dougie had chosen well.

It was dark now. Clark was on his second cup of coffee when he looked up to see two guys right outside the site. Dougie and Sanford. Finally. He got up fast, left a ten-dollar bill, and jay-walked fast out into the street, weaving through the lanes of stationary traffic. When he reached the other side of the road one of the guys was already in a car, lights on, the second guy, taller and burlier than the other one, was just getting in. It wasn't Dougie and Sanford, just a couple of construction workers. 'Hey man, I'm waiting for Dougie. He inside?'

The burly guy shook his head, no. Looked to his buddy. The buddy shook his head.

'I'll just wait. When's the build get finished?'

The second guy was in the car now. 'Probably eight months.'

Dougie had told him three to four months.

'What's the delay?'

The man looked at him, what's it to you. Shrugged. 'That's the schedule we have.' He grimaced at Clark, closed the door, and the car joined the traffic.

Clark almost flipped them the bird.

He went across the street and paged Dougie with the number of the payphone and then waited by the phone. The rain was getting worse. It was six o'clock by the time he realized he must have made a mistake. They were going to meet at Sanford's place first, then head over to the site later, take a peek inside. It would be better without all the work going on around them. That made more sense. The rush-hour traffic, red and white light trails, was backed up East and West. Great. In this traffic it was going to take an hour's drive to get to Sanford's.

He had the *Peter Pan* in the trunk of the rental, that and a few other pieces. He'd spoken to Dougie on the phone. Dougie was pretty cool about it, especially when he explained to him that Lomax had some problem on his site. Soil or something. Dougie said he could probably give him $100K of his money back for the *Peter Pan* and the others. Then, once he had done his 'big deal' – he hadn't told Dougie what it was – he could pay the $100K back into their store investment account so he still had $500K invested. That way he wouldn't lose out. Clark had said to Lomax he'd have the money for him within a week. Lomax didn't say it, but it was obvious some of his investors must be leaning on him, trying to shoehorn their money out of him. That meant they had an inkling that things were not going to pan out too good on that development. Maybe that's why Gudsen had left the firm earlier that summer. Clark was glad he hadn't invested in that scheme.

Clark couldn't have Lomax working himself into a frenzy, panicking. He could ruin everything. Lomax was starting to become the meltdown type. A man whose reason could soon desert him. Hadn't he married that cheerleader, barely out of high school? Want, want, want over reason.

The other day when he'd called to try and get some of his money urgently back off Clark, Lomax had told him he thought his ex-wife might have reported him to the Feds. Clark figured that was probably revenge, but whatever it was he didn't want the Feds at his door. And if they were at Lomax's then it would just be a matter of time before they were at his.

Almost an hour later, and a couple of wrong turns, Clark was over the other side of the canyon, outside Sanford's. He still hadn't gotten a page back from Dougie, but through the railings and shrubbery he could see lights on downstairs, so someone was home.

The pedestrian gate was closed, although the gate to the drive was wide open, but there were no cars in the drive and none out on the street except for Clark's. Shit, don't say they'd headed down to Hollywood just as he was coming here? He knew he should have paged them he was en route. He wasn't driving back down to Hollywood, not in that traffic – he'd only miss them again. He'd ask the house-boy, Raoul, wasn't that his name, if he could just wait inside, maybe use the phone and page them again. Besides, Sanford might even have one of those portable phones Raoul could reach him on. Clark would have loved one of those. It would have been so useful when he was standing out in the pouring rain.

Even over this side of the canyon it was raining. Hopefully the sun would be shining tomorrow. What's the point of LA without sunshine? Clark didn't want to wait in the car in case the security patrol came past. He wanted to keep as far below the radar as possible. He was a few feet from the house when he noticed light bleeding out onto the path from the slightly open front door. Clark didn't want to just push it open, so he rang the bell. It sounded like a jackhammer. He listened. No one was coming. He pressed it again. When it had drilled through his head one more time, he heard a strange moaning. Deep moaning, coming from somewhere near the door. Clark pushed the door open a tad, peeked around it. Sanford was lying there in full tennis whites, feet towards the door, face down in a pool of blood that ran out from his head onto the white glossy floor.

'Jesus, Sanford! Sanford?! It's Cliff. Don't move. Don't move.'

Sanford tried to move.

'Just stay still. You got a towel in here, man? I'm just gonna get a towel . . .'

Clark yanked open the zipper on Sanford's sports bag, pulled out packs of tennis balls, half-empty bottles of Evian. At the bottom he could see some small tennis towels. He pulled them out and scooted over on the floor towards Sanford's head.

'Sanford, you got to stay awake.'

Clark pressed the towels, one after the other, onto Sanford's skull until they were too soaked with blood to use.

'You're gonna need some stitches in that, man. We gotta get you to a hospital.'

'No hospital.'

'You need the hospital.'

'No hospital. Dentist.'

'Dentist! Sanford, you need to get checked out. You're not making any sense.'

Sanford was pointing off into the living room. 'Book.'

'What book? I need to dial 911.' Clark was already making his way over to the hall phone. 'Did you trip, coming in? Hit your head on this?'

Clark looked at the marble hall table. There was no blood on it, no signs of it having moved, or anyone having struck it with their head. Out of the corner of his eye, he noticed something sparkle. He looked closer now. There was a short trail out of one of the doors off the corridor. A trail of glass.

He was over at Sanford again now, phone in hand, pulling the cable out as far as it would go, so he could call and sit next to him in case the dispatcher asked him any questions about his condition. 'Did someone hit you with something, Sanford? A vase? A glass vase?'

Sanford shook his head, splattering blood everywhere. 'Dentist.'

'OK. OK. I'll call them.' Clark moved to the living room. On a side table, next to another phone, was a large address book. Maybe they were a relative or something. He flicked through to D, Dentist. Eric Davies. It was the top entry.

He went back out to Sanford, who was still clutching the towel to his head, but he was sat up now, cross-legged, like a Buddha in the blood. 'I'm calling the dentist. And when I do, I'm gonna call 911 right after. See if they'll send an ambulance, and maybe the cops.' Clark thought he'd peel away if the cops were coming. Just leave Sanford there. 'Where's Raoul?' Sanford still had blood running down his head and into his mouth. 'Press harder.' He pushed Sanford's hand down harder against his skull. His face was getting paler. Jesus. Clark grabbed the box of tissues from the hall stand and started wiping Sanford's face clean, see if there were more injuries under all the blood.

'Raoul, day off. Thursdays. Off.'

'What the hell happened here, Sanford?'

Sanford was staring off, following the trail of glass.

'You're lucky I came back this way. I was waiting for you and Dougie. Now I know why you weren't there. Where's Dougie? He's not at the building site.'

'Building site?' Sanford's body started shaking. First his shoulders, then his torso, so much so he started rocking back and forth. Clark thought he was crying with the shock and then a great laugh, accompanied by yelps of pain, rose up from deep inside Sanford's Buddha belly.

'Stay still, buddy. We don't want to make this worse.'

'There is *no* building site.'

'What do you mean? I was just there. I met two of the construction guys. There's definitely a building site.'

'Not ours.'

'Sanford, I don't know what you're talking about. Perhaps you should just keep quiet for a while.'

'Not ours! They took my money. Took yours.'

'Took our money? What do you mean? Who took our money?'

'Dougie.'

'Dougie?'

'And Travis!'

'Sanford, you should really rest.'

'And they stole *Alice*.'

'You're just messed up, Sanford. Talking nonsense.' Clark didn't want him to talk any more, didn't want to hear.

Clark's gaze followed Sanford's towards the door off the corridor. Broken glass crunched underfoot. Oh no.

Sanford pointed to his head, 'Who do you think did this?'

Clark was getting a real sick feeling at the pit of his stomach. 'Dougie and TJ? How do they even know one another enough to do something like this?'

'Juvie.'

'Juvie? Dougie and Travis?!'

'Thirty years ago. Ow.' Sanford pushed the towel into his head.

'Thirty years? Why didn't you warn me?'

'I thought they'd gone straight.'

'Jesus, Sanford. What the fuck were you thinking? Obviously, they're pretty fucking far from straight!'

'They've got *Alice*.'

'Fuck *Alice*, Sanford! Just fuck *Alice*! They've got *my* money. *All* my money.' Clark took a breath. Now his head was hurting. 'Really, Sanford? Really? *All* of it?'

Sanford nodded, wincing. 'All of it.'

'You don't have any? Nothing?'

Sanford shook his head. 'They got mine too. Cash. A mil.'

'Jesus. Where do you think they've gone?'

Sanford shrugged. 'They took my cars. Both of them. That's why they hit me. To get the keys for them and *Alice*.' He stared at Clark out of glassy eyes, as the blood kept dripping down his head. He grabbed Clark with his other hand, pulled him in close. 'They stole *Alice*!' And then he started to sob, deep heartbroken sobs.

Clark sat staring at him, unable to believe what he was hearing. And then he thought back to the auction, TJ showing off his address on the outside of the catalogue, but he was an auction regular who should really have known better. Never kid a kidder. It wasn't Clark who had conned TJ, it was Clark who had been conned. The way Dougie just appeared like that, from where? Clark had been watching the room. But they had obviously been watching him and Dougie must have been stood behind him in the auction room, or even on the payphone outside running up the price of first Clark's lot and then TJ's, the one Clark had bid eighty K on. Eighty K! It was too much of a coincidence that TJ got up and moved away like that at the end of bidding on Clark's item. So theatrical. 'Peter Pan, the little boy that never grew up, like all of us.' Isn't that what he'd said? The douchebag. Clark had been a fool, a total fucking fool. He had made himself a mark, even dog-earing the catalogue page and wandering around the auction house with it open on that page and gazing at the *Peter Pan* lot in its glass case just a few feet away from his own lot. The way Dougie had drawn him back to Sanford's. Shown him how the other half live, high on the hog. Showed him *Alice*. That was Dougie's prompting. It hadn't been Sanford's idea at all.

Want. Want. Want. Over reason.

Clark just wanted to scream at Sanford, smash him over the head with something else. How could he not have warned him? The only good thing about the sorry mess was that Sanford Winkleman, for whatever reason, perhaps loyalty to his crook of a brother, or maybe because he'd bought *Alice* with money he didn't want the IRS to know about, whatever the reason, didn't seem too keen on involving the authorities. Clark just had to ensure it stayed that way. But he had to get out of there and fast whilst keeping Sanford placated and totally on side. No one back in Abraham City or in the books world could ever hear about this. If they did, Clark was as good as finished. This was bad, but not unsalvageable: he would hear from the Faith in the next forty-eight hours to confirm their purchase of the Letter of Accession, and the collection of accompanying letters. They had agreed a tentative price of $2.2 mil. But if Clark got embroiled in the mess Dougie and TJ had left behind, it wasn't beyond the realms of possibility that news would travel back to the Faith and kill that deal dead. The Faith did not embrace scandal.

He would do what Sanford wanted.

He picked the address book back up out of the blood and tapped out the dentist's number on the dial pad.

39

November 4th 1983, 8am

Abraham City

Last night, after Patricia's little top-of-the-news story which featured select footage of Judge Laidlaw's warrants being executed and a seemingly impromptu interview with lead Detective Sinclair, somehow, against the Captain's yelling, Marty had managed to calm him down. Told him that he was working a plan, there'd be a result in twenty-four hours, or he'd die trying. The Captain looked a little disappointed the latter might not come true. Marty had told him that the past thirty-six hours without a bomb was pretty good news. And then the phone rang. The Governor. It had been almost a week since the first bomb. He'd want answers. The Captain, face still set on growl, shooed Marty out of the office and reached across to pick up the call. Marty was glad of the interruption. He wanted to go downstairs to the basement and work on putting all those pieces of paper together. Al was already down there, helping search the fingerprint records, get it done quicker. The fingerprint on the Lomax/Hartman IOU was their best lead yet in finding Hartman. If that didn't work, Marty knew they'd have no choice but to contact the Feds to find its owner and once the Feds were involved they'd take over the entire case and give the Captain the chance to fire Marty out of the department.

The deli had repaired their window. Outside, a decorator was sketching out DAILY DELI onto the window, preparing for it to be filled in with paint. Clark watched as they entered, polite smiles. They must be curious. They had been respectful on the phone, but they knew detectives didn't tend to call people at 7 am. Not unless it was urgent, or fatal. It was only just 8 am, but they were meticulously turned out. Gloves, tweeds and those long green waterproof overcoats you see in J. C. Penney marked 'English Country Style'. It was almost as if they'd been fully dressed and ready when the phone rang, not long after dawn.

'I'm Rod.'

'And I'm Ron.'

They sat down. He remembered them from Mission when they were younger, maybe twenty-five or so . . . and he was just a teenager. They didn't shake hands then either. But they smiled politely. Still did.

The Rooks each ordered a glass of hot milk and a slice of banana loaf. They told Marty how good it was. How they got it every morning on their way into work. They looked out the window over to their store. It was boarded up. 'We have to leave it like that, for security.'

'So many valuable things inside,' said Ron.

'It must be very difficult.'

Both men nodded sadly. 'Our father's store,' said Rod.

'And his father's before him. Our family's been here since before the city even had a name.'

'You'll have it back together soon.'

Rod clamped his hands together. Closed his eyes.

Ron leaned forward. 'Your summons intrigued us, Detective. How can we help you?'

He had called them just as soon as he'd finished piecing it all together. He and Al had worked through the night, taking it in turns to get some shut-eye while the other one kept working on it.

'Is it about the bombings?' said Ron.

It was about the bombings but he didn't want to tell them that just yet. He had a few questions to ask them first.

'We gave a statement to the detective who spoke with us, while we were waiting for the paramedics to tend to us,' said Rod.

'We weren't badly hurt or anything, not like poor Mr Angel. We could wait a while.'

'Hobbs?'

'Yes, that was his name.'

'We told him that we hadn't seen anything that morning,' said Ron.

'Yes, thank you. I've read your witness statements.'

'We hope it was of help?' said Rod.

'We'd really like to help catch whoever did this. They damaged so much of our stock, wrecked the store,' said Ron.

'What I'd like is your expert opinion on something,' said Marty.

'Is it a coin?' said Ron.

Marty shook his head. Ron looked disappointed.

'He's coins. I'm documents. Manuscripts. Books. All of it,' said Rod.

'Not that I don't know anything about them.'

'No. It just makes it easier for people to tell us apart, if they know what we sell. We split the store right down the middle, to make it even easier.'

Marty thought it might be impossible to tell them apart, except for their speech patterns which were just a tiny bit off-rhythm from one another. But if they didn't speak they were identical.

Marty pulled the large sheets of card up off the floor, from where they were propped between the table and the wall. He'd sat at a six-seater table, just so he could spread these out all over it. He could have asked the Rooks to come to the station, but he wanted to keep it under wraps for now. He knew the deli wouldn't get busy until the other stores opened at nine.

Ron was picking up the fragments of letters. His brother had homed in on the letter Whittaker had tested and said was signed in human blood.

They were silent for a minute. Marty didn't speak, just nodded over to the waitress for another fresh juice.

Rod spoke first. 'Where did you get these?'

'I can't tell you that. I'm sorry.'

Marty thought he knew exactly what the documents were. He could read a lot of what was written there, despite the water damage, the charring through the pages. He just wanted to be sure. He had to be sure.

'You must know what this is. Your father, he would have spoken of this,' said Rod.

'Please, Mr Rook. Tell me what *you* think it is.'

Marty was no expert any court was going to listen to. If he had to he would call one or both these guys as experts. He also couldn't lead the experts to their answer. He had to hear it from them, unadulterated.

Ron was reading over his brother's shoulder now. 'How can this be?'

'What do you think that letter is, sir?'

'It's the Letter of Accession.'

'The Letter of Accession? That can't be it,' said Ron.

'No. It can't. This isn't right. Can't be right,' said Rod.

'And why do you think it isn't right? Ron? Rod?'

'But you know why, Detective,' said Rod.

'Please. I have to hear you say it.'

'Because we're the real Faith. Not them. Not Reno, not the so-called Real Faith, not the children of Rebecca and her son Jeremiah, but us, the children of Elizabeth and her son Abraham.'

'And that's what it says there, on that Letter of Accession? That Robert Bright chose Jeremiah to hand his Faith on to?'

'Yes. From what I can read,' said Rod.

'These letters, eleven of them. Back and forth between the wives, disputing it all. They stop a few days before the war of succession began,' said Ron.

'Can you tell me if you recognize the handwriting of the women, of Robert Bright?'

'Well, the women, yes. But there's no extant handwriting to make a comparison with Robert Bright.'

'So this could be anyone's writing?'

'Yes,' they both said at the same time.

'Is it in keeping with the period? Would you believe it was genuine?'

'Examining it in these conditions, and with these letters with it – they came together, I presume?' said Rod.

'Yes.'

'Then they're real,' said Rod.

'Or someone's playing a very clever trick,' said Ron.

'What makes you say that?'

'Why do you have them? That's what I'd ask you, Detective? Why don't the so-called Real Faith have them? Surely, it'd be of benefit to them?'

'Great benefit.'

'How come the Police Department has them?' He smiled at Marty. 'That's a rhetorical question.'

'Well, we'd assume that, yes, they should be with the Real Faith. I can tell you one thing, they didn't have possession of them, at least, not last. Which, of course, begs the question: why didn't they have them?'

'Have you spoken to anyone over there?'

'Not yet. I was waiting to hear your thoughts. Also, do you know why they would be going to a newspaper?'

Marty pulled out the envelope, what was left of it, a fragment out of a square typed label. They could see *Desert Times* clearly. 'By Hand' printed above it. But whoever it was made out to just had a random e and a capital F left visible. 'And do you know who this might be? Anyone at the paper interested in documents?'

The men leaned over it together, and almost conferred silently before saying together, without a beat, 'Debra Franklin.'

'Is that the one that's anti-Faith?'

'A real troublemaker, Detective,' said Rod.

'So, if somebody wanted to create mischief, that's who they'd send this to?'

'No one better,' said Rod.

'Is that what you think it is? Mischief? It's not genuine?'

'I'm not sure until I can get it tested,' said Marty. 'But I'm always extremely dubious of things that show up miraculously after a hundred and fifty years of being missing and, in this case, no one ever seeing them before. Am I right?'

'Your father taught you well,' said Rod.

'God rest his soul,' said Ron.

Hands clasped together. Eyes closed.

297

Marty nodded, thank you.

'No one has any record of the Letter of Accession. Nothing. The Faith likes to think of it as just that, faith in our path,' said Rod.

'The One True Path,' said Ron.

'If this is real, what do you think it would be worth?'

'Oh, millions,' said Rod.

'How many millions?'

'Really, however much someone would be prepared to pay for it. But at least two million.'

'Have you heard of anyone offering it for sale?'

'No,' they said together.

'But that would be very confidential,' said Rod.

'Yes. Imagine if the others got a hold of it,' said Ron.

The others. Reno.

'That's true, Detective. It would destroy us.'

'Worth killing for?' said Marty.

'What do you mean?' said Rod.

'Somebody might not want this becoming public property.'

'Someone in the Faith?' said Rod.

'I didn't say that.'

'You didn't have to,' said Rod.

'If I had a document worth a good sum of money, who would I go to at the Faith?'

'Well, we're a good conduit.'

'And if not you?'

Rod held his hands up. 'Dear Peter. Peter Gudsen. He always helped choose documents for us.'

'He was the librarian?'

'Not a librarian. An archivist,' said Rod.

'Did Mr Gudsen like to collect books – have a collection, do you know?'

They both looked at one another. Rod nodded, Ron spoke. 'Yes. It used to be coins. But he switched to books, manuscripts. Bibles, mostly. He always thought of them as investments. Also, first editions.'

'He bought from you?'

Rod looked around. The deli was still quiet. 'Yes. Yes he did.'

'But also from Clark,' Ron chipped in.

'Clark Houseman?'

'Yes.'

Houseman.

'If Mr Gudsen was unable to help, who else would help select documents and books on behalf of the Faith?'

'Disciple Laidlaw.'

'Alan Laidlaw.' They both nodded.

Marty had kept the covering letter he'd put back together. He had known, within just a few words of piecing it together, who was its author. More specifically, who the real author wanted it to appear to be. The phrasing was perfect, the handwriting even more so. But something was very wrong about the covering letter. Alan Laidlaw would never betray his Faith. It stated that the Faith was trying to buy the Letter of Accession and hide its truth from the world. The letter wasn't signed and the name of the author wasn't anywhere on it. But it wouldn't have taken a reporter long to find its alleged owner. And with the writing so perfect it would be hard for Laidlaw to deny. No smoke without fire.

Houseman was its courier. But that couldn't be all.

'Anyone else you know of, able to select documents for the Faith to acquire?'

'Not until they were going to do the deal. Or if it was very important.'

'Who would it be then?'

'Either the Order of the Twelve Disciples or the Triumvirate, you know: the Supreme Leader and Disciples Laidlaw and Browne.'

Was that so?

'Is Clark still in the hospital?'

'I'm afraid so.'

'Poor Clark.'

'Do you know if Mr Houseman might deal in documents of significant monetary value?'

'Clark?'

'Yes.'

'Not exceptionally high value. Nothing like this. If this were real, of course.' Rod looked at the Letter of Accession.

'And he does bring a lot of things to us.'

'He buys from us also, Detective. Regularly. Most weeks he's in.'

'What's the highest-value item he's ever brought to you?'

'Oh, probably just over twenty thousand,' said Rod.

'What about the *Peter Pan*?' said Ron.

'The novel?'

'Yes, Detective. But that was a fake. It doesn't count,' said Rod.

'I guess so. Perceived value wasn't what you meant, was it, Detective?' said Ron.

'When did he bring you the *Peter Pan*?'

'Oh, recently.'

'Could you be more precise?'

'Probably a few days before Halloween.'

'This Halloween?'

They both nodded.

'Did he say where he got it?'

'A yard sale, I think. On the road. He's always out on the road. Buying and selling.'

'He was very disappointed it wasn't real. He tried to hide it, but I could tell,' said Ron.

'Yes,' said Rod. 'It would have been worth a hundred and fifty thousand retail if it was.'

'Did he say how much he paid for it?'

'Five hundred bucks I think.'

'That's a lot for a yard sale.'

'Funny, that's what I thought,' said Rod. 'But you find all kinds of things traveling. Often, people don't know the value of what they've got. It was signed and everything – you know, by the author. I imagine they knew full well they were selling him a dud.'

'Have you ever had reason to doubt any document Mr Houseman has brought to you? Or other books, coins. Anything.'

'Clark!?'

'No, Detective, we haven't,' said Ron.

'Clark dealt with our father, even before we took over the business full-time.'

Marty hoped he didn't take too sharp a breath. 'Do you know a Mr Hartman?'

'Mr Hartman?' said Ron.

'Cliff Hartman?' said Rod.

Cliff.

'Have you ever met this Mr Hartman, Rod?'

'Oh no, Clark and any other dealer would never let us meet their sources. They keep us well apart,' said Rod.

'In case you cut out the middle man.'

The brothers both smiled.

'Do you know if he lives locally?'

'I don't think Clark ever said,' said Rod.

'Thank you, gentlemen. You've been very helpful. Could I just ask you one more question? Do you have any idea who might want to kill you?'

'Kill us? What on earth makes you say that?'

'The car bomb was parked outside your premises. Deliberately, we believe.'

The twins looked at one another, shook their heads. 'No, Detective. We don't know anyone who would want to kill us.'

'We live our life in a good way.'

'Sometimes that's the problem,' said Marty.

Marty gathered up all the documents, paid for their breakfasts and left the Rooks sitting at the table. Identically silent.

*

Marty was barely two steps out onto the sidewalk when he saw Al, smiling, standing next to a cruiser. A large, bald man in his forties in back.

'Who's he?'

'Meet Red Faber.'

'Red Faber?'

Al held his right thumb up. 'Mr Fingerprint, actually Thumbprint. Same name as the old White Sox pitcher under Comiskey. Hard to forget. Parents must have been a fan, 'cos this guy sure ain't him. Red's dead. This one's beat up, but alive. Come see for yourself.'

'White Sox. Thought I knew the name from somewhere.'

'I saw it on the investors list,' said Al.

'He's an investor?'

'Yeah, small used bills only,' Al laughed.

'All untraceable.'

'You got it. He invested four K.'

Al pulled Red out of the cruiser.

'How did you get that black eye, Red? Stood too close to a bomb, maybe?'

'You can't arrest someone for having a black eye.'

'Yeah, shame.'

'He says he was in a bar fight in Callaghan's. You know, over the county line.'

'I know.'

'I called the manager. You know him? Mikey.'

'Sure.'

'There was no fight in there anytime in the past week or so. Unusually.'

'Maybe he had a run-in with his old lady and just doesn't want to admit she won. Let's see your hand.' Marty grabbed the guy's right hand. Scratches visible on the knuckles. 'You got a couple in. How many she land?' Marty looked at the guy's face, at the yellowing eye. 'Not that many, huh? Why was that, surprise? Is that what happened? You jumped this Hartman character for Lomax someplace he weren't expecting you . . .'

'I don't know anybody called Hartman.'

No, but the rest of it was correct, huh.

'Shoved the paper in his face. Got him to sign. Is that all you used?'

'Nope.' Al took out a .45 from the back of his waistband. 'He might have had help from his little friend. Loaded. One in the chamber.'

'Expecting trouble, Red? Something tells me you're going downtown. And maybe straight to jail if that violates your parole. He on parole?'

'How did you guess? Rap sheet as long as your arm,' said Al.

'I told him,' Red nodded towards Al. 'That's my old lady's.'

'Except there was no old lady anywhere around. No women's clothes in the wardrobe. Nothing. So, the law assumes the gun's yours. She got it registered, your old lady?'

Red didn't answer.

'He was halfway out the drive with the car all packed up when I got there.'

'Someone warn you we might be coming, Red? Tell you to run? What happened, didn't get the message in time?'

'I dunno what you're talking about.'

'Model citizen, huh?'

'Not according to his rap sheet. I don't know where he got the four K to invest, but I doubt it was his army pension.'

'He got army bomb experience?' said Marty.

'Wasn't in any of the bomb units. But, 'Nam? Who knows what went down over there,' said Hobbs.

'Who told you to run? Was that Lomax?'

'I'm not saying nothing. You can lock me up if you want.'

'I love to make people's wishes come true. Don't you, Al?' Marty nodded towards the cruiser.

'You're a regular fairy godmother, Mart.' Al shoved Faber back in the car, banged on its roof and watched as it took off towards the precinct.

Al turned to Marty. 'It might just be a weird coincidence, but

Houseman's got a bruised-up eye. At least he did the other day.'

'Injury from the bombing?' said Marty.

'No, I thought so, but just thinking about it, it was starting to yellow. It had been there a couple of days at least.'

'Well, this one is a few days fading,' said Al.

'Then I think the elusive Mr Hartman just moved well and truly out of the shadows.'

40

October 27th 1983

Rooks Books

He had to know. Had to. And they had told him. Straight. Right between the eyes. And they had all laughed about it together. Everyone makes a mistake. Not him. Not Clark. What were the Rooks talking about? It wasn't five large, it was $580,000. Gone. Just like that. Only quicker. And with it, part of his dreams.

He tried to focus on the call that should come later today. They would have had their time to pray, to seek guidance. He tried to tell himself that everything would be OK. That they would say yes, and that showing the Faith up for what they are, frauds, would compensate him for the loss of his LA dream and all his money. If today worked, he would make over two million bucks.

Two million.

Plenty money to repay Lomax and go start his own collector's store wherever in the world he wanted to. But it was no good, he couldn't stay in the store, couldn't make small talk with the Rooks, not now. He could feel something beginning to overtake him. He had felt it before when he had become Rebecca, when he had dug deep into her soul and Elizabeth's to write those letters. Had felt the conflict of the sister-wives. Felt their rage and now it was welling inside of him. Their rage, their hatred, mixing with his own. He could feel it sucking him in, like the booze and the vortex had sucked him into other worlds, other lives. He had to get out of there. He had to.

He'd parked in the rear car lot, so he could make a quick get-away and hopefully not bump into anyone on the street. He had just got to the car when he saw a flash of movement to his side, and someone jumped him.

Before he could even react he was being dragged into the rear entrance of the empty store next to the Rooks'. Then yanked up by the collar, and as he got to eye level with the big bald guy his head was knocked sideways by a killer right hook. He stumbled backwards and pulled the guy with him, the guy lost his footing and almost followed Clark to the floor. Clark landed heavily, but managed to shoot his leg out quickly, unbalancing his attacker, who slammed hard into the wall. Clark tried to scrabble to his feet, but he was too slow and before he was even up on his knees the guy was on his back, pressing his face down into the cement. 'I'm broke, buddy. You picked the wrong guy. Check the wallet, there's nothing in it.' It was true: the wallet *was* empty, but he had a wad of cash tucked into his inside jacket pocket. Hopefully this Neanderthal wouldn't find it.

'He told you to pay the money back, didn't he?' said the thug.

Lomax.

'It's coming. I told him. These things take time. I'm not a magician.'

'You don't have any more time, Houseman. We're sick of your excuses. He can't pay us back until you pay him back.'

He slammed something down next to Clark.

'Sign it!'

'Sign what?'

Why was he asking questions? This goon would beat him to a pulp and probably enjoy it. Clark had been down in the den, at breakfast, had a drink. That was a lie, not at breakfast, *for* breakfast. He thought it must be making him irrational. The guy dug his knuckles into the back of Clark's neck. Hard. Grinding Clark's cheek into the ground. Shit.

'That's the uplift you promised him, plus a year's interest, payable no matter what. You had your chance.'

He shoved a pen into Clark's hand.

Clark stared at the flimsy paper, to where Arnold's name clawed back everything he owed. And then some.

Cold steel at his temple.

He wrote the rest of the signature tiny, illegible. But its capital letters he wrote large. Large C. Large H.

Cliff Hartman. Just like all the other lines in the ledger Arnold had used. Why wasn't he using that?

No more cold steel. Footsteps, moving away. An engine. A screech of tires as the goon pulled onto the street.

Peter Pan was open on its spine, pages ripped out, fluttering away across the lot. He picked it up, walked slowly, painfully over to the garbage. He wished he'd shown Sanford that day, maybe after his head had been stitched up, but he'd split out the side door right when Dentist Davies arrived. He could have asked Sanford's opinion, would have found out earlier that it was a fake, not even risked coming here. But he had just wanted to get out of there.

It must have spooked them, him asking Dougie to use the *Peter Pan* as a lien to get some of his money back.

All that glitters isn't gold.

They must have thought he'd rumbled them somehow. Made them hasten their plan. Grab what they could and scram.

Trash or recycling.

He opened the trash can and threw *Peter Pan* in.

He couldn't even remember getting back from LA the previous week. Or how he'd managed to drive himself down to San Diego and get himself through the airport and on a plane back to Abraham City. The booze on the plane was free, it wasn't a Faith airline, so it was flowing for the ninety minutes' flying time from San Diego.

He had checked in with Ziggy. The Faith hadn't phoned all week. Today was their deadline. And now he sat, staring out the diner window, willing the phone to ring. Willing their call to travel through the airwaves and Ziggy to appear and urge him to the phone.

'Hey man, what happened to your eye. You look all beat up.'

It was Kenny. He plonked himself down opposite.

'Tripped over Jack's skateboard.'

'You got him skating already? Radical. Go Clark. Did you order?'

'The usual.'

'I'm thinking of going for the full rack of ribs. Chicken. Onion rings. The works.'

Kenny always went for the works when he knew Clark was paying.

It was a shame the diner was too quiet to try putting him in a trance again.

Clark pushed an envelope of cash towards Kenny.

'Thanks, man. Appreciate it.' He tucked it inside his back pocket. Kenny had run a few signed first editions down to Scottsdale. Some nice signatures, personalized. They'd made a few grand. Clark looked out the window.

'What's up?'

'Just waiting on a call.'

'A watched phone never rings. Isn't that what they say?'

'No. That's a kettle. A watched kettle never boils.'

'Hey look!'

Over on the counter TV they were running an advertisement for a documentary. 'The Hitler Diaries, that's some crazy shit, isn't it? All that money for something fake. People are whacko.'

'Why?'

'Five million bucks or something. *The Times* of London and that German paper. How the hell would Hitler have time to write a diary during the war? I don't have time to write a diary and I'm not invading countries and killing everyone.'

'Churchill did.'

'Did he?'

'And more pages than that. And, if the buyer believes it's real, then it is.'

'Is it?'

'That's what they're paying for, belief, not reality.'

'That guy's going to jail.'

BANG, BANG, BANG.

Clark turned to see Ziggy banging on the window next to them.

'Jeez, what's with him?'

'The phone. I gotta get it.'

'Maybe you should get a real secretary,' said Gloria, refilling Clark's cup.

'He tried: they were all out of blondes.' Kenny laughed loud at his joke.

Gloria wagged her finger out the window, to Ziggy. He

frowned. Wagged back. She smiled.

'Hey, what about your schnitzel?'

'Keep it under the warmer, can you?' said Clark.

He was up now, out of the booth. Heading fast toward the door. 'I'll be back in a minute. I might even order some pie.'

'Really?' She watched him as he ran out of the door and along the path towards the phone, Ziggy following behind.

Clark grabbed up the phone from where Ziggy had left it balanced carefully on top of the box.

'Brother Clark? It's Alan Laidlaw.'

Alan Laidlaw. It must be good news if he was calling. If it was bad news he would have expected them to get Peter Gudsen to call. 'Disciple Laidlaw. How are you?'

'Good. I wanted to ask you a couple of questions about the documents.'

'Please do.'

'We have sought the Lord Prophet's guidance through prayer. We held a vigil here at the Mission last night. The Twelve Disciples prayed in unison throughout the night. This is a most difficult situation. The Lord may judge us on our decision for all eternity.'

'Yes, Brother. He may indeed.'

'The Letter of Accession, Brother Clark. What's to say there's not another one out there somewhere?'

'You mean the Jeremiah letter, not the Abraham letter?'

'Yes, or even another one of these?'

'Why would there be another one of those?'

'We think this might be a fake.'

'A fake? Absolutely no way that letter's a fake. It came through Cliff Hartman, an exceptionally reputable contact I've used many times before, with no problems. He's exceptionally thorough, famed for it.'

'I don't doubt it. But after we had sought the sanctuary of prayer, it gave us time to think clearly. Reflect. We had a round-table meeting afterward. We thought perhaps those in Reno might have worked this Letter of Accession and the accompanying letters into the hands of a reputable dealer like yourself and your colleague. Knowing that they would most likely find their way to us.'

'No, Disciple Laidlaw. The letter and everything that accompanies it is a hundred per cent genuine. It's been verified by two independent experts.'

'Just like the Hitler Diaries.'

The fucking Hitler Diaries.

'The Disciples have all been following the revelations about those. It makes us err on the side of caution.'

'But these aren't fake. They're authenticated as genuine.' Clark tried not to raise his voice.

'For the past few months, the Hitler Diaries were authenticated as genuine, son. And now look. Who's to say it's not Reno feeding that newspaper reporter stories? And it's them that have forged this document in the hope that we would buy it, and shame us, revealing to the world that we are engaged in some kind of cover-up to hide the origins of our Faith. Or disguise them.'

'But if they'd have forged it, wouldn't Reno have kept it themselves and been shouting from the rooftops that they were the true religion?'

'No, not if showing us to be deceitful would be a superior game plan. Imagine, they humiliate us and then the document itself confirms them as the true religion. In doing so, they have destroyed us and elevated themselves to what they have always claimed to be . . . the Real Faith. It would be quite the master stroke.'

Wouldn't it.

'I would side with the experts, Disciple Laidlaw. They know their business. If they are wrong about this, what else are they wrong about?'

'Perhaps that's why, after what's happened in Europe, so many libraries around the world are carrying out inventories of what documents and manuscripts they hold, compared to what ones they think they hold. We might be doing that ourselves soon.'

Clark felt a shiver down his spine.

He could already gauge the Faith's answer, but polite ritual meant he had to ask. 'What was the Disciples' conclusion?'

'We can't proceed now, Brother Clark. We just can't. Sorry to disappoint you. It's just not the right time. I will leave the documents at the main desk, there's a lockable closet there. Please just pick them up whenever it's convenient.'

Clark had barely mumbled thank you when he heard the dial tone.

He felt short of breath, nauseous. He thought if he moved he would be sick, right there, over his own shoes. Keep it together. He picked up the phone and dialled Debra Franklin. It went straight through to voicemail. He waited for the tone and began to speak. He finished by telling her that the informant would have the documents couriered to her office this week. That they were extremely valuable and the informant would need the receptionist to sign for them. Clark would put a note in that the Faith were trying to buy these documents to cover up that Reno was really the heir to Robert Bright. But he wouldn't write it in his own hand. He had a far better plan than that.

He wasn't going back into the diner. He couldn't. Couldn't ever. He knew what he had to do. He had to destroy them, before they could use their knowledge to destroy him. The Faith thought they were all-knowing, all-powerful. They didn't know shit. Clark would show them they knew nothing. No Lord Prophet or travellers from planet Lumina were going to save them. Not now. Not ever.

He jumped in his car and floored it.

People up ahead.

He slammed his brakes on, he could smell the rubber. He almost ate the steering wheel. 'What the fuck?' He looked up to see a trail of people crossing in front of him. A man led them. His hand up, guiding them across the road, and halting Clark. He stared in at him. Clark looked along the line of people, three women following the man, strange clothes and a trail of children in their wake. He looked back to the man. Robert Bright. Clark honked the horn, floored the gas, they scattered. When he looked in the rearview, there was no one there.

41

November 4th 1983, 9 am

Abraham City

Marty had stood in the centre of the room. It was so clean, so empty, it was as if someone had scrubbed the whole place down ahead of surgery.

There was an array of bookcases. All empty. A cupboard under the sink, also empty. A tall chair sat at an empty make-shift desk, next to a workbench which was obviously new, and replaced something the surface of which might have given up its secrets.

'I don't understand, Detective.' Edie Houseman looked more amazed than Marty. 'But this is where Clark always is, when he's home, working on something or other.' Together they stared at the empty walls.

Down here, under the house, there was no noise, not a sound. He must have liked it like that. Needed the silence to work.

All work and no play makes Clark a dull, dull boy.

Marty knew then, knew that whatever had gone on in this room, it was his mind, the mind of Clark Houseman and whatever he had created here in this dungeon that held the key to all the death and destruction that had gone on the past week.

Marty had sent a reluctant Edie off to fetch Whittaker from the kitchen, told her to stay up there with the others and send her sister down here in a minute.

Whittaker's feet stopped on the wooden stairs. He whistled.

'Wow, this place is clean.'

'Isn't it.'

'What you hoping to find, Mart?'

'Anything. You still looking for that blast cap?'

'We are.'

'Maybe it's here. Somewhere.'

'Really? He's done a pretty good job of the clean-up. Smell that? Bleach, ammonia and who knows what other household products. He's a good few steps ahead of us.'

Marty just hoped that Houseman wasn't too far ahead, because they needed to catch him.

He turned the handle and swung the door open.

How different to last time. No longer in a coma, now hooked up to just one machine, Clark was sat up in bed eating grapes with his good hand, on his lap a week-old copy of the *LA Times*. He smiled at Marty as if expecting him. Perhaps he was. The doctor had refused permission last night, citing some test or other.

'Good morning, Detective.'

Marty didn't like to think he looked like a cop. Not that he was ashamed, far from it. He just didn't want to look like a job. It was rare for people to peg him as a cop. He wondered if Houseman had really been in a full coma the other day. Perhaps he had been semi-conscious and heard every damn word they'd said. And perhaps *Good morning, Detective* was Houseman's way of telling him this. His way of firing a shot across the bow. He wasn't going to be a walkover. Marty hadn't thought he would be. And now he knew for sure. Marty didn't speak until he sat down at the side of the bed.

'Good morning, Mr Houseman.'

'Please, Detective. Clark.' Houseman held out the bowl of grapes.

Marty shook his head. 'No thank you, Clark.'

Houseman smiled a wide smile. It was almost as if he didn't have a care in the world. If he hadn't recognized him, Marty would have thought he was in the wrong room.

'I wanted to ask you some questions, sir.'

'Clark, please. Sorry I couldn't see you then. The doctor said no. No visitors. My wife's coming this afternoon. Edie. I hope she brings the papers. They're not allowing me the TV or newspapers, except this. Too traumatic apparently.'

That smile again.

'It's not a problem, Clark,' said Marty, smiling right back.

'It's about the bombing?'

'That's right, Clark. About the bombings.'

Marty didn't want him getting worked up too early. Didn't want to ask questions that would put his back up, close down the session. 'You just let me know how you're feeling, at any time. We can stop.'

'Thank you, Detective – they said I had a brain injury. Swelling. I could have died.'

'Did you see anyone hanging around near your car, Clark, that day or the days before?'

'I'm sorry, Detective. My memory's shot.'

'Do you remember what happened at the time of the explosion? Were you in your vehicle?'

'I'm so sorry, Detective. I can't remember a thing. All I remember is having dinner with Edie the night before. Around eight pm. She'd just got back from a few days at her sister's. The rest is an absolute blank. Mercifully.'

Strange thing to remember in a vacuum of memory loss.

'You don't remember bringing your wife breakfast in bed the morning of the bombing?'

Clark was quiet. He was thinking. Thinking that Edie had obviously told them that. And knowing what the next question would be. Clark shook his head. 'I don't think so.'

Marty wasn't going to let him close it down so easily.

'She said you often did that if you had a sale to celebrate, or an anniversary, something like that.'

'Yes.'

'What were you celebrating that morning?'

'I can't remember.'

Because if you could, you'd probably remember that you were just saying you had something to celebrate, so you could wake your wife up to give you an alibi for the morning of the first bombings.

'You'd made a good sale, maybe the day before, or perhaps that week sometime?'

Marty was leading him to a dead end. If Houseman was clever he'd find a way to turn around, back up.

'I don't remember.'

'Really? How far back can't you remember? What's your last memory before the bombing, apart from the dinner?'

'Maybe a few days. It's all a bit hazy that last week. Just patches of flashbacks.'

'Do you recall being attacked, perhaps a few days prior?'

'Attacked?'

Marty nodded.

'No. I don't recall being attacked. Was I really attacked?'

'I believe so, Clark.'

'Do you recall perhaps reporting that attack to the police?'

Clark shook his head. No.

'Is there a reason someone might want to attack you? Perhaps if you could tell us that we could find the person responsible.'

'Do you think it's the same person?'

'We're looking at several theories right now. Can you remember, right after the explosion, you said that someone was trying to kill you? Do you remember that?'

'Did I?'

'Yes, Clark. Can you recall why you might have said that?'

'No.'

'Even though you were attacked and then bombed in the space of a few days.'

'The doctor says it's the trauma, the memory loss.'

'Can you tell me where you got the documents in your car?'

'What documents?'

'In the trunk of your car. There was an exceptionally valuable collection of documents.' Marty looked at Clark, waited for him to tell him what they were. He couldn't claim to forget something he must have been involved with for months before the explosion. If he could claim months' worth of memory loss, how could he have said someone was trying to kill him less than a few minutes after the bomb had exploded? When he was referring back to either the bomb, the attack or both.

'I don't remember any documents. In the trunk? Are they OK?'

'No. I'm sorry. They're ruined.'

'Do you know what they are? Maybe that will help me remember. Can you describe them?'

'The explosion shredded them into thousands of pieces.'

'How terrible.'

'But my colleague and I put them back together.'

'You did?' The very briefest of tremors, shock, crossed Clark's face. He was sat up straighter in the bed now, leaned more towards Marty. 'What was it?'

Al arrived, almost on cue, moved silently to the other side of the bed. Nodded hello to Clark. Clark didn't offer him any grapes.

'The Letter of Accession.'

'*The* Letter of Accession.'

So he remembers something.

'Well, not the ideal one the Faith would have wanted to have. But one worth two million dollars anyhow.'

'Two million dollars? It's a shame I can't remember it, isn't it?'

'Would you know where you got it from?' Marty took out the letter, in a baggie, flicked through the others quickly. 'This letter and the collection along with it, any idea?'

'No. Was it in something? An envelope? Maybe that has a return address on it? Maybe even a receipt or a letter or something with it?'

A letter . . . or something.

'No, no letter.'

'I'm so sorry. I don't. People send me stuff all the time.'

'Stuff worth two million?'

'Even more than that. I check authenticity of documents. It's not always to sell. Shame I can't remember this.'

'Do you keep records, perhaps at your office?'

'I don't have an office.'

Marty smiled to himself at how Houseman's memory was only faulty when he didn't want to answer.

'At your home?'

'Dealers don't like *records*. Most of what I deal in is very confidential.'

'Would you be able to put us in contact with Mr Clifford Hartman?'

'Mr Hartman?'

'You know him?'

Marty knew what was coming.

'I'm sorry. I don't remember. I must have had an address book. I hope it wasn't in the car.'

'We didn't find one in there.'

'Why do you want to speak to this Mr Hartman?'

'We think he's the dealer for this document.'

'I don't remember a Mr Hartman. But what has that got to do with the police?'

'It's a fake.'

'A fake? No, that's impossible. A fake worth that much?' Clark's eyebrows knitted together. 'But I thought you were investigating the bombings.'

'So did we,' said Marty. 'But we think that this Mr Hartman might be responsible for the bombings.'

'Really? What makes you think that?'

'You did, Clark. Don't you remember? Right after the explosion, that's what you told me.'

Did Marty see a flicker in the eye, just a flash of something? Satisfaction. Clark leaned back on the bed.

'I have no objection to you searching my home, Detective. It might help my memory. If you could find my records, such as they are. And, if it helps, I could take a lie-detector test.'

'I don't know how that would help, Clark. If you have memory loss, it might not be reliable.'

'Oh.' Was that disappointment in the slight downward movement of the chin? Whatever it was, he quickly recovered. Chewed another grape.

'I'll let you rest, Clark.' Marty was up now. He turned back to Houseman. 'I hope you get better soon, Clark. Oh, some friends of yours wanted me to send you their very best wishes.'

'Oh, really?'

'Yes. Wonderful folks. The Rooks.'

A flash of darkness swept Clark's face quickly replaced by a megawatt smile. 'How kind of them. Thank you, Detective.'

'My pleasure, Clark.'

Marty felt Clark's eyes bore into his back all the way out the door. Al was waiting outside the room with Grady's kid.

'He hasn't had the papers, no TV, no visitors, phone? Nothing?'

'No, Detective, just like you said. Nothing and no one but the medical staff in and out since he woke up.'

'Good. Thanks.'

'Detective! Detective?' Marty and Al both turned around. It was the nurse that had been tending to Clark on the first day. She was holding out a phone. 'We have a call for you. A Detective Renaldi.' Marty and Al both looked at each other.

'Venice Frank? Tracked you to here? He's damn good. Tell him I told you that,' said Al.

Marty took the phone off the nurse. 'Thanks.' She nodded, smiled. She still had a great smile.

'Frank, Marty, what on earth. How long's it been?'

'Too long,' the deep voice on the phone said. 'We missed you at the Christmas party. You should try and come out for this year's. It's at some smart hotel they built overlooking the beach.'

322

'I'll tell Al. But this isn't social, huh?'

'No. I got someone here wants to talk to you.'

'To me?'

'Who is it?'

'A walk-in. Ziggy Bookman. He's worried about a friend of his. One of the victims in that case you got up there.'

'Who the hell's . . .' And then he remembered Burkeman, as Carvell had called him.

'He thinks he can help you, help his friend. There's a guy he thinks might be responsible.'

'Oh yeah.'

'Yeah. His friend gave him money, told him get out of town, it's getting dangerous. He's out of control.'

'Who's the friend?'

'His friend's Clark Houseman. He said he thinks he knows who tried to kill Houseman and killed the others.'

'He got a name, the bomber?'

'Yeah. What was it again, Mr Bookman?'

Marty heard Frank pass Ziggy the phone. Ziggy whispered into the receiver. 'Clark doesn't let him out much. I think he's bad. A bad man.'

'Who, Ziggy? Who's a bad man?'

'Cliff Hartman.'

Marty looked at Al, smiled – then, back into the phone, 'Who warned you to get out of town? Clark?'

'Yes, he said Cliff Hartman was out of control. You need to catch him, Officer. He's a murderer.'

'We will, Mr Bookman. He gave you money? Clark?'

'Money and a little Bible owned by . . .'

'Edgar Allan Poe?'

'You're clever, mister. That why you're a detective?'

'And how much money, Ziggy?'

'Five thousand dollars. Cash.'

'Clark must have been a good friend.'

'The best.'

'What day was all this, Mr Bookman, can you remember?'

'My mother's birthday. October twenty-eighth.'

October 28th. Two days before the first bombing.

'You gonna catch Bad Hartman now, Detective?'

'We're gonna catch him now, Mr Bookman. Thanks to you.'

42

November 4th 1983, 3 pm

Old Canyon Road

The Mustang had slipped and slid all the way to the top. Up here there was nothing that hadn't been abandoned long ago. Marty parked near the old ski chalet. What was left of it. It had gotten hit by a mini avalanche back in the late 1950s and no one had bothered to rebuild it. The hotel a couple of hundred yards away was long abandoned, rendered obsolete when a swanky resort opened up the other side of the canyon, attracting the rich and famous for the skiing in winter and rehab in summer. It was the state's answer to Aspen.

The sky was a brilliant blue, the snow pure up here, a fresh powder had fallen and it was ready to ski. On the ridge overlooking the old hotel parking lot were thousands and thousands of evergreens. Marty didn't want to get out of the car, not just yet. He wanted to set the postcard in his mind. He had been up here many times. Mostly on his own looking for Liss. Even if it had been a horrible death, this would still be a beautiful resting place.

They had promised heavy snow later, it might even block his way out down the canyon pass. He hoped he would find what he was looking for before the snow came. Marty knew if you wanted to catch a killer you had to think like one, but this was more than just murder. Fake documents, the Faith, large cash transactions, hundreds of thousands of dollars missing, a bust property investment firm and who knew what else. What he did know was that Clark Houseman had in all probability been beaten up by Red Faber, who undoubtedly was paid for this by Lomax as the paper had ended up in his safe. No doubt to replace the ledger the former Mrs Lomax had stolen and given to Peter Gudsen. Did everything else that ensued, the bombings, stem from this one action? Marty doubted it, but it was all he had now. Lomax's most precious object, Bobbi, had been taken from him, so you could say the hatred for Lomax was greater than for Peter Gudsen, despite the nail bomb that had killed the latter. Houseman had owed Lomax, at the end, almost $700K. Lomax, under pressure from all sides, was an easy mark for Clark to fit everything on. Clark loved his family, according to Edie, he doted on the kids. Just from that it was easy to think that there was no way on earth he'd be building bombs right underneath where they all slept. Even if Edie and the kids were away for a few days before the bombings, like she'd said, most likely they weren't assembled until right when Clark needed them. And where did he test them? It had to be somewhere remote, somewhere away from the congested, residential sides of the canyons. And where better than what Clark would have known was empty land, not likely to have passers by, for the very end of the Old Canyon Road was impassable thanks to a major landslide over a decade ago.

Marty looked up. A proud sign announced 'COMING SOON 500 NEW HOMES', and to the side of it a cheesy life-size photo of Arnold Lomax and emblazoned on that 'SELLING FAST'. Where better for Clark to practice, a part of the canyon where you wouldn't come unless you were lost or up to no good.

If there was anything visible, any bomb dummy runs, all evidence of it had been covered by the snow. But when he looked at the snow, in what he supposed had been a flat part of the ski chalet's yard he could see that there were visible pockets, where it looked like it had sunk a little into the ground. Marty had seen those kind of depressions in snowy ground before, on his search for Liss. It usually meant something was underneath that was warmer than the rest of the earth, or that the earth underneath had been turned recently, or – and this was the one he never liked to think about – that there was something buried there, just near the surface.

Thirty minutes later he had sweated his jacket off in the low winter sun.

'Looks like you could do with some help.'

Marty looked up. It was Al. They had dug together before. Dug while searching for Liss. And now who knew what they were digging for. 'Snow's a bitch, and the ground's rock hard.'

Al was unfolding a sheet of paper out of his coat pocket. 'One-eyed guy came up trumps. Recognize anyone?' Marty looked at the sketch. 'I just faxed it to the department. They're going to circulate it urgently, see if anyone else recognizes our Mr Houseman, or is it Hartman?'

'Looks like Hartman's quite the forger.'

'Yeah, matched only by Houseman.'

'Let's get Hobbs or someone to go over to the original Mrs Lomax. Ask her if this is who she saw meeting Gudsen at the Faith Mission that night.'

'You think it was him she saw?'

'That's my gut. Let's hear her say it though. I think the Faith are in with Houseman somehow, Al, although they'll be wishing they weren't now.'

'Speaking of Hobbs. He called. Frank Renaldi sent through

a twelve-page fax with all the details of Ziggy's dealings with Clark Houseman and his associate Cliff Hartman. It's quite a read, apparently.'

'Useful?'

'Sounds like it. Calls, transactions, names. Good work, Mart.'

'Good work Ziggy Bookman.'

Marty knew Al would start digging alongside him and wouldn't stop until Marty did. That's how it had been before. So maybe now was a good time to call a halt. There was nothing here. He was pissed about Houseman, they needed physical evidence to tie him to the bombings. Sightings and statements weren't enough. This was a capital case. Marty drove the shovel hard into the ground. It was softer here, less compacted by the cold, and so he drove it in again. It hit something which forced Marty's shovel back deep into his hand. 'You son of a . . .' Marty peered into the ground, saw a little spot of something lemon-colored. He dropped to his knees. Al was next to him. 'What's that?'

'I dunno. But somehow I don't think it belongs here.'

Marty scraped away at the soil covering it. A cooler box. He grabbed the handle and pulled it hard and fast up out of its burial place.

He sat up on his knees, hunched over it, about to open it. Al grabbed his shoulder: 'Don't! We should call it in. Who knows what the hell's in there.'

'You think the bomber left us a little surprise?'

'Could be, although it's not in a ribboned box.'

They both laughed.

'I can't see any wires. But maybe they're all inside,' said Marty.

'Yeah. Why spoil the surprise.'

'I've got an idea.'

'What?'

'Step back. Come on. Right back. Just in case it goes up.'

They moved back twenty yards. Marty threw himself down onto the powder. Pulled out his .38, straightened his right arm, rested it on his left, bent in front of him. Al looked at him. 'Come on, you're not going to try shooting the lock off. I'll radio Tex.'

'Tex? He'll blow up half the mountain.'

Bam.

The bullet took off the first clip-lock and the force of the impact pushed the top half off the cooler box, twisting the second clip-lock off and exposing the contents. Covers and pages of books blew in the wind.

Marty and Al made their way back over to the box. Marty picked up a large velvet case that took up half the top of the chest. He clicked it open.

'Coins?'

'I'll give Houseman his due, he's diverse.'

'Follows the dollars, I guess.'

'Looks that way.'

'What's he thinking, burying all this up here?'

'Planning on coming back for it one day, I guess. Lomax must have told him, or somebody did, that the land was toxic, not likely to get anything built on it. He took a gamble they were right.'

'Well, he's not coming back for anything. Ever.'

'What's all that?' said Marty.

'Lot of old books, signed some of them. Letters.' Al picked up one of the letters.

'Who's that one from?'

'George Washington,' said Al.

'Who's it to, Elvis?'

'No. Von Steuben, that was his military guy, wasn't it? In the Revolution?'

Marty was staring to the far side of the abandoned hotel. 'What's with all that glass smashed out of there? It wasn't like that before, last time I was up here.'

'Vandals, maybe?'

Marty moved away, towards it. 'Close that lid up, Al. Put this one in your car. And then we'll start digging for the rest.'

'There's more?'

'Oh yeah. Eight, I think, in total. Look at the way the snow is uneven over there.'

'Like graves.'

Marty could see Al regretted that line the second he said it. But he couldn't dwell on it.

Al pressed the books and letters back down into the chest. Hoisted it up and carried it like a sleeping child towards where Marty was clambering through panes of broken glass in the wooden window frames. In front of him he could see the blue tiles that surrounded the long empty pool. 'Watch it, Al, there's all broken glass out there buried in the snow.' Marty pointed off. 'Go round over that way. There's less of it.'

*

A few minutes later they both stood beside the empty pool. Nothing but blue tiles, on the walls, in the pool. Everywhere blue. Crumbling and cracked. Almost the entire place was splattered with blood. The pigs it had come from, at least several of them, were blown into hundreds of decomposing lumps that almost covered the bottom of the empty pool.

Marty nudged Al. 'What's that down there?'

'What?' said Al.

Marty jumped down into the pool, pulled out a handkerchief, plucked something metal off the tiled floor. Held it up so Al could see. 'A blast cap.'

'The missing one?'

'He must have dropped it in here, not realized.'

'Lost it before he had time to wipe the prints?'

'That would be good.'

Marty's foot kicked something. He looked down. A pig with a nail through its eye. Just like he'd seen Gudsen that day. He turned away.

'How's Houseman looking now, Mart?'

Marty turned to Al, smiled. 'Like a dead man walking.'

Al helped pull Marty back up out of the empty pool. 'You better get Whittaker and some of his boys up here, Al. Help us extricate that stuff from the ground.'

*

After Al and Whittaker's team had taken off back to the precinct, Marty sat in his car, the door open, his feet rested in the snow. He rolled a cherry menthol. Lit it. Inhaled. It was so good. Sharper up here, at this altitude.

Liss.

Everyone thought it was short for Felicity.

Happiness.

It wasn't. But she had brought him that.

331

Liss was the name she'd called herself, as a toddler, somewhere in her mouth losing the A in Alice.

He looked out, over the ridge of a million evergreens that ran as far as the eye could see.

The light was fading.

The snow was falling.

He took another hit, closed his eyes and thought of Alice.

Tomorrow morning he would charge Clark Houseman with the killing of Peter Gudsen and Bobbi Lomax.

I can see the city as I rise above it.
All I know is here somewhere.
Something stops me, maybe gravity.
And, as earth fast approaches, I feel the warmth
of its air beneath me,
Feel the heat and its efforts to devour me.

Funny, I can't hear anything.
All I taste is sulphur, with a hint of mercury.
As I fall to earth, I don't smile,
I think
No Man Knows My Name
And then I smile.

Cliff Hartman, Halloween 1983

Abraham City, several years later

Clark Houseman: Abraham City had to move Clark's trial upstate to ensure he would receive at least the appearance of a fair trial. To avoid the death penalty Clark pleaded guilty and now earns pin money in jail writing love letters to other prisoners' wives, girlfriends, and sometimes boyfriends, in their hand, but not with their words. The inmates call him Cyrano.

Edie Houseman and her children moved to Wyoming to be near her younger sister, who has cable. After divorcing Clark the day after he pleaded guilty, she married a cattle rancher and now has five children, two boys and three girls.

The Rooks rebuilt their store with the help of the good citizens of Abraham City and continue to trade.

Arnold Lomax finally co-operated with the authorities and Judge Laidlaw signed an order for him to repay his investors in full. He also signed another order to seize and sell any of Clark's forgeries as curiosities and also to sell his genuine first editions in order to facilitate repayment to his creditors.

Since 1983 **the Faith** has expanded into forty-seven further countries and each day a silent prayer is offered by members the world over to planet Lumina for its deliverance from

Clark Houseman and his heretical intentions. Clark didn't like to think that by attempting to destroy the Faith he had strengthened even its weakest links.

Betty Gudsen never remarried. Her boys all graduated Summa Cum Laude from the Faith's university.

Sanford T. Winkleman is still looking for *Alice*, his brother and Dougie Wild. He has hired a private detective agency to assist. When he finds them, he'll hire a hitman.

Ziggy lives on Santa Monica Beach, just down from the pier, and reads a book a day, mostly crime fiction, except for Sundays when he reads two.

Kenny got the hell out of Dodge. And stayed out.